TOUCHED BY DARKNESS

NICOLE LECLERCQ

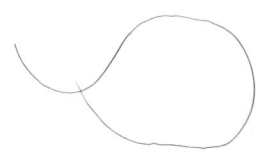

ACKNOWLEDGEMENTS

First, I'd like to thank Claire Chilton for her support and advice. I'm immensely grateful for her knowledge and time.

A huge thanks to Sarah Strous, Jennifer Ellis and Linda Kirkemo for helping me find all the little errors that cropped up in my story. Their input and suggestions made this into a better, stronger book.

And lastly, thanks to my mom for being there whenever I need guidance.

First published in the United States by Ragz Books 2015

This edition published by Ragz Books 2019

Published in the United States by Ragz Books

Design & Illustration by Claire Chilton

Artwork by Tony Mauro

ISBN 13: 978-1-908822-47-5
ISBN 10: 1-908822-47-3

TOUCHED BY DARKNESS

NICOLE LECLERCQ

www.ragz-books.com

PROLOGUE

Jonathan Stratton salivated as he watched the vampire's fangs pierce Erin Holland's bottom lip. He drew closer to the computer monitor that glowed in the darkness of the room. He frowned when the back of the vampire's head shifted and blocked his vision. Stratton moved his fingers on the keyboard. A few commands later, he was able to zoom in on Erin's face.

She was so still. Her face was pale, near ghostly, and her eyes were shut. Her hair floated about her in a golden veil as she lay sprawled on her back on the dusty church floor. The white pentagram beneath her had not been able to protect her from the magic blast that had just knocked her unconscious. Nor was it protecting her from Dane Lynch drinking from her.

Stratton chuckled when he noticed Dane's hand on Erin's breast. The hand slid to her waist before it stopped.

No, please don't stop now. This is excellent, Stratton cheered in silence.

The best footage ever.

Dane lifted his head, looking down at Erin. Her lips had parted. There was blood on them. Dane glanced at the black-haired witch lying in front of the crucifix. The young witch was still passed out.

Stratton grinned.

But you're not safe Dane, because I did witness your actions.

Dane licked his lips, removing the blood glistening on his mouth. He bent down once more. The way his hand kept rubbing Erin's throat, making her swallow, it was obvious to Stratton that he was feeding her his own blood. Dane waited for the blood exchange to be complete before cradling her in his arms, sheltering her.

Even better.

He should have known that Dane would mark Erin as soon as he had the chance, bind her to him so that she could never escape him.

It must be quite a thrill to have someone with Erin's powers as a blood slave, Stratton mused. Dane had always been smart enough to get what he wanted, even if he had to cheat or threaten.

Stratton's expression hardened as he recalled Dane threatening him. Fighting the rage building inside him, he clenched his fists. Dane wouldn't get away with ordering him to break off his plans for Erin.

Stratton zoomed out to look at the other girl on the floor. The young witch might be of use to him. He should have her further investigated.

When he saw Erin stir slightly, his gaze immediately returned to the blond woman. She did not open her eyes and therefore was unable to see the way Dane stared at her with dark, hungry intent.

Erin seemed to have more color in her cheeks.

Stratton and Dane were both focused on her, eagerly waiting for her to wake up.

They didn't have to wait long for Erin to open her eyes. When her shoulders tightened defensively, Stratton smirked.

Her tongue slid over the open wound on her mouth. Her eyes were wary.

"Do you know, my dear, whose blood you're swallowing now?" Stratton snickered.

When Erin attempted to get up, she lost her balance and fell back, shaking her head as if trying to clear it. Stratton's lips curved in an ironic smile.

Lack of blood can do that to you.

She finally noticed Dane staring at her and raised her hand, about to touch a lock of his dark hair. He grabbed her fingers before she could succeed, putting her hand against his chest instead. He kissed her forehead, pretending he cared.

Stratton grimaced, his eyes glued to the screen.

Just wait. She'll soon discover that you're not so caring after all.

Almost as if she heard the warning, Erin got up, leaving the arms of Hope Acres' master vampire. She didn't get very far, collapsing on the floor before starting to vomit blood.

Dane was quick to assist her.

"You don't want her to get rid of all your blood, now do you?" Stratton sneered aloud.

Dane kept trying to hold on to her, but Erin was determined to reach her witch friend.

"If you don't let me go, I'll make you," Stratton heard Erin snap at Dane.

3

TOUCHED BY DARKNESS

Yes, let her go.

After a short argument, Dane finally released her.

On wobbly legs, Erin moved toward the young woman, shaking her softly. The witch's lashes lifted, and she blinked a couple of times as she slowly awakened.

"Well, did it work?" the witch asked.

Stratton's gut clenched, waiting for Erin's response.

You'd better hope you failed, little witch!

If Erin had managed to lose her powers, he was going to hurt someone. When the detective had informed him that Erin's new roommate had bought myrrh, sandalwood and rosemary incense in a magic shop, he had immediately realized what they were going to do. If he had believed for even one second that the witch would be successful in undoing the ritual Erin's father had performed, instead of placing hidden cameras in the Devereaux church on Halloween, he would have taken her out.

Concentrating on the sound of the high-tech receiver, he took a deep breath, concerned that he was about to find out that the time and money he had invested in Erin had been for nothing.

Sure, Erin had proven to be immensely entertaining when she had eaten the psychiatrist he had arranged to have her kidnapped. But he wasn't done with her yet.

Erin started calling out at the creatures in her head. Apparently, she couldn't hear them because she smiled briefly before she confirmed that the ritual had worked.

4

Stratton swore under his breath. As he stared at the screen, a red haze of anger started pulsing through him.

The witch had just signed her own death warrant.

Stratton was so furious that it took him several minutes before he realized that the witch had already fled the scene.

Then Dane uttered the words that saved the witch's life.

"*I can still smell the leopard.*"

"I guess we're still on," Stratton murmured. Perhaps the voices in her head had been vanquished, but her powers were still there, waiting for him to use them.

Even though Dane and Erin started to argue again, Stratton was lost in his own thoughts. The argument wasn't about the blood exchange, so he could still use the footage. He considered what he was going to do with it. He couldn't wait to show it to Erin, but informing her of Dane's betrayal right after it had happened was no fun. Besides, he liked nothing more than to test people, and he had always wanted to play one of his pranks on Dane. If only he could make Dane break down.

Once the other vampires witnessed Dane's break down, Stratton wouldn't have to educate his following anymore of their error in thinking they could leave him and join Dane. It had been five years since he had overheard two vampires plotting to seek refuge at Dane's.

Did Dane know? Did he do something to encourage others that he would be a better master?

It didn't matter. Dane was pathetic, and soon everyone would know.

Stratton sighed when Dane finally left the church. He leaned back in his chair while he continued to observe Erin.

He couldn't help but think back to the last time he had watched her. She had been naked, fearless and shining with power as she had confronted the enemy from her childhood. She was such a pleasure to watch. But if he wanted her to shine like before, he had to put her through hell first. She thrived on danger.

He couldn't wait to meet her in person. Puzzled, he zoomed in on her mouth when he heard her talking to herself. Or was she talking to someone else?

He frowned when Erin started laughing.

"I'm even relieved to hear Gideon," Stratton heard her say.

Gideon was the warlock who had died during the massacre that had nearly killed her. So not only had the ritual not been successful in removing her powers, but the ghosts of the creatures were haunting her still.

Erin, however, flashed a smile of relief. She seemed happy, oblivious to what Dane had done to her, oblivious to what Stratton had planned.

Stratton chuckled. "Let's have fun."

ONE

"A survival week in December?" Erin shivered with apprehension. The thought of taking her ghostly companions to a remote, rural place to mingle with her innocent colleagues was not an appealing one.

"Team buildin'." Frank's smooth southern accent broke off into a laugh at the concept. "Nikko called it a team-buildin' week. It could be kayaking or skiing. It will boost up our morale. Don't you want to lift up your spirits?"

"My spirits are fine, thank you very much."

"*Finally, she acknowledges us!*"

Erin winced as her half-sister's voice echoed through her mind. Sometimes it was difficult to hold a conversation when the souls of her supernatural family were chatting away as if they were in the room with her, not trapped inside her head.

"Besides," Erin continued, ignoring Leila's interruption, "a week away with Nikko and Sheila? I can only imagine it will hurt our morale, not improve it."

"*And there she goes, back to ignoring us,*" Gideon

complained.

Erin sighed. Because of the cacophony between her ears, she had trouble focusing on her conversation with Frank.

Surviving a ritual killing by her crazy, voodoo priest father when she was seven had left her with many scars. But the four other victims becoming a part of her—trapped inside her body like her own personal demons—was an ongoing punishment.

Right now, it was hard to recall why she'd been so upset at the thought of losing the voices last week when she believed that she had exorcised them from her mind forever.

After the silence, she had discovered that she missed her annoying, phantom sidekicks.

It was hard to believe how happy she had been when the voices had returned shortly after. Temporary insanity, that was all. Like some kind of traumatic bonding.

What was it called? Oh yes, Stockholm syndrome. I got so used to them taking over my body that I missed them invading my life and ruining it!

Gideon was the worst. She considered his obnoxious behavior part of his sinister warlock personality.

Closing her eyes, she gently started to press and rub her temples. Frank's touch on her back startled her.

"Are you alright?" he asked. "Are you really that worried about the survival week?"

Erin shook her head. "I'm fine. It's just a slight headache."

"*A headache! So that's what we are to her,*" Gideon grumbled.

"*Shut up, Gideon.*"

At least some of the voices defended her.

"You don't have to worry about a thing. I'll protect you. I'm very strong you know," Frank boasted while he flexed his muscles.

"And who'll protect you from me?" Erin muttered.

With his large, imposing form, Frank could make people wet themselves with a single glare. In spite of his brutish physique, he was the most kind-hearted person she knew.

He grinned, unaware of how easily she could tear him to pieces.

She wanted to tell him. She wanted to tell him everything. Frank was not just a colleague. He was a friend.

"Are you sure you want to be workin' overtime tonight with that headache?" A glimmer of sympathy appeared in his eyes. "You know, you shouldn't be workin' double shifts just so you can afford a pretty dress. Dane Lynch should accept you for who you are."

"I know that I don't *have* to buy a dress. And, you're right. I never thought I'd be someone who would bother getting all dressed up for some guy, but at least I'm paying for the dress myself."

Frank's lips curved in a smile. "That's true. You're probably the only person I know who would date the wealthiest creature in Louisiana without having at least some bling bling to show for it. I don't even think my Janice would have been that noble."

"Creature?" Erin asked. "Not man?"

He flushed. "I'm sorry, *chère*. That just slipped."

She frowned. "You think of Dane as a creature?"

He immediately shook his head. "I didn't mean it like that. It's just… They make me nervous."

Would I make you nervous?

"I'm glad that you're finally datin' someone and that he makes you happy. It's nice, but…" A shadow passed over his face. Then it was gone, replaced with a strained smile.

"But what?"

"…But I wish that he wasn't, you know, a vampire. I want you to go out with a normal person. Janice even has a friend she thinks is perfect for you. Like her, he's a teacher. Please don't tell Dane Lynch I said this. Last thing I want is to piss off Louisiana's most powerful vampire."

Erin's gaze flickered away from him. She hid the pain she felt at Frank's words. He didn't know that she didn't fall into the "normal" category either. Should she jeopardize their friendship by revealing her "otherness"?

"I guess I just need to get used to it, that's all."

She stared at him in silence. He shrugged before facing the screen once more. "It's like you've become a different person. It's not just you letting down your hair or the make-up…"

Self-conscious about her recent changes, Erin touched her face. "It's only a little bit. It's not too much, is it?"

Frank immediately shook his head. "*Non, ma*

soeur. But why are you askin' me if it's too much? Before Dane Lynch, you didn't care about other people's opinions. Nikko asked ya lots of times to do something about your appearance, and you told him to go to hell. It's like that vampire turned you into someone weak, insecure."

"*He's right,*" Altman said. The fatherly vampire caught inside her head sounded even more serious than usual.

"And I thought you couldn't stand Dane Lynch," Frank carried on. "Vampires can use mind control, right? What if that's the reason you're with him?"

"He did not glamour me," Erin said. "I would know."

Wouldn't I?

Why didn't Altman reassure her?

Erin instantly recalled a situation where a vampire had tried to use mind control on her. "Vincenzo tried to glamour me at the hospital last month. It didn't work. I guess I'm immune. Also, I do say *no* to Dane, occasionally. Like I said, I won't let him buy my dress."

"Why don't you just wear this lovely security guard uniform when you go out? He's seen you in it before, and you're still dating."

She laughed. "Technically, you know that we haven't gone out on a date yet, right? Tomorrow night will be our first official date. That's why I'm saving for that dress."

"It's a good investment since you'll need it again next month. I can't believe I forgot to tell you. There's some kind of gala at the end of the team-

11

buildin' week at one of Stratton's hotels in Las Vegas. We're allowed to invite our partners. Janice will be thrilled! First, they'll put us through hell, but a party is fun, *n'est-ce pas?*"

Erin smiled politely, but she couldn't help but worry. "Why are they organizing this for security guards? This must cost a fortune. Have you ever done something like this before?"

"We did a cooking workshop once. I wasn't sure how that would help me with my work. A physical activity makes more sense."

She sighed. What if the team-building trip was going to be so tough that she would have to pretend to be weaker than she was? Perhaps she was being paranoid, but after having just been kidnapped and recorded while she ate her attacker in leopard form, she thought it wise to use caution.

She half-listened to Frank as he talked about how excited he was about the gala. She was tired of having to pretend to be normal. The vampires and werewolves weren't hiding what they were anymore.

But what if my only human friend thinks I'm just a creature *too?*

"We might see famous people at the casino. Of course, Jonathan Stratton will be there. Maybe you could bring your vampire."

"I'm not sure Dane would like to meet my colleagues. I don't think he's into social events. Actually, I don't think I'm into social events either— Too expensive! I can buy a simple dress. I can't afford anything fancy."

Frank shook his head as he got up. "You could

still ask your new roommate to pay part of the rent. I'm sure that she wouldn't mind."

Erin pulled a face. "She's doing so much cleaning in my flat I feel as though I should be paying *her*. Besides, she's only just started her new job, and the pay is lousy. I don't want to take her money. She needs to save it, so she can rent a place of her own as soon as possible. I would rather have her live with me for a short period for free, than for a longer time and get paid a fortune."

Frank chuckled. "Not so much fun having a roommate, eh? I'd gladly offer you money, but I know that you'd never accept, so I won't bother. I can offer you something else though. It'll be a long day for you. Why don't you let me do the first round, so you can relax a bit?"

"I love you," she joked while staring at the security monitors.

"Are you sure you're alright?"

Erin lifted her gaze at the concerned tone in Frank's voice to find him standing in the doorway, watching her. His brow creased into deep lines with worry.

He cleared his throat. "Never mind. See you later."

She waited for him to leave before she got up to go to the bathroom. She approached the mirror and checked her make-up. Her cheeks were remarkably red, clashing with her pink lipstick and purple eye shadow. She didn't need make-up, so why had she suddenly decided to wear it? She shouldn't change herself for someone else.

TOUCHED BY DARKNESS

"*What's the matter, honey?*" Erin's mother asked.

Erin looked around, but the bathroom was empty.

"*You look fine,*" Leila said.

"Thanks, but Frank's right. This isn't me." She opened the tap and started splashing water on her face to remove the eye shadow.

"*Erin, you're being silly. Just leave it,*" Leila sighed.

"*She's always being silly, Leila. You should know that by now,*" Gideon grumbled.

Erin shrugged. "And you're always whining, Gideon. What else is new?"

"*It doesn't matter to Dane if you're wearing eye shadow or not. Hell, he probably won't even care that you're going to buy a dress. All he'll care about is seeing you without it,*" Altman grunted.

Erin's lips twitched. She agreed. She loved seeing Dane in jeans but having seen him without them… A weakness assaulted her, accompanied by an arousal that came just short of painful. She blamed her half-sister's leopard hormones.

"Thanks, Leila," Erin muttered under her breath. Unfortunately, the echo in the bathroom was loud enough for her half-sister to hear.

"*Now what did I do?*" Leila asked.

Erin ignored her, letting thoughts of Dane take over. His smell was so divine that she wanted to lick him, set her teeth in him…

A woman entered the bathroom, interrupting Erin's thoughts. When the stranger greeted her, Erin caught herself blushing in the mirror. She grabbed a towel to dry her face and hands before rushing back to her office.

Frank left the hospital at five o'clock sharp. Erin returned to the office with a hot cup of coffee after her third patrol of the hospital that day. She didn't really like the drink but hoped it would help keep her awake. She took a sip and shivered. If the caffeine wouldn't stop her from sleeping, the taste would. She sat back and looked at the security monitors in front of her. A couple of visitors were walking toward the elevator on the second floor, a doctor was flirting with one of the nurses on the fifth floor, and a cleaning lady was mopping the floors on the third floor. She sighed, slumping back in her chair.

I'm bored. During the day, she had always had Frank to keep her company. She hadn't realized how much she would miss him. She turned her head to the side and took a deep breath. The chair had a lovely, leathery smell. Rubbing her left temple, she closed her eyes. *Just for a few seconds.*

A rustling sound woke her up. Erin frowned at the walkie-talkie on her hip. The only person she had ever talked to on the walkie-talkie was her colleague Frank.

Since she was the only security guard on duty, she was surprised someone tried to reach her on it. A little worm of worry wriggled into her mind as she wondered if the night was going to be more eventful after all. Talking about being careful what you wish for…

TOUCHED BY DARKNESS

"Hello?" A stranger's voice crackled through the speaker, whispering softly. Erin couldn't determine if it belonged to a man or a woman.

She took the device out of the holder and put it in front of mouth. "This is Erin Holland speaking."

"Where's Steve? We need Steve here straight away!" It was a man's voice. "Send him to the fourth floor, now."

"Steve is on vacation. I'm repla—" A loud bang interrupted her.

"Oh fuck." Erin lowered the walkie-talkie in dismay.

"I don't give a shit who you are. Get up to the fourth floor, now!" the man shrieked. The banging sound became repetitive. "Hurry!"

A chill spiked through Erin's veins. For as long as she had been working in the hospital, she had feared that someday she would have to assist the doctors in the psych ward. Her mouth tightened, her knuckles whitening as she fisted her hands. She would *not* stop someone from escaping that hellish place. They could threaten her with a million lawsuits, but she refused to do so.

"*Go on,*" Altman ordered. "*Maybe it's not so bad. Not everyone is like Doctor Quirkhart.*"

"*Some people really do belong in a psychiatric hospital,*" her mother said quietly.

Well, she *hadn't* belonged there, and if she had been held against her will in such a place, others could be too.

Still, she ran out of her office, rushing up the stairs. The electronic card to unlock the door to the

16

psych ward was already in her left hand before she reached the floor.

Steeling her spine, she entered the hallway. She first noticed the two men in front of her. One was a blond man in his early forties and the other a younger, black-haired man with glasses. They were both wearing doctors' coats. Three nurses were hovering in front of a door whereas the men were leaning against it. Obviously, someone was trying to break out of the room.

"Finally!" the black-haired doctor cried out as soon as he spotted her. Then he hitched his breath.

Erin narrowed her eyes. "What's going on?"

"What do you think?" a pretty nurse snapped as she glared over her shoulder while trying to use a table to barricade the door.

Erin frowned when she recognized the girl. The nurse was the woman that Victor had told Erin he had once gone out with, and the memory of Victor was enough to cause Erin to clench her jaw in anger—Victor, her neighbor, her friend, the werewolf who had betrayed her. He had abused her trust and handed her over to a psychotic psychiatrist for his twisted experiments. Tasting an acrid film on her tongue, she continued to move forward.

Animal growls echoed from the room, causing Erin to wonder who or what was trapped inside it. Unease gnawed at her gut as she stopped in front of the group. She looked through the cracked window and took a step back as soon as she stared straight into a wolf's copper eyes.

Immediately she thought of Doctor Quirkhart

and his testing on her, trying to take her powers, seeing how he could change into a leopard himself.

Gritting her teeth, she glowered at the hospital staff. They were no better than her old psychiatrist. Instead of helping them restrain him, she should let him loose on them.

They deserved it.

"What are you doing standing there? Help us keep this door shut!" the younger doctor shouted at her. "Or maybe you should call a *man* to help out."

She scowled as she leaned against the door while the banging continued. A piece of cement next to her head broke off and fell on the floor. The whole doorway started to develop cracks.

"The door isn't going to hold him much longer," the other doctor warned.

"Well, maybe you should have thought of that before you decided to lock him in."

She noticed a spark of surprise in the doctor's eyes and wondered what he was playing at. "What?" She sniggered. "Aren't you keeping him here for your sick tests?"

There was a hint of genuine confusion in his eyes, and she realized that maybe she had misread the situation.

The doctor panted he put his hand against a small hole that had started to form in the wall. "What tests?" The hole quickly started to turn into a larger gap. "Billy works here as an intern. He was attacked last month. The wolf had bitten him several times, and he was lucky to have survived it."

"Yes. Lucky," Erin muttered.

"He came here and locked himself up voluntarily. He was worried he might harm someone if he wasn't locked up somewhere during the full moon."

"Do you perhaps have some drugs you can use to sedate him?" Erin asked.

He snorted. "Yeah, sure, there are lots of drugs here. But who is brave, or stupid enough to approach a werewolf in this state?"

"*If you go in there, you might get bitten.*" Erin shook her head at her mother's redundant comment.

"*You already turn furry occasionally,*" Gideon stated. "*A wolf bite won't make a big difference.*"

"*Yes, it would. Because then Erin would have to answer to the alpha of the Hope Acres' pack. No one would voluntarily do that,*" Altman said.

"How about calling the alpha of the Hope Acres' pack?" Erin asked the doctor. "Shouldn't he be involved?"

The man grunted as he continued to try to keep the door in its hinges. "Billy made us promise not to do that. It had to be one of the werewolves in Crispin's pack that had attacked him. He was terrified about seeing that wolf again."

Dane would know what to do, Erin thought.

It was tempting, very tempting to call Dane for help, so tempting that she froze in sudden wariness. For a woman who had been so pleased to finally be allowed to exercise control over all aspects of her life when she had gotten out of the asylum—with the exception of her current job where she did often feel trapped—she didn't want to rely too much on someone else.

TOUCHED BY DARKNESS

Tired of following Dane's orders, she decided to be reckless and do the one thing that Dane would forbid if he knew what her intention was going to be.

"Give me the drugs," she told the doctor. "I'm going in."

"What? No!" the man exclaimed, horrified.

"It is my job," she said impatiently. She turned and faced the door, annoyed that they were wasting time. Perhaps the doctor thought it wasn't right to have a woman defending him against one of his patients, even if technically Billy wasn't a patient. It didn't matter. Erin was a security guard, and she fought her own battles.

"Let her do it," the other doctor mocked. "Obviously she feels as though she has something to prove."

Erin refused to respond to the man's taunts. A pulsing fist of nausea grew in her throat as she held out her hand for the drugs. She couldn't help but think of the irony of the situation. The last time she was on that floor she had been the one getting drugged against her will. Tonight she was the one doing the drugging.

The black-haired doctor dropped the syringe in her open palm. Everyone stepped away from the door and watched as Erin put her hand on the door handle. Meanwhile, the banging had stopped.

Erin frowned as she peeked through the window of the room. In spite of the glow of the moon, bright enough to light up most of the room, she wasn't able to see the wolf.

"*Erin, are you sure this is a good idea?*" her mother

asked.

Because of the curious stares of the hospital staff, Erin decided not to answer.

Of course this was a bad idea. Where was Billy? What if he was hiding next to the door, waiting for her to open it and ready to pounce?

Blowing out a breath, she sucked in another, the action shaky.

She opened the door.

A growl of rage filled the stale air of the hospital an instant before the werewolf's body slammed out of the room and into Erin, taking her down. She hit the ground so hard that her breath whooshed out of her on impact. She dropped the syringe and cursed as it rolled out of her reach. She heard the people around her scream.

She had to use both hands to keep her attacker from mauling her to death and forgot all about the syringe. She grabbed the creature's neck and pushed its muzzle away from her face. The strong smell of wet dog made her gag.

The werewolf snarled as its eyes met hers, primitive and devoid of civilized thought, a rabid animal. She heard the fabric of her uniform tear as the werewolf's claws ripped through the sleeves.

"*Careful*," her mom warned.

"Hell no," Erin said. Her knee swung up and connected with its balls. Grunting with pain, the large creature fell off her. She got up and kept it in her sights while crouched, eyes narrowed, her breathing heavy now.

"Hey, er, security guard?" a man behind her said.

TOUCHED BY DARKNESS

"I've got the tranquilizer here."

Erin looked down at the hand of the blond doctor holding out the syringe. She turned to grab it. Without warning, her body lifted, picked up as if she weighed no more than a feather, and she was flung forward. She could not evade the glass door as she plowed into it. Glass crashed and shattered around her. It bit across her shoulders as she went through the door. She landed on the linoleum floor. The nurse shrieked.

Still dazed from the blow, Erin did nothing as she was jerked upright and thrown into the wall hard enough to knock her teeth together. She saw flashes of light before her vision cleared enough to see the werewolf dart forward. She summoned up enough strength to kick out high with her feet, catching it in its face.

Blood spurted from its nose.

She lunged at it and inflicted a blow near its right shoulder.

A roar of rage tore from its lips.

She smashed her fist in its throat.

It gagged and jerked away.

Adrenaline coursed through her veins, and her heart raced but not from fear. Her leopard was emerging.

Erin let her leopard rise to the surface, her senses expanding as she concentrated on letting the wolf feel the energy of her animal.

A moment later, the wolf sniffed the air, and its eyes turned even more chaotic and panicked, a rabbit caught in the headlights of something monstrous.

"Who's the predator now?" Erin whispered.

Triumph rushed through her as she hit the wolf's muscular form like a freight train. Not realizing that she had partially shifted, she struck at the werewolf with her left arm, intending to give him another blow.

The werewolf made a high-pitched sound as her claw tore open its right cheek and part of its neck. Blood stained the front of Erin's uniform, bursting across the fabric like a painter's spray.

"Shit," Erin murmured as she knelt on the werewolf, one knee shoving hard into its stomach. Relieved that her right hand had remained in human form, she held it up. "Syringe," she said.

She kept her eyes on her prey while someone put the tranquilizer in her hand.

Panting, the werewolf looked up at her, mesmerized. Or was it terrified? She pulled the cap from the needle with her teeth and plunged the needle into its neck. She depressed the syringe.

"Erin, what are you doing?"

Erin was so shocked to hear Dane's angry voice that she froze. Turning from the wolf, she looked up. "Dane?"

While she had been fighting, the corridor had cleared out. The only person remaining was the blond doctor.

"What is it?" the doctor asked. "Do you need me to help you hold him down?"

"I'm at the hospital. Erin. Where the hell are you?" Dane's voice again.

"Fuck off, Dane," Erin said.

TOUCHED BY DARKNESS

The doctor narrowed his eyes at her.

She jumped when something bit the back of her right wrist, a vicious sting hard enough to bring her focus back to the creature beneath her.

Her stomach lurched. She suppressed a scream as she pulled her arm from the werewolf's muzzle. She elbowed it sharply in the stomach, but it shook off the blow and snapped at her as if it hadn't even felt it.

"Billy, stop it! That's not you," the blond doctor cried out.

"When is the tranquilizer supposed to work?" Erin asked.

The doctor knelt down beside her and finally helped her with restraining the wolf while waiting for the drugs to work.

"Straight away," he replied. "The tranquilizer is very strong. He'll be out for the rest of the night and should wake up in human form."

The large wolf kept staring at Erin, its large glistening eyes pleaded with her for deliverance. Pity choked her throat.

"Soon you'll be able to sleep," she said. "And when you wake up, you'll feel better."

Shortly after, the werewolf passed out. Erin continued to hold him.

The blond doctor looked at her in admiration. "That was amazing. Are all female werewolves stronger than the males?"

"Wrong question," a cold voice behind them said.

Goose bumps rose across Erin's flesh as she realized who had arrived.

"The question should be: '*What makes you think you can endanger yourself like this without there being any consequences?*'"

Erin's head snapped up.

Dane smiled at her. His eyes glittered like hard stones, and the chill that crept up her spine felt like the crawling of a thousand spidery legs.

TWO

Erin's stomach shriveled in on itself as she got on her feet to confront Dane. She told herself not to let him intimidate her, yet her hand was fisted so tight, she was cutting half-moons into her palm.

"W-what are you doing here?" Her voice hitched as she walked up to him. "I thought our date was set for tomorrow."

"Did you just tell me to fuck off?" Dane's tone was as tough as flint, and so was his expression. She shivered in apprehension. His mouth was set in a grim line.

She heard footsteps behind them and knew that it was the blond doctor even before he coughed to draw their attention.

"Are you alright?" the man asked.

Dane responded by putting his arm around her waist in an outrageously proprietary way. "Obviously she isn't." His tone was blade sharp. "You're covered in blood."

"It's not mine," Erin said.

Dane pointed at what remained of the glass door. Shards, dark tipped with blood, were jagged in the frame.

"Okay, some of it's mine. I'm not really hurt." She peeked at her right wrist. There was a smudge of dried blood, but she couldn't see any cut flesh, not that she wanted to take a closer look. The blood had to belong to that werewolf from when she had slashed open its cheek. Its teeth must not have pierced her skin after all.

I must have imagined it.

She let out a sigh of relief.

Such drama over nothing.

"I'll be the judge of that." His large hands gripped her waist, and he picked her up and set her on the counter. He lifted the fabric from her stomach, intent on examining every part of her. "He tore holes in your clothes. It's a miracle he didn't tear holes in you too."

She flinched when she saw the tiny pieces of glass stuck inside her skin.

"Fucking hell! Because of your quick healing the glass is turning into a part of you." He looked up at her, his eyes narrow and unforgiving. "I'll cut it out of your skin before it becomes a permanent part of your body."

"And have you drool over my blood!" She arched one eyebrow. "I'm fine. We're in a hospital, remember? I'm sure one of the doctors can handle—"

"And what's this?" he interrupted, peeling away the stained sleeve of her right arm to reveal the crimson mark on her wrist. When he started rubbing at the stain, his actions removed the dried blood.

Erin drew a deep breath when she saw the

smooth skin underneath. Definitely no bite marks. Her eyes hadn't been deceiving her.

"Not what you were expecting?" he asked mockingly.

Annoyed, she shoved her hand against Dane's chest. His mouth was on hers before she could do more than part her lips to respond. He branded her with his kiss. His tongue arrowed into her mouth with one swift thrust, and Erin's body took over.

She heard footsteps fading into the background before realizing how unprofessional her behavior was. The realization broke the spell and sent anger rocketing through her. "You have nothing to say about what I do with my life." She pushed him away and glared at him.

He stared at her with a hungry intensity that sent a quiver along her nerve endings.

"I propose we compromise."

"Compromise," Erin repeated. When she realized that they were drawing the doctor's attention, she lowered her voice. "Whatever for?"

"Well, you did tell your lover of one week to fuck off, and that may have hurt his feelings," Dane explained dryly.

She shook her head in blatant disbelief. "What feelings? So far we've only slept together once, and if that means you're going to act crazy possessive and butt in when I'm working, then I don't even want to have an encore."

"Someone should butt in with your work. Look at you, all because of your stupid pride. You should have let me buy you that fucking dress. And this isn't the first time that your job gets you covered in blood. I recall you were pretty happy with me 'butting in' the last time."

She stiffened. "I'm not going to defend my job to you."

"You should quit. You can live with me where I can keep an eye on you."

"*He wants you to live with him,*" her half-sister Leila cheered. "*Do it, do it, do it! I know you want to.*"

Living with him does make me happy. Damn, I need my head examined.

"*No, you don't want to live with him. He'll put you in a cage. You didn't leave the asylum to let him take over,*" Erin's mother warned.

"*She doesn't even like her job,*" Leila said. "*I wouldn't mind being a kept woman.*"

A kept woman.

That settled it.

"I'm not quitting my job," Erin said.

"We will talk about it tomorrow on our date."

She crossed her arms across her chest. "I'm not so sure I want to go on that date anymore."

"Don't kid yourself that you can get out of our date or get out of discussing what happened here tonight."

She gave him a hostile look. "What's there to discuss?"

"We'll talk about it tomorrow."

She noticed the blond doctor observing them and experienced discomfort talking to Dane with a stranger listening in. On the other hand, she was probably safer having the conversation now than

29

when it was just the two of them.

"*We can't be together if you have me worrying about your safety all the time,*" Dane said telepathically.

"You want to break up?" *Please don't!* "And stop talking in my head. What the hell? Is that some kind of side effect of sleeping with a vampire? Because then we shouldn't sleep together anymore."

"What!" Dane's expression grew black. "Hell no! Listen, I realize that you're probably fed up with having voices in your head and may have been surprised with hearing an additional one," he acknowledged.

"Did I hear correctly?" she asked. "Did the master vampire of Hope Acres just apologize to me?"

"Not quite," he said. "But I'm not sure I'm thinking clearly. I'll continue with my examination of your body tomorrow night to reassure myself."

"*He can do a thorough examination of my body any time,*" Leila said.

Erin felt color seeping up her neck, into her face. "I don't hear what you're saying. I'm still in shock over you apologizing."

"As long as you don't expect me to apologize for kissing you. I could never apologize for that."

"Hmm, I guess we're both suffering from side effects then."

"So... Are you willing to risk more side effects tomorrow?" he challenged her.

Heat rippled through her. "Let's just see how the date goes first, right? So... we're good?"

Throwing her a grin of pure delight, he turned around. "You'll see." Before reaching the stairs, he called out, "I'll pick you up at seven."

The words were a sultry promise, and Erin shivered with longing as she watched him leave.

When she felt a hand on her arm, she had to suppress a primitive growl. She looked up and found the blond doctor staring at her. Something in her gaze must have revealed how she felt, because he immediately withdrew his hand.

"Here," he said as he handed her a leaflet. "I also wrote my number on it. You can call me anytime."

She frowned when she read the title on the leaflet.

Abusive Relationships.

She didn't know whether to laugh or cry. Gideon and Leila did though, because they started to snicker, and she could have sworn that even her mother joined in the fun.

Erin sighed. "Ha ha, very funny."

"No, it's not funny at all," the doctor protested. "I specialize in these kinds of relationships, so I recognize the signs. It's never too late to leave. Although, it may be difficult to reject the master vampire of Hope Acres. But as a werewolf, you should be able to get support from the werewolf community. Can't you ask Crispin for advice?"

"What makes you think I'm a werewolf?"

"Sorry. Your claw gave you away. But, thank God you're a werewolf. The situation is bad enough with Billy. I would hate it if we were responsible for creating another one."

"I didn't get bit." She showed him both her arms. "See, no marks."

31

TOUCHED BY DARKNESS

The doctor shrugged. "It doesn't matter. You're already one anyway. But please think about what I said. You can get help. And don't forget to go to the ER to get that glass removed."

Erin merely raised an eyebrow at him and turned around without responding. The doctor's remarks didn't warrant a response. Before she reached the stairs, she walked past a bin. She threw the leaflet away. The doctor had probably witnessed her chucking his leaflet, but she didn't care about offending him.

It was all nonsense.

I'm not a werewolf, I never got bit and Dane's not abusive. He's the sweetest ... She snorted.

Yeah, right. I'm fucked.

Her roommate shrieked as soon as Erin opened the door to her studio apartment.

"What the hell happened to you?" Pauline asked.

"You should see the other guy," Erin said as she unbuttoned the top of her uniform.

"Oh my God." Pauline walked up to her and took the torn and bloody jacket from her before she could throw it on the floor. "The dried blood has made your clothes all hard."

"Yes, and they smell awful." Erin cringed. "Sorry, I smell awful."

"Someone attacked you? Who was it? Do you need me to do a spell?"

"Whoa, calm down, Pauline." Erin raised her

32

hands. "I thought you weren't going to do any dark magic anymore."

"Er, of course not. A tracking spell so we er, we can tell the police where he is." Red fire flamed across Pauline's cheeks.

"Say that once more, but now as if you mean it." She winked at Pauline. She looked down at her dirty bra glued to her body and had trouble removing it. "Yuk, it's stuck. I'm making myself gag. I need a shower."

"Nobody stopped you walking around like that?"

"Yeah, right. Would you stop someone on her bike who is covered in blood?"

"Okay maybe not, but what happened?"

Erin sighed. "One of the orderlies had been attacked by a werewolf, and tonight he shifted for the first time. I needed to subdue him. He didn't want to be subdued."

"Why was he at the hospital? Don't they have some kind of community to police their own?"

She nodded. "Yes, but I understand why he didn't want to join them. I wouldn't want to be part of a pack where one of the members attacked me."

Pauline frowned. "I think it's irresponsible. He could have created more werewolves... Oh my God, what if you're going to become a werewolf too?"

Erin walked toward the shower, muttering, "Not you too." She slammed the bathroom door shut.

"Did he bite you?" Pauline asked through the closed door.

Can't I have a moment's peace? At least she didn't follow me inside.

"Don't worry, Pauline. I don't have a mark on me," Erin called out as she turned on the shower. She closed her eyes and put her head under the water jet. The sound of the water blocked any sound Pauline might have made.

Several minutes passed before she turned off the shower. She examined her right wrist once more. There was no mark.

Thank God.

She then inspected her stomach. Now that one of the ER doctors had removed the glass, that part of her also felt smooth as silk as if nothing had happened.

Nothing happened. I'm fine.

She grabbed a large shirt from the laundry basket. Ordinarily, she would never put on dirty clothes after having taken a shower, but she knew Pauline felt uncomfortable around nudity.

I miss having an apartment to myself.

Reluctant to leave the bathroom and having to answer more questions, she leaned against the sink and closed her eyes.

"*You can't hide in here forever,*" Altman said. Of all the voices in her head, the vampire was her favorite.

"I'm so tired of these questions," she whispered. "First Dane, then that doctor and now Pauline. They're all hounding me. I just want to go to bed."

"*You should go to bed. It's the middle of the night,*" Altman said. "*Tomorrow is early enough to think about possible ramifications.*"

"You sound just like Dane. Do all vampires talk alike? Ramifications, consequences... Nothing happened."

34

"I'm sure you're fine," her mother said.

Erin forced herself to smile and opened the bathroom door.

Pauline had turned off all the lights and was lying on her mattress.

Thanks to her leopard senses, Erin had no problems seeing in the dark. Not that she had to worry about tripping over clothes or shopping bags now that she had Pauline as a live-in-maid. Resentment against Pauline and her obsessive cleaning churned inside Erin. Erin wished she had time to herself and that was impossible now that she had offered to let someone she hardly knew share her one-bedroom apartment with her. She felt a stab of guilt as she thought about what Pauline had gone through before and how she had tried to help Erin.

She walked up to her bed and sat down on it. She could tell by Pauline's uneven breathing that she wasn't asleep and had been waiting for her roommate's return so she could continue her inquisition.

"Erin?"

I shouldn't be a jerk.

"I'm sorry if I exaggerated about your appearance. I er, I'm really glad that you're letting me stay here," Pauline said.

Erin slid under the covers. "I'm not kicking you out."

She smiled when she heard Pauline's sigh of relief.

"Is it okay if I ask you one more question?" Pauline asked.

35

"You just did… I'm sorry. I didn't mean to snap at you. What is it?"

"You er, you said you didn't have a mark on you. But is that because you weren't bit?"

"I wasn't bit," Erin said.

"Oh thank God! I thought it could be hard for you to get a mark anyway with your leopard genes. You mentioned once that you heal quicker than us normal folk."

She swallowed the lump in her throat.

I do heal quicker.

"Good night, Erin."

"Good night." Her voice cracked, but Pauline didn't seem to notice.

She turned to lie on her side and closed her eyes. She shivered involuntarily. She had one last lucid thought before sleep took over.

Did I feel its teeth pierce my skin?

THREE

"Just because you ran off to join your blood slave last night doesn't mean that we're going to leave you alone," Karma said as he strolled into Dane's basement.

Dane shot to his feet as the words *blood slave* caused a jolt of horror to swirl inside him like a tornado. He watched the gray-haired vampire approach his desk.

How the hell does Karma know about Erin? Did he tell anyone? Does Erin know?

"Oh, was it a secret?" Karma drawled. "Don't worry. I don't think anyone else realized why you were acting like a man possessed yesterday. Did you leave without saying anything because you sensed that she was in some kind of danger? So, what'd happened to the poor girl?"

Gritting his teeth, Dane refused to answer.

Karma laughed. "They're supposed to worship you, not the other way around."

"I wouldn't know."

"Your first blood slave?" Karma studied his face. "I warned you to stop focusing on less important things, or at least wait until we're gone."

TOUCHED BY DARKNESS

Erin isn't important.

But she was always in the back of his mind, and during the day, as he had lain restless, the image of her haunted him. Now that Erin had become his unwitting blood slave—thanks to his quick thinking—he discovered some side effects he hadn't taken into account when he had created the blood bond.

Suddenly, their blood connection alone wasn't enough. He wanted more from her. He wanted her to be with him of her own volition, not because of something he had forced upon her while she was passed out. He needed her to love him.

He sighed. The blood exchange affected him more than he had expected. It was eerie to feel emotion and realize it was hers. The connection between them was now every bit as powerful as the volatile chemistry he sensed whenever they were together. He could not recall the last time he had felt so little in control, especially of his physical desires. What was it about Erin that found a way around his brain and tapped into feelings he had put into cold storage centuries ago?

"Hello, Earth to Dane Lynch?" Karma smirked, a smug knowing twist of his lips.

It took a great deal of effort, but Dane swallowed his annoyance and settled back into his chair. "You promised me that the council would leave me alone."

"Yes." Karma waved a report at him. "But nobody gets out of the paperwork."

Dane pinned him with a glare.

Karma chuckled. "So, are you going to tell me what happened with your blood slave?"

He considered telling him that it was none of his business, but Karma seemed to have some experience with the blood bond. He could use his expertise. "Erin was trying to subdue a werewolf. It's her work. She keeps getting in trouble."

"That's all?" Karma shrugged. "Just tell her to quit her job. She'll want to please you and be happy about it."

Erin following orders…

He thought of Erin's face in the harsh fluorescent hospital light. She had looked exhausted, not happy at all with his arrival. Curling locks had framed her face, giving her an angelic appearance that had been a stark contradiction with the blood covering the rest of her. The blood had matched the evil look she had thrown his way. "She'll refuse."

Karma frowned. "Really? Well, with your reputation, you can always get her boss to fire her."

"Jonathan Stratton owns her company."

Karma raised his eyebrows. "I didn't know that Stratton owned companies in Hope Acres. Did he hire her just because of your relationship with her?"

"No, she's been working there ever since she got here. I didn't even know her then. Stratton hired her because of her father. Have you heard about Oliver Merenda?" When Karma shook his head, Dane explained, "That's her father. Twenty years ago, he tried to kill Stratton in order to take away his power, but he disappeared before he could be punished. Stratton wanted to get back at him through her. In fact, I'm sure that if I asked him to fire her, it would only make him more eager to hold on to her."

39

"Sorry," Karma said, but there was laughter in his deep voice. "Maybe you can tell her about Stratton's history with her father? Or you could offer her a better job. One that's safe. Do you need help with building that shopping mall? I heard there have been some protests."

"Yes, but I don't want to put her in front of an angry crowd either."

"Is security all she knows? If so, she's bound to get into trouble. You can't keep running off every time she's having problems at work."

"You're right. She should get out of security." Dane smiled. "I'm overcomplicating things. I should just get her a higher education. Studying is safe."

"And I suppose her being indebted to you for paying that education is a nice bonus." Karma sniggered. "So now that we've got that settled, shall we finish this?"

Karma put the file on his desk. Reluctantly, Dane picked it up. In silence, he read the account of how he ended up killing Gregorio, the previous master vampire of Hope Acres. The account was accurate, so he signed it without any protest. He handed over the file, and Karma grinned as he took it.

"Now that was easy. Don't you wish now you had signed this straight away before running off to your security guard?"

Through gritted teeth he said, "Good night, Karma."

Karma walked to the door. "Don't bother getting up. I'll see myself out. Good luck, Dane. You'll need it."

He waited for the sound of the front door to close before he mumbled, "Good riddance."

Dane turned on his computer. He opened his mailbox and narrowed his eyes when he spotted an email from Jonathan Stratton in his inbox. He double-clicked on the message. A chill ran down his spine when he read "Surprise" and noticed the file attached.

He knew that whatever was in that file, he was going to have to go to war with Stratton. Part of him reveled in the battle ahead. His previous victory over the Las Vegas master vampire had felt empty, not very satisfying at all. It had been too easy since Stratton had hardly put up a fight when he had told him to stay away from Erin.

As soon as Dane saw the first image on the computer monitor, he knew why.

Stratton had never been defeated.

He stiffened when he saw a close up of Erin. The camera had zoomed in on her while she was unconscious, and Dane knew straight away what he was about to watch. Anger welled up as he saw himself exchanging blood with Erin while she was passed out. The film lasted for only three minutes but it felt like a full-length movie. He made himself watch it twice before he grabbed his cell phone.

He hesitated. Getting Stratton to fire Erin now would be impossible. Obviously, Stratton had decided to continue whatever horror he had planned with Erin and thought he could blackmail Dane to step aside.

He thought wrong.

The best way to deal with a blackmailer was to

reveal the secret he was trying to hide.

Fuck! If he had any doubt about his feelings for Erin, the terror he experienced over her finding out about the blood exchange taught him exactly how much she affected him. Why would he care that she should know? He never cared about anyone's feelings but his own before he met her.

But he did care. It wasn't just because he worried that their bond was too fragile, too fresh, or that he knew she didn't need him as much as he needed her. It was the knowledge that she would be upset once she found out about his betrayal, and that thought burned as if a knife had been thrust and turned into his gut. He hoped that over time, the bond would tighten, making it impossible for her to leave him.

Considering how she had been able to stand up to him the previous night, that time would not be soon.

His second option was to kill Stratton, which was his favorite choice. Stratton had many enemies wanting him dead, and he had proven to be very hard to kill. That didn't mean it was impossible. Dane hadn't seriously tried it after all.

He decided to ask Brock to do some investigative work on Stratton. Perhaps he could form an alliance with his enemies. His lips curved when he thought about going to the Council. They would probably approach Stratton to sign a couple of documents, stating that from now on he would try to act like a good, little vampire.

Another solution was to blackmail the blackmailer. Stratton was still pretending to be human and even put gray highlights in his hair to pretend he was aging. Alas, Dane realized that Stratton didn't do this because he was afraid to out himself as a vampire. Stratton was someone who enjoyed messing with people's heads, and this was just another one of his pranks.

He needed to find a secret that Stratton really wanted to keep hidden. For that, he needed time. While he was trying to find a way to outsmart him, Stratton had a free hand to play with Erin.

A chill slithered through Dane's veins, and his lips thinned. "No, I won't allow it," he vowed.

He took a deep breath before dialing Stratton's direct number.

The phone rang four times before he heard a familiar click.

"Dane, you're up early." He could hear the smile in Stratton's voice.

"Stratton." Although Dane's voice seemed casual, a darker, calculating edge simmered beneath the surface. "I got your message."

"Splendid." He heard laughter echo through the handset.

Dane's frosty gaze locked on the screen in front of him. "Get to the point."

"What point? I just thought you looked so sweet together. You might want something to remember it by. You know what, maybe I should send a copy to Erin too. Yes, I should have her email address somewhere."

"You won't do that," Dane said.

"Oh, why wouldn't I?"

"Because I know you. You like dragging things out. Holding this over my head for a while would give you more satisfaction than sending this to Erin straight away."

Stratton sighed. "Yes, you're right. I suppose I could wait to tell her, unless you give me a reason to tell her now."

"Why don't you come over so we can discuss it?"

"Oh, how primitive." Stratton chuckled. "No, I'm happy discussing this over the phone."

I'll bet.

"Fine," Dane said.

"What's 'fine'? You mean that you will give me a reason to tell her now?"

"No, I won't." Dane kept his voice low, but his cold tone carried.

"Splendid," Stratton repeated. "Well, as always, it's been a pleasure talking to you. I'd love to chat some more, but I have some *plans* to prepare for our favorite security guard."

Stratton disconnected before Dane could think of a reply. Gritting his teeth, he felt fury raging brutally though him. Stratton would not get away with this. Dane needed to find a way to have the upper hand before Stratton not only got between him and Erin, but also, before he found a way to harm her. He knew that the sadistic, Vegas vampire was inventive enough to find ways to torment her.

He thought about his date tonight with Erin and knew that he was not going to be on his best behavior. She might get upset.

Tough, Erin needed to accept him as he was. He

was going to let off some steam. His lips twitched. The night could end on a happy note after all. Not allowing Stratton to get to him was the best revenge he could think of.

But he shouldn't let his date with Erin distract him. Stratton had to be destroyed. For that, Dane needed knowledge.

Dane deleted Stratton's email and switched off his computer. He left his desk, walked up the stairs and stopped in front of Brock's room. He knocked once before opening the door. He didn't wait for Brock's permission to enter.

Brock left his bed as soon as he entered. In silence, he put on his trousers, leaving his ebony chest bare.

"I want you to investigate Jonathan Stratton," he instructed his second-in-command. "I have to know everything you can find on him; his routine, his skeletons, anything. Even if you think it's irrelevant, this is priority number one."

Brock grinned. "Finally, I'll start working on this straight away."

He studied his suddenly eager-to-please assistant. "You're looking forward to going to war with Stratton? You think you're up for it?" His eyes narrowed a fraction, causing Brock to stiffen with anger.

"If you're having doubts about my competence, maybe you should get Erin Holland to be your second-in-command."

He sighed inwardly. He knew Brock was trying to hide his insecurity by acting out. It grated on his nerves. Brock should have gained more confidence in his new position by now.

When Dane remained silent, Brock swallowed nervously. "Uh no, I'm not really looking forward to it. But I know you can fight him and win. I wish someone had taught that bastard a lesson ages ago, not that you should have done something before. He never did anything to you. It's just that he's been getting away with too much shit for far too long."

After a nod to Brock, Dane left the room.

Stratton has *been getting away with too much shit*, Dane silently agreed.

Stratton was a known sadist who enjoyed finding out people's weaknesses and confronting them with it.

Dane had heard of a vampire Stratton sired about fifty years ago, whose daughter he had kidnapped for fun. The five year old had been talked into acting as if she had recently been turned into a vampire. The act had been so convincing that the mother had attacked Stratton in despair. Of course, she hadn't been able to do any real damage. Stratton had not been amused that someone had dared to assault him, so he had punished her by really siring her daughter. The child vampire couldn't survive and had to be killed. After that, the Council officially announced that siring anyone under the age of sixteen would be a capital offense. Such a statement should never have been necessary.

Yes, Stratton had been getting away with too much crap, but it stopped now. He wouldn't tolerate Stratton causing Erin any distress, and he would not let Stratton interfere with their relationship.

He pondered over the situation. He had to be realistic. For now, he had no choice but to give in to his blackmailer, which meant he had to back off while Brock tried to find incriminating information on Stratton. The Las Vegas vampire was so twisted, it should be easy to find. But Brock had to hurry with the investigation.

His white knuckles stood out as he fisted his hands. His intentions of getting Erin to quit her job tonight needed to be postponed for the time being. He shook his head, annoyed with himself. They would have to find other topics to talk about instead.

What would she cherish most in the world? he wondered. *And could I give it to her?*

Almost automatically, his mind moved to what *he* cherished most in the world, and he froze when the answer came to him without any pause.

Erin.

The realization terrified him. What if she was taken from him? What if she left him?

For the second time that evening, he said, "No, I won't allow it."

FOUR

"*You're so quiet. Do I look so ghastly?*" *the young woman asked. She stood in the center of the room while a dressmaker was finishing off her pastel pink outfit.*

"*You're stunning, Jane, and you know it. Your coming out party will be sensational. You'll have men fighting to be on your dance card.*"

"*And will you let them, big brother? Or will you scare them away?*" *She coyly batted her lashes at him.*

"*You're a gently bred lady, Jane. Don't let me hear about you flirting with any rakes.*"

The dressmaker styled Jane's gown and then stepped away to admire her work. Jane's outfit had a fitted bodice with a skirt that fell from just beneath her breasts to the floor. Catching the skirt to hold it wide, Jane turned on one toe.

"*I feel like a princess. Thank you, Dane!*" *She then ran up to him and put her arms around him. "You're the best brother.*"

He closed his eyes, enjoying the familiar warmth, her silky soft hair against his cheek, inhaling the smell of her, pure vanilla. "Oh Jane. I've missed you so."

When he opened his eyes, he discovered he was holding Erin in the Devereaux church instead. She was unconscious,

48

her complexion deathly white. He brushed a lock of her
blond hair behind her right ear.

He stared at her. Excited.
Excited?

"Erin?" A woman's voice startled her awake. "Erin, wake up."

Erin abruptly sat up, momentarily confused by her surroundings, the time, her company.

She focused on the person who had spoken. "Oh, hi Pauline. What time is it?"

"Late. Wow, you look exhausted. You really shouldn't work double-shifts anymore."

"Yeah, I'm trying to cut down my daily werewolf attacks too. It plays havoc with my complexion." Running her fingers through her hair, she stood up from the small bed, her body feeling tense and stiff, and her muscles aching.

"Maybe you should cancel," Pauline suggested.

"Cancel?"

Pauline laughed. "Don't tell me you forgot about your date!"

Erin groaned and rubbed her eyes. "Canceling sounds brilliant. How much time have I got?"

"Less than an hour. Don't worry, I'm a miracle worker!"

"Why aren't you saying anything? Is it too short?" Erin asked Pauline. A minute had passed since she had walked out of the bathroom, and her roommate still had not uttered a single word.

Erin wore a red dress with short sleeves and a skirt that stopped just above the knees. A gray wrap covered her arms.

"I *am* a miracle worker! Well, apart from the shoes. You really can't wear sneakers with that outfit."

Erin shrugged. "I haven't got any other shoes. Besides, I want to feel comfortable. I'm nervous enough as is it."

"Part of being a woman, I'm afraid. Here." Pauline gave her a pair of black high heels. "Try these on."

To please Pauline, she took off her sneakers and squeezed her feet in her roommate's shoes. They were at least half a size too small. She was about to remove them when Pauline blurted out, "You look hot."

Erin walked up to the mirror and took in her new appearance. Pauline was right. The high heels completed the picture. But Erin couldn't help but tease her roommate as she cocked an eyebrow at her. "Hot to you or hot to him?"

A blush stained Pauline's cheeks, and she folded her arms across her chest. "Just because I named your cat Willow doesn't mean I'm gay! I'm a witch, that's all."

A knock on the door interrupted their conversation. A chill of exciting dread shot through her. She thought about the vivid dream she had just woken up from.

He'd acted so gentle, apart from the ending. That had been just weird.

Pauline grinned and winked at her. "Go on. Let's

see if he's wearing jeans on your date."

Erin frowned and whispered, "Don't embarrass me." She straightened her shoulders and tried to ignore the nosy witch hovering behind her.

"Good evening," Erin began with the sort of cheery enthusiasm she imagined appropriate for a first date. As she caught sight of Dane, her eyes widened in appreciation of the picture he made on her doorstep.

"*Yum, yum,*" Leila cheered.

"*Leila…*" Erin's mother warned her stepdaughter.

Erin hoped they wouldn't talk throughout the entire date.

"Good evening," Dane echoed, his low-pitched voice making the ordinary greeting a caress.

He cordially inclined his head, and she shivered. He said nothing about her appearance. He merely smiled, taking in the whole of her with barely leashed hunger. He took a deep breath, as if tasting the air.

"Nice outfit." Pauline chuckled.

Erin shot her new friend a warning look, hoping she wouldn't humiliate her.

Dane looked gorgeous in his black shirt and jeans, his hair slightly disheveled by the wind. The clothes made him appear sexy and mysterious—a dark knight. Irresistible.

He held out his hand. "Shall we?"

Erin cleared her throat before she tentatively placed her fingers against his, smooth and electrifying. "Of course."

She let him lead her out of the apartment, and they left her ramshackle building. She thoroughly enjoyed touching his arm, and her only regret was that she wasn't able to touch more of him. She unconsciously tightened her grip when they reached his sleekly designed automobile. He assisted her, and as she swung her bare legs inside, she glanced up, and her breath caught. The bluishness of his eyes seemed to snag her gaze. The tension in his jaw told her that he was just as affected by her as she was by him.

"So, where are we going?" she tried to ask nonchalantly as soon as he settled into the seat behind the wheel. She was afraid she failed. She didn't feel nonchalant tonight. Instead, she felt an alarming combination of elation and anxiousness. Goosebumps rose across her skin, and she tightened the wrap around her.

"It's a surprise."

She gazed outside at the dark trees flashing by. They drove for about fifteen minutes in silence before he turned to the right, and they parked down by the riverfront. A large red riverboat awaited them.

She shut the door of the dark blue Mercedes and walked across the empty parking lot, Dane a silent presence by her side. He reminded her of a tiger. Quiet, just before it struck its prey to sate its voracious appetite.

The sky above them was black, the air hot and heavy with moisture, promising rain in the evening heat. Her gray shawl slid down her back, and she let it stay there. As they approached the dock, she could hear piano music.

Carefully, she stepped onto the shaky boardwalk toward the entrance. Dane solicitously held the door for her, ushering her in ahead of him.

A tall African-American woman wearing a long white dress welcomed them. "Monsieur Lynch. We are honored to have you and your partner as our guests this evening."

His partner. She didn't even look at me.

Erin smiled.

Who can blame her?

"Will you please follow me?"

They went through a narrow hallway, walking behind each other. Her fingers clenched as Dane put his surprisingly warm hand against her naked shoulder. His touch made her shiver. A week ago, he had introduced her to sex, and now she could think of little else.

They entered a large dining room. Flames leaped in the fireplace to her right, the golden glow illuminating a female pianist. The tables were set beautifully with lit candles, but there weren't any other people.

Their hostess stopped in front of a table that was the furthest from the entrance.

Dane held out Erin's chair while the hostess put the menu on her side of the table.

Dane sat down in front of Erin, glancing past her for a moment. He seemed pleased that from his seat, he could keep an eye on the doorway. Erin wondered if that was really necessary as their hostess walked away.

"Oh wait. She forgot your menu."

He grinned. "No, she didn't."

She drew a sharp breath and felt blood rush to her

face. "Oh, of course. So you're just going to watch me eat? You're not going to eat anything tonight?"

She saw his eyebrow quirk and his mouth twist. "I hope not."

God, how many times was he going to make her blush? "I told you before that I didn't want you to bite me."

"I remember what you told me. Why don't you have a look at the menu?"

Erin frowned, realizing that although Dane acknowledged he knew what she wanted, he refused to reassure her that he would abide by her wishes. She peered at the typical Louisiana Creole dishes on the menu. "I usually think it's a bad sign to eat somewhere if I'm the only one."

"I don't want to share you with anyone."

She glanced at him. Her eyes narrowed as she studied his serious expression.

"Not even with work?" she asked.

"I want you safe," he said, his expression unreadable.

The hostess walked up to them with a bottle of wine and smiled at Erin. "Mr. Lynch has chosen this wine. Would you like to try it?"

Erin was briefly tempted to say "no", that she was old enough to decide for herself what to drink, but her inclination to please him silenced her. She nodded and took a sip after the woman put a drop of wine in her glass.

"Thank you. It's nice," Erin said.

"Have you decided what you'd like to eat?" the hostess asked while filling up the rest of her glass.

"I'd like the trout meunière amandine, please," Erin said as she handed over the menu.

"You lied," Dane said as soon as the elegant hostess had left their table. "About the wine."

"Oh, yes, sorry. It's all right. I've just not really developed a taste for it yet."

He picked up the glass and took a sip. "I'll finish it." He winked at her. "Just like a normal human being."

"*There's nothing normal about him*," Leila said.

Erin frowned. She'd hoped the voices in her head would stay quiet tonight.

He grabbed her hands and held them.

At first, this confused her. It seemed uncharacteristically romantic. But then she remembered what he had said during their night together a week ago about the magic of his touch. He'd told her that when he put his hands on her, the voices went away.

She grew instantly suspicious. Had he heard what Leila had said and wanted to shut her up?

And am I complaining?

She remembered all the other embarrassing comments the others had made in his presence and would rather not discuss them.

Maybe ignorance really is bliss.

"A normal human being," she repeated. "With a normal life?"

He slid his hands to the inside of her wrists, stroking them, making her melt. "Perhaps," he replied. "Would you like a normal life with me, Goldilocks?"

TOUCHED BY DARKNESS

She had to swallow past the lump in her throat before she could respond. "My er, my work has an event next month. We can invite our partners. You could join me if you like. We first have to do team-building exercises, but then we go to Las Vegas and have this fancy ball hosted by Jonathan Stratton. Ouch!"

Dane's grip had tightened. She struggled, but he wouldn't release her.

"Hey." Her voice came out husky. "You don't have to join me if you don't want to."

He loosened his grip but didn't let her go. "I don't want you to go."

She sighed. "I won't give up my job. And a ball might be fun. Maybe we'll get to meet Jonathan Stratton."

"We've met." A flat statement.

The hostess returned with Erin's dinner, and after that they both tried to unsuccessfully steer the conversation toward lighter-hearted subjects.

Erin was finishing her cup of tea when Dane stood up and held out his hand. "Do you want to dance?"

She hesitated. She had never danced before. It wasn't as if she could have learned dancing at the asylum. On the other hand, if she was going to attend a ball, it might be good to practice with only Dane and the pianist as witnesses.

The pianist was singing what appeared to be a romantic French song. Erin accepted Dane's hand as he led her to a small dance floor. Drawing her toward the center of the floor, he guided her into a steady rhythm.

He pulled her against him, close enough to smell his earthy scent. Her muscles tightened, and her cheeks heated up.

"Just relax," he said. He kept his eyes on her, leading her perfectly in time with the music. His other hand slid around her hip to rest in the small of her back and pull her closer. She hesitated, failing faintly in her stride, and then she found her pace.

"I love holding you," he murmured after a moment, his tone deep and almost caressing. He dropped his forehead to hers, nuzzling her cheek, so a hint of stubble rasped against her skin. His arm closed around her waist, his chest against her breasts. When he shoved his leg between hers, the shocking intimacy of his conduct sent a tide of heat through her.

Being so close in front of the pianist was positively indecent, and yet she refused to back away from his powerful embrace. She rested her head on his firm shoulder and squeezed her eyes shut, absorbing the exquisite sensation while she drank in his virile aroma. She simply didn't want to move away.

The song ended, and another started, this time in English.

He surrounded her.

I don't want to go.

"We're not going anywhere," he said.

"Oh, did I say that out loud?"

He chuckled, a deep, rumbling sound that resonated in her head, her heart and deep inside her womb.

He gently grasped her elbow as he guided her off

the dance floor and toward the exit.

Their hostess smiled at them as they passed her. "Your room is down the stairs, at the end of the corridor to your right."

Erin waited until the woman couldn't hear them when she asked, "So you planned on us sleeping together tonight?"

Dane quirked an eyebrow. "Weren't you?"

"I didn't know what to expect. What would I know about dating? This is my first date ever. I was more worried that you'd want to fight because of what happened with the werewolf last night."

He grabbed her waist, stopping her. "Just because we didn't argue about your reckless behavior last night, doesn't mean I'll stand idly by while you put yourself in harm's way."

"You're acting like I'm to blame for what happened."

He ignored her comment, as if he thought it was too stupid to acknowledge and passed her to unlock the door to their room. As he entered the room, he took her wrist to pull her in with him. A tiny muscle ticked along his jaw, and there was something blazing in his blue eyes, something that was about to be set free.

He looks like he's going to eat me alive. Should I worry?

"I, eh, I think we should probably go," she stammered. She found her breath was getting shallower. Yet in spite of his dangerous mood, she didn't really want to leave.

He shut the door behind them and turned the

lock. "We're not going anywhere."

Swiftly Erin stepped away from him as if scorched by his presence. His blood froze as he remembered how near the reckless girl had come to getting hurt. If she had been bitten, she would have become part of Crispin's pack, where women had little say in what happened to them. Her talking back would have killed her if she had managed to survive the first shift.

Struggling to collect his temper, he blew out his breath in frustration.

Why didn't she care about how close she had come to getting hurt?

Because of Stratton's recording of the blood exchange, he couldn't force her to quit her job for the moment, but he hated this feeling of helplessness.

A sudden urge to master Erin overwhelmed him. As he approached her, she crossed her arms tightly over her breasts, unwittingly forcing them up, creating a distracting image that he couldn't help but appreciate.

He stopped in front of her, setting the heels of his hands on the wall, successfully ambushing her. Long, blond unruly curls fell down her back while her golden eyes watched him warily. He reached out, one finger twining in a tight curl that fell over her shoulder.

Mine. His last rational thought before he dragged her against him, cupping her bottom with both hands and thrust upward, pressing his hips against hers. Her breath caught. She moved her arms, her fingers wriggled against his chest, but she didn't push him away. *Yet.*

He lowered his head. She was quick, her lips managed to evade his mouth, but he wasn't giving up. He pushed her backward until she couldn't move anymore, effectively trapping her body between his and the wall behind her. He grabbed her face, desperately trying to rule her with his kiss. She had to understand his absolute control, but the feeling of her nipples pushing against his chest fired him up, and he found himself wanting to seduce rather than conquer.

"Give in," he murmured into her ear.

"W-what?" Her voice sounded dazed as his lips slid to her cheek, her neck. His tongue tasted her skin. He caught the lobe of her ear with his teeth, closing them gently on her skin. Her head fell back, her body melted as a shattered moan escaped her throat. He inhaled, catching the scent of her arousal, and he felt a surge of triumph. Impatient to feel her soft skin against his naked body, he released her.

She watched him as he tossed his shirt aside. He unzipped his jeans next, his cock springing free as he pushed them down his hips, while her golden eyes were fastened on his every movement.

She lifted her chin in defiance and moved backward.

Oh damn, she's thinking again. Her face flushed with color, and he heard her draw in a shuddering gulp of air. In silence, he followed her until her back hit the wall once more.

She curled her fingers into tight fists. He caught

one, carrying it to his mouth. He brushed his lips over the soft skin of her knuckles. Her hand shook, but she didn't pull herself free.

"Let's not fight tonight. Don't you want us to focus on more pleasant matters?" As soon as he had said it, Dane realized he'd never asked for sex before. He never had to ask for anything he wanted. He took, always, until Erin. It was the kind of realization that unsettled him. For a moment, he struggled to keep his hand from squeezing hers. He was close to taking what he wanted, Erin's feelings be damned, before his iron control reasserted itself.

He kept his eyes locked on hers while his lips grazed the inside of the wrist he continued to hold. He raised his other hand to stroke his fingers along the curve of her shoulder.

She lifted her left hand, the one he wasn't holding, and reached up. She grabbed his shoulder, squeezing it before wrapping her arm around his neck. She arched herself upward against his body, and his mouth curved when she shivered. Her cheeks were flushed when he ground his pelvis against hers.

Her golden eyes dilated with desire.

"That's it, Goldilocks." His voice held satisfaction.

The contentment in his tone must have broken the spell because she flinched. She pushed at his naked chest, and she jerked at her arm.

"Not just yet." His voice hardened as he grasped her other hand too and raised both her arms over her head.

Not until I've left my mark upon you.

TOUCHED BY DARKNESS

Clasping her wrists with one big hand, he anchored them against the wall. She struggled, and his grip tightened. Leaning close, he lightly brushed his mouth over hers and sensed a tremor going through her. He then nipped her bottom lip before drawing the soft flesh between his teeth. His fangs lengthened in anticipation.

When he drew his mouth away to stare down at her, she gazed up at him with huge, bewildered eyes. The fight had left her. This time he didn't let her see his triumph.

"I said, no biting," she whispered.

Holding back the dark passion within him, he drew in the scent of her hunger. A fire smoldered in her eyes, and he smiled, shaking his head at her. He had never seen a woman more ready to be bitten.

His left hand continued to hold her immobile while he let his right hand wander. His fingers played at the edges of her left breast. He nudged the strap of her dress over her shoulder, pushing her dress lower until her nipple was unveiled. He filled his hand with the lush mound. While slanting his lips across hers once more, he shaped the firm flesh, his thumb raking over the tight nipple as Erin arched against him and shuddered in pleasure

The edge of his hand touched the marred skin just under the swell of her breast, and for a brief moment, his gut tightened when he thought about the sword that had pierced her skin when she was a small child. An emotion he suppressed. Tonight, he would only focus on ecstasy and making her his.

His mouth left hers, kissing her jaw, her neck,

moving down until his lips brushed against the rounded top, licked over it. His fangs scraped the taut peak, and he smiled when he could hear her moan.

No biting, my ass.

He examined her face. Her golden eyes darkened, a wild glitter of hunger flickering in them as her little pink tongue moistened her lips. She didn't protest as his large, broad hand moved down until it reached her knee before it turned around to slide her dress up her thighs until his fingers arrived at the damp center of her cotton panties. They moved subtly, pressing against her clit as it throbbed for attention.

Staring into Erin's golden gaze, he watched her sensual nature take over as he slid his hand underneath her panties, cupping her possessively between her thighs for a full minute before he continued to rub his middle finger against the tight entrance. The sweet flow of her juices coated his fingertips. He removed his hand and lifted it to his mouth. A little gasp parted her lips, while he licked his fingers.

"Hmm, I want to have more," he murmured. "Can I have more, Goldilocks?"

For a second, she looked confused. But then by the widening of her eyes, he realized she understood. It also meant that he had to let go of her hands now.

She couldn't pretend anymore that she had no choice but to give in. He saw the struggle in her eyes but sensed that her passion would outweigh any rational thought.

"Shh," he whispered as he released her. "I just want a taste, Goldilocks."

She stood frozen as he got on his knees and

ripped her panties into shreds, not wanting to give her another moment to choose whether or not she should be stepping out of them.

He wedged his broad shoulders between her thighs, holding her open to him as his gaze met hers. Staring up at her, he parted the swollen folds and laid his lips to the sweet pink sensitive flesh of her clit.

Her hips arched.

Holding her thighs immobile, Dane held her in position as he placed kiss after kiss against the sensitive knot of nerves. The taste of her was intoxicating. Thrusting his tongue inside her, he fucked her with it, groaning at the spicy, sweet honey meeting his tongue as she cried his name, her hands tightening in his hair, pulling him closer.

He wanted to give a triumphant shout. She had surrendered to him.

Mine.

Gripping his cock, he straightened until her feminine heat brushed against its head. He hooked one arm under her bottom and lifted her. She parted her thighs, and he shoved himself between them. His hips shifted, his engorged crest pressed inside her.

His penetration was fast and rough.

"No more restrictions," he vowed, his voice thick with emotion. "No more putting yourself in danger." With each word, he thrust, pushing himself deeper and deeper into her. "You're mine."

The fingers of his right hand curled in her hair, digging in, so the tension angled her head to the right and exposed her neck to the heat of his mouth closing over her jugular. He sank his fangs into her sweet, pale flesh.

He heard her cry out. He didn't know if it was in protest or acceptance. It didn't matter. He fed. The taste of her filled him, overpowered him.

Grim-faced with his effort at control, Dane moved his left hand between their bodies, urging her toward the climax she needed, stroking her fevered skin until she found a breathless release.

Seconds later, his body joined her as a seemingly endless stream erupted from the head of his cock. He leaned against her, continuing to push them against the wall while he tried to regain his strength. He only needed a few seconds before he managed to stand on his legs and carry her to the bed.

He didn't want there to be any doubts about tonight. He put her down on the bed, his eyes intent on her. He was ready for her again, and he noticed her nipples had hardened. She was ready for him too.

"No restrictions," he said again as he parted her legs and took her for the second time that evening.

Dane lay on his side, watching Erin sleep. Exhausted, she had settled her soft, warm frame against his side. He brushed her hair from her neck, rubbing his knuckles against her skin.

He had kept his promise. He had branded her and hoped his mark would stay visible on her body after that night. He had no regrets even if he expected her to complain about it as soon as she woke up.

Reluctantly, he left her warm body and walked to

the small round window looking out across the river. Using the flat of his hand, he wiped the condensation from it and studied the trees on the shore. Moss hung in long silvery webs, swaying gently from the twisted cypress branches lining the river.

The sun was about to rise. He didn't want to wake her, but he didn't feel comfortable leaving her to wake up without him either.

She should move in with him, and then these situations would be avoided. If she lived in his house, it would be harder for Stratton to reach her. But then she wouldn't go to work either. He smiled. She would probably fight him tooth and nail if he was to lock her up in his mansion, but he found the image of her as his captive very appealing.

He shook his head. Locking her up should be used as a last resort. It would probably take years for her to forgive him if he did that. It would be easier if he first tried to rid the world, once and for all, of Stratton. Unfortunately, Stratton always surrounded himself with bodyguards. It would be impossible to get close to him.

Unless… Unless Dane allowed Erin to go to the ball in Las Vegas, and he joined her as her partner.

If Stratton wants to mingle with his employees, he will have fewer bodyguards to protect him. Forget about Brock's research and blackmailing the blackmailer. Stratton must die. I'll kill Stratton at the party, he vowed. *And I'll kill him before he gets to tell Erin what I did to her.*

FIVE

E rin stood under her shower in a daze. Exhaustion weighed on her. Was she weak because of the loss of blood from Dane's voracious feeding last night? Why had she allowed him to take her blood? She should have struggled. She should have railed at him. Instead, she had given herself up to him.

She staggered as she stepped out of the shower, grabbing the sink to regain her balance. After drying herself, she swiped her towel over the glass and studied her reflection. She looked no better than before the shower. Her face was starkly white with shadows under her eyes. Her right eyelid wouldn't stop trembling, and she blamed Dane. In dreams, her mind had replayed the night with him.

She examined her neck. At least her body hadn't completely betrayed her. In spite of his promise, he had not been able to leave his mark on her. She touched the skin over her pulse. It was unblemished.

But what if there are other consequences?

"Altman... Dane bit me last night. Do I, uh, do I need a rabies shot?" Erin whispered. She didn't want Pauline to overhear.

"*No, but you may need one for that werewolf bite,*" Gideon said.

"I. Didn't. Get. Bit. Besides, I wasn't talking to you," Erin said. "So shut up."

"*No, of course you won't need a rabies shot,*" Altman replied. "*But some people do get addicted to the bite, so you should try to limit the times you let Dane bite you.*"

"I didn't *let* him do anything," Erin snapped. "He, uh, he overpowered me."

Leila snorted.

"Okay, so I didn't really fight back. But I won't let him bite me again. Thanks for the advice, Altman. I sure don't want to get addicted to getting bit."

"*I don't think you need to worry about that. Biting is usually quite harmless,*" Altman explained. "*Just make sure that you don't bite him. Don't drink his blood.*"

"Gross!"

"*Thank you very much!*"

"Uh, sorry, Altman. I mean, it's gross to me. You were a vampire. You had no choice."

"*I wouldn't mind setting my teeth in him,*" Leila joked. "*Even if I weren't a were-leopard. So…how was it? Did he rock your world?*"

Erin sighed. "Forget I asked."

After putting on a shirt and white panties, she left the bathroom.

Pauline was in the kitchen singing while she was preparing their lunch, or breakfast. It was nearly two o'clock, and Erin had only been up for twenty minutes.

She opened her mouth to ask Pauline what they were going to eat but slipped, quickly reaching for the wall to steady herself. This time, her notebook was responsible for her imbalance. She picked it up, surprised to find it lying open on the floor, especially since she had deliberately hidden it from her roommate.

"Do you know what this is doing on the floor?"

Pauline stopped singing and glanced around the corner. A blush heated her cheeks. "No. What is it?"

"Oh, come on. You must recognize this. Gideon must have told you about it."

"N–no. Gideon has never talked to me. And I–I don't like your tone. I'm not lying. I did not touch it."

Erin frowned. Was she overreacting? "It was underneath my mattress. I guess it could have fallen on the floor while you were changing my bed. Thanks for that, by the way."

Pauline shrugged, but Erin couldn't help but notice the curiosity in her gaze.

"*But Pauline is such a neat freak,*" Gideon taunted. "*Wouldn't she have noticed something lying on her spotless floor? She notices specks of dust, so something as big as that shouldn't escape her notice, should it?*"

"What is it, a diary? I would never read your diary," Pauline promised. "My father read mine once, so I know the feeling."

"Uh, no. It's more like a spell book. Some of it is mine, but some spells are black magic. I have a sort of arrangement with Gideon. We agreed that sometimes I allow him to theoretically work on a spell."

"Oh, cool," Pauline said, confirming Erin's suspicions.

TOUCHED BY DARKNESS

She blew out her breath in frustration. "No, it's not cool! That's why I was hiding it. I don't want to do any dark magic, and I don't want others to do it either."

Pauline's brows drew together in confusion. "So why are you writing them down then?"

"Because Gideon can take over my body while I'm asleep and do black magic anyway. He just hopes that if I write them down, one day I'll need to use one of his spells so badly that I won't worry about anyone or anything getting hurt. In exchange he promised he wouldn't possess my body."

Pauline nodded, but Erin could see the doubt nagging at her friend.

"I'm sorry I didn't trust you. I just didn't know if I could trust Gideon. But I'm relieved that he didn't show himself to you. So maybe that tells me I should have faith in him too."

"*Of course you can have faith in me,*" Gideon said.

"That's okay. I understand. Do you want to have lunch now?" Pauline asked.

"Sure," Erin said as she followed Pauline to the kitchen. She smiled. A diary, that sounded logical. She had to have more faith in her roommate, especially with how helpful she had been.

Erin woke to the sound of her radio alarm. She pried her eyes open and turned to see Pauline sleeping on the mattress on the floor. She sat up, switched off the alarm, stumbled from her bed into the bathroom and stuck her head under the faucet to clean her mouth. Pauline didn't have to go to work until noon, so she could stay in bed.

Lucky girl.

After a quick shower, Erin got dressed and moved to the kitchen for a drink. She opened the fridge when she heard a plaintive meow. She walked up to the window and lifted the curtains.

"Shh, you don't want to wake Pauline," she said in a soft voice.

The cat put her paws against the window and moved them up and down the glass. She meowed again.

"All right," she whispered. She pushed the window upward, and the curtains aside. The cat jumped inside and landed on the floor with a loud thud. The animal crouched next to Pauline's mattress, watching Erin intently with her green-gold eyes. Erin dropped the curtains and reached down to scratch her cat's head when the animal suddenly flattened her ears and arched her back, her fur standing on end.

Erin blinked in surprise. The cat hissed at her, while her tail thrashed back and forth. She froze, flicking her gaze to Pauline, who was beginning to wake up.

"What?" Pauline mumbled sleepily. "Willow?"

The cat struck with incredible speed. Erin felt a sharp pain and made a high-pitched sound as teeth pierced her skin. She yanked her hand out of the cat's mouth and saw blood well up. There were jagged teeth marks on her hand.

She gasped. "What the hell?"

"Did Willow just attack you?"

Erin rubbed her sore hand. The cat moved toward Pauline, sat on her mattress and stretched out on the cushion beside her.

"Traitor!" Erin said. "She already favors you over me. Have you been giving her special treats, or something? Bloody hell, she's never done that before."

"It's probably because I named her. You should call her Willow too."

Erin narrowed her eyes at her pet and approached her cautiously. "Is that it, Willow? Are you upset because I haven't called you by your name?"

The cat's tail twitched, and she growled while she kept her gaze fixed on Erin.

In surrender, she raised her hands up high. "I give up. I'm going to work."

"Sorry. I hope I didn't ruin your cat," Pauline called out as Erin left.

"I hope so too. I'll see you tonight."

Erin watched the monitors while Frank did his rounds. It was ten o'clock in the morning, but she felt as if she had already worked a double shift. The cat's—no *Willow*'s—weird behavior occupied her mind. The only time she had seen Willow hiss at someone had been when Victor had shifted into his werewolf form in her apartment.

Werewolf… Could I have been bitten after all?

She shook her head. Maybe Pauline was right.

Yes, her new roommate had ruined the cat. That explained it. She smiled, pleased that she had found a logical explanation for Willow's attack.

She yawned indelicately and rubbed the palms of her hands over her eyes. She then ran her hands over her hair and propped herself up to stare at the screen once more.

Must. Stay. Awake.

Behind her, a man cleared his throat. She turned around and saw someone wearing a white coat standing in the doorway.

"Hi uh, can I come in?" the man asked in a shaky voice. He appeared to be Erin's age, but in spite of his youth, he was quite bald, skinny and sporting a beard.

"Uh, are uh, are you Erin?" He saw her nametag. "Ah, yes. You are. Okay." He approached her, his expression wary, a mixture of fear and sadness in his eyes.

She noticed his hands shaking.

When he caught her staring at them, he shoved them in his pockets. He looked as though he hadn't showered, shaved or changed his clothes in a week.

Does he have sweat patches?

She frowned, alarmed.

"Come sit down," she said. "You're making me nervous."

He walked over and sank down onto the office chair. He had taken his hands from his pockets and was tapping his fingers on her desk. He stared at them. "I uh, do you know who I am?"

She had a sneaking suspicion.

Yes.

"No," she said.

He started rocking his body back and forth. "Oh God, oh God, oh God." He shut his eyes.

"Are you all right?" she asked. "Do you need some water?"

He shook his head. "No, no, no. I can't tell you. But I must. I can tell you. I'll tell you."

He opened his eyes and met her gaze. Fear crawled up her spine.

"My name is Billy Blair. I'm the werewolf you had to subdue Friday night."

She sucked in her breath. "Okay."

"I eh, I keep seeing images of that night. They keep popping into my head; the screams, the smell… I didn't really need to see your nametag. I remember your scent, and your taste. I remember blood filling my mouth. But a lot of that night is a blur, so I'm not sure exactly what happened."

"You didn't bite me."

It came out in barely a whisper, but Billy's hands immediately grabbed hers. So much relief washed over his face. "Really?"

She nodded. He smiled, and then his face completely fell apart. Tears glistened in his brown eyes, and he squeezed her hands. "Thank God," he choked out. "I kept thinking that I bit you. I could have sworn that I tasted blood. Oh, I felt so guilty."

She swallowed and nodded, though she couldn't get rid of the dread tightening her chest.

"I mean—I'm still guilty for attacking you. And I'm sorry about that. But it could have been so much worse. I could have created another monster."

She wanted to comfort him, but hesitated to touch him. "You're not a monster."

"I hate it. I have to live with them now. I'm like a prisoner. I had to beg them to let me go to the hospital today. But I *had* to see you."

Anguish blocked her throat and tightened her airway. "Did—did you tell them why you had to go to the hospital?"

Oh God. They'll force me to live with them.

She couldn't breathe around the growing knot.

He shook his head. "No. They were already angry and punished me for not going to them immediately after I got bit. If I had told them that I'd bit someone when I should have been with them, the punishment would have been so much worse. And thank God I kept quiet because you're okay."

He grinned and stood up. "Thanks. And again, I'm so sorry for attacking you."

She forced a smile. Billy waved before walking out the door.

"*Maybe you can check if you weren't bit after all,*" Erin's mother said.

Erin moaned, dropping her head on the keyboard. "Not you too, mom."

"*He said he tasted blood,*" Leila added.

"Well, he wasn't exactly lucid. He said so himself. And I didn't have a mark on me. I don't want to talk about it anymore."

After that the voices remained quiet while Erin sat there, staring at the monitors without seeing anything, worry nagging at her.

SIX

As soon as her shift had ended, Erin rode to the forest beside the bayou, her refuge. She stepped off her bike and scanned the area. The forest swarmed with life, with sounds of birds and frogs. Night insects hummed in great abundance, bugs that dived and darted. Somewhere in the distance, a snake or a branch fell with a splash into the water.

The night called out to her. Clouds covered the sky and added an air of unknown to the evening. She took off her uniform and dropped it next to one of the moss-covered cypress trees standing in the water. She longed for her leopard to emerge. She couldn't be both leopard and werewolf, right? She closed her eyes and focused on the leopard in her mind. But instead of seeing an animal covered with pale, orange-brown fur and solid black spots, the image of a yellow-gold wolf appeared.

It's all this werewolf talk, that's all, she told herself.

She suppressed the wolf and called out to the leopard. Heat shimmered through her body. There was a curious disorienting feeling before her skin rippled with fur as her body changed. With her shifted body lower to the ground, the scent of dead leaves and soggy moss was much stronger. Her claws dug into the soft earth as she trotted through the dense vegetation, enjoying the freedom of the leopard's body.

The wind stirred, and the trees rustled. She could smell, feel and hear everything. The night was alive, and she felt wild, free. She started to run, when a shiver of anticipation caught hold of her. She could smell them, an irresistible fragrance that shot straight to her animal brain, bypassing reason and reducing her to pure instinct. A silent call hung in the air. Lured by it, she inhaled the wind to locate the source, and she found it.

She followed the scent, running fast, swerving in and out through the trees. Sheer euphoria rushed through her veins as she got closer to her target.

She froze as she reached her target, hunkering low and sniffing the air.

Wolves.

She wished she could turn around, hide before they spotted her, but she was too late.

A pack of large black wolves stared at her, long and intently before stalking forward. Their sheer, overwhelming size terrified her. Since they appeared to be twice the size of a regular wolf, they had to be werewolves. Behind her, a beast with gray fur appeared.

Erin retreated slowly, but the gray werewolf stopped her escape.

A vicious growl tore from his throat.

All four black werewolves in front of her opened their mouths, their lips curled up, displaying their incisors. One of them howled, and a cold chill went up her spine. In the distance, she heard another howl like a trumpet of war. A heavy weight pressed against her side, and she turned her head to see the black wolf sniff her.

She growled.

The black werewolf looked up and bared its teeth, its yellow gaze fixed on her. It reminded her of how wolves hypnotized their prey, giving some kind of predatory stare that the victim instinctively understood and accepted. She seemed to grow calmer and stood still while the other werewolves closed in on her.

A wet nose touched her fur, and it broke the paralysis. She lashed out with her claw and hit the nose, scratching it open. The werewolf howled, fell down, and she jumped over its body to run as fast as she could.

She ran with her heart racing, the humid air stinging her lungs, and the sounds of a pack of werewolves closing in on her. Her mind whirled. She knew she could never outrun a pack of wolves, and she needed a miracle *now*.

Usually when Erin was in leopard form, the feline took over. As if it sensed that it could not escape on its own and needed help, it now allowed Erin's human brain to think of a solution. Unfortunately, panic flooded Erin too.

"*You need to hide,*" Erin's mother said. Erin reached a clearing at the edge of the bayou, and she stopped. She listened. The frogs and insects had gone silent. Alligators slithered in the dirt, the sound loud in the silence before they slid into the water and disappeared beneath the muddy depths.

Where are the werewolves? Are they playing some kind sick of game?

Erin knew wolves enjoyed a hunt just like any other predator, but they didn't seem to have the patience to let their prey wait in terror. The silence caused dread to spread in her stomach.

"*Hide where? Wolves' sense of smell is highly developed,*" Leila said. "*Like that of leopards.*"

"*Yes, yes. Leopards are brilliant, Leila. Maybe she can swim?*" Altman suggested.

Erin looked down. The water looked murky, almost oily.

Can werewolves swim?

"*How about she climbs a tree?*" Leila suggested.

Erin looked at the trees around her and didn't waste a single second. She picked the biggest one, an oak, and climbed up the large tree as fast as she could.

"*They could still smell her though,*" Leila said.

Oh God, what if they surround the tree and wait for me to get down?

"*She needs an invisibility spell,*" her mother proposed.

Erin knew invisibility spells, but they needed to be spoken, not thought. Erin focused on shifting back to her human form, when her mother started to recite a spell:

"*Hide her from those who seek,*
So none may smell her or hear her speak,
No prints of hers on the ground,
She shall not make a sound,

TOUCHED BY DARKNESS

She won't be found,
So none can touch her, so none can see,
As is my will so mote it be."

As soon as Erin's mother finished reciting the spell, all sounds around Erin became muted. She could still see the forest around her, the water below and the tree branch she was sitting on, but where before the branch had been creaking, it now held her weight without any sounds of protest. She couldn't even hear herself breathe.

She considered descending when the werewolves arrived at the clearing. The group was now larger. Instead of the five werewolves that had previously encircled her, Erin now looked down on eight large werewolves. Five wolves were black, the other three gray.

Some were sniffing the ground next to the water, whereas the others were looking up the trees. One of them stood next to the tree Erin was hiding in, but it didn't sense her.

In less than a heartbeat, an eye-blink too quick for Erin to register, they were in human form, all naked men.

"Where is she?" a man with gray hair asked. "She can't just disappear like that."

"Her scent is gone," a teenager said. "It's like she vanished into thin air."

"I don't smell gasoline, so she can't just have driven off."

"Do all leopards smell like that?" the teenager asked.

"No," the gray haired man replied. "I've encountered were-leopards before, and she was different. It's like she has the wolf in her."

"How is that possible?" one of the other men asked. "It seems unlikely. If she has, why didn't she shift into wolf form? Maybe then we would have been more welcoming."

Some men laughed. "Oh yeah, I sure as hell would have been welcomin'."

Erin's throat was fast closing as the men below her continued describing what they would like to have done to her.

"Shut up," the gray-haired man said. "We must tell Crispin. If she didn't shift because she's just been bit, we will need to find her before the next full moon. We can't have a first time werewolf roaming free. We have three weeks to track her down."

"A female werewolf, I call dibs!" one of the men cried out. He ran away with three other men chasing him. The other men shifted back into wolves before running after them.

Erin waited at least ten minutes before she dared to climb down. She hurried to her bike, and after checking that the werewolves weren't nearby, shifted back to her human form.

"*So you have three weeks to find out if they are right,*" Altman said.

"*Three weeks from now, so that's December seventh*?" Leila asked.

"December seventh," Erin repeated. "Shit. Isn't that the week of the team building?"

Jonathan Stratton had just finished talking with his banker on the phone when Margot Sloane walked in. He noticed she was still avoiding his gaze. Her trembling hands caused the papers she was holding to shake.

You'd better not wrinkle them.

"Here's your mail, and Mr. Roberts has just returned a signed copy of the agreement. I only need your signature now," she said, her voice sounding strained. She put it on his desk and stepped away.

He suppressed a smile as he picked up the contract. He noticed her casting furtive glances toward the door. Oh no, he wasn't going to let her off the hook that easily.

"Ms. Sloane, could you please come here?" His secretary's body was stiff, coiled with tension as she slowly walked up to him.

"Why?" she croaked, her voice wavering with the remnants of her terror.

"I thought I'd told you that I wanted you to put signature flags when you ask me to sign a document, so I don't have to waste time searching."

Ms. Sloane nervously swallowed and wrung her hands. "I—uh, I thought that wouldn't be necessary if there's only one page where you need to sign. I—uh, it's open on the signature page."

"Ah, but how would I know that there aren't any other pages you want me to sign?"

"But there—" She stopped.

"But there what, Ms. Sloane? Come on. Speak

up."

"But there are only three pages," she whispered.

His jaw tightened, and he shot her an angry glare. "Time is money, Ms. Sloane as you very well know. It doesn't matter if I have to check three pages or three hundred pages. They are two pages too many. I find this very disappointing. You wouldn't want to disappoint me, Ms. Sloane."

She laughed, a harsh, dry sound that assaulted his ears. "No, Mr. Stratton. I wouldn't want that."

Deliberately he used the pen that had the words "blood writer" engraved on it to sign the contract. He saw her looking at the pen in horror and sensed her need to cry. But she held it in check, stubbornly refusing to submit to her emotions.

"Oh, Ms. Sloane." He sighed. "Have some pride."

Her shoulders dropped in defeat. She stuttered a shaky breath, her hands tightly clenched.

"Is that all, Mr. Stratton?"

"Scan this document and return one copy to Mr. Roberts. I don't want to be disturbed for the next hour."

His secretary nodded quietly, took the contract and left his room in a hurry. He shook his head at her escape. As if he would ever let her leave with all the knowledge she had of his affairs. Last month, he had been informed of her job application with one of the other successful casinos. He had then made sure that she understood just how valuable she was to him, and that even the thought of leaving him would have consequences. As usual, he had to teach her the hard way. He just hoped he hadn't now damaged his secretary. Good and reliable help was so hard to find.

He grinned as he examined the blood writer pen. Ms. Sloane knew what it represented. He had taken the pen from John Tennant who had wanted to write a book about him. John Tennant wouldn't be writing any books about him, nor about anyone else for that matter. He usually had someone take care of these matters, but this had been personal so he had enjoyed crushing the writer himself.

And now, there was another personal matter he had to attend to. He grabbed the phone. His call was answered immediately.

"Mr. Stratton. What can I do for you?"

"I'm just calling to check if you have prepared everything for the team-building event?"

He heard the man on the other side of the phone inhale a deep breath as if gathering his nerve, though Stratton knew better. His employees never spoke up to him. "Uh, yeah, it's all set. But, uh, I think someone could get killed."

Stratton groaned. "I'm not paying you to think."

"Oh, no. Okay. Uh, goodbye, Mr. Stratton."

Stratton hung up and rubbed his temples.

Good help...

If people got killed, he knew he wouldn't be blamed. But he wasn't expecting anyone to die. He had faith in her.

She won't let it happen.

Erin's heart raced as she ran up the stairs. She reached for the door handle, paused when she noticed that her hand trembled.

"They could be wrong," she told herself. "There aren't many were-leopards around so what does that guy know about what I should smell like? It's probably been a really long time since he smelled one. He doesn't know anything."

After her little pep talk, she straightened her shoulders, put the key in the lock and twisted the cold metal handle. In silence, she entered the room, her legs so wobbly she barely made it to the bed where she collapsed as Pauline came out of the bathroom.

Pauline's eyes widened with surprise. "I didn't hear you come in. You look awful. Are you okay?"

Erin saw Pauline peering at her shoes.

"Uh, maybe you should take them off? You don't want to dirty your sheets."

Erin stared at her roommate for a long moment. Then she chuckled. First, a barely audible sound as if she was trying respectfully to control her amusement. Then she lost all control and started laughing.

"Are you finished?" Pauline demanded. "I'm glad you find me so entertaining."

The laughter disappeared, and Erin wiped tears from her eyes. "I'm sorry, Pauline. I wasn't really laughing at you. Well, maybe I was, but I didn't mean to. I've just had some disturbing news."

She heaved a long-suffering sigh and closed her eyes, attempting to get a grip on herself.

"Remember when I told you about that fight I had with that werewolf at the hospital?"

TOUCHED BY DARKNESS

"You mean the werewolf that didn't bite you? Sure. Why?"

"Well, uh, I may have been bit after all." Erin opened her eyes and looked at Pauline. She forced a smile. "Yes, I think I must have had a similar expression on my face when I realized that I may now also turn into a wolf once a month."

Pauline shook her head. "Why do you think you were bit when before you said you weren't?"

"I may have been in denial. Hell, you gotta love the irony here. I came here to become a normal human being, but instead I get even more different."

"But why do you think you'll become a werewolf? Do you suddenly want to eat raw meat, feel the urge to pee against a tree, what?"

"Well, I remember the werewolf putting its teeth into my skin, but it didn't leave any marks, so I just thought I had imagined it. And it threw me through a window, so I was already covered in blood, and I cut it up pretty bad too."

"Good."

Erin smiled. "Thanks for your support. And as to why I have now changed my mind: First, Willow hissed at me this morning, and the only person I've seen her hiss at was Victor, and he's a werewolf. Then I went to the hospital where I met Billy the orderly aka the werewolf I had to subdue, who remembered tasting my blood. Only he wasn't sure because it was his first shift, so he wanted to check and to apologize. Afterwards, I went for a run as a leopard. But before I shifted into a leopard, I saw an image of a wolf in my head. I got confused."

"But this can all be explained," Pauline said as she walked up to Erin's bed and sat down beside her. "It doesn't mean anything. Willow probably hissed at you because I spoiled her. Billy doesn't remember anything, but he may have wanted to bite you so much that he started to hallucinate, and you only pictured a wolf because you're scared."

Erin sucked in a shaky breath. "I, uh, I forgot to tell you that during my run I was drawn to a scent. I-it belonged to a pack of wolves, or I should say werewolves. I couldn't think. It lured me to them. They surrounded me, smelled me, and then one of them said he could smell the wolf in me. I managed to get out and hide but I heard them say that they were going to tell their alpha about me, and that they would try to find me."

"Oh shit," Pauline muttered.

"Yes. Shit."

"Well, you're not alone in this. I'm here to help you. I can do some research. We'll watch werewolf films together. Werewolves, don't they have a problem with silver?"

Erin shrugged. They'd had movie nights at the hospital, but they never showed any horror movies. They probably didn't want to upset their patients.

"Yes, I think so," Pauline continued. "And I have a silver knife, so we can try it out. Well, at least I think it's silver." She stood up and searched her bag.

"Why do you have a silver knife, or even a regular knife? I have cutlery."

"It's just a keepsake," Pauline said. "Ah, found it! Ain't it pretty?" Pauline handed over what appeared to be a twelve-inch knife with a wood grip and a deeply engraved design. Erin took the handle and examined the text on the blade with suspicion. She didn't recognize any of the symbols.

"Where did you get this? Do you know what it says?"

Pauline grinned. "I took it from Selena. I have no idea."

"I'm not sure I'm comfortable holding this. Did she use it in any of her rituals?"

Pauline laughed. "Oh, don't worry. I've never seen her use this one. But it looks real, right? I think there's a hallmark here." She took it from Erin. "Ah yes, see? It's a tiny lion."

"Okay," Erin said. "So it's probably silver. But what should I do now?"

"You hold the blade." Pauline held it out to her again. "I remember seeing a film with Christina Ricci as a werewolf where she touched a silver pie knife, and then I think it hurt her. I'm not sure. It's been a while."

"*Are you sure you want to do this?*" Erin's mother asked.

"*Do you want her to remain ignorant? You're not protecting her that way,*" Gideon complained.

Erin briefly hesitated before grabbing the blade with her left hand. Pain speared through her chest, and she fell on the floor, gasping for air.

"Let go. Let go of the knife," she heard Pauline call out.

Erin didn't know what happened, but she felt as if she was no longer in control of her body. As soon as she touched the knife, her hand had automatically squeezed it and kept on squeezing it. The weapon seemed glued to her hand, continuing to burn as if someone was prodding her with a hot iron.

Pauline sank to her knees in front of her. "Why aren't you letting go?" she cried out.

Erin gasped as Pauline tore the weapon from her hand. The world went a little watery as tears welled in her eyes. Her mind was dim as she slowly sorted through her muddled thoughts.

What the hell happened?

Sweat beaded her forehead, and she swallowed back the nausea that rose in her throat. She tried to suck in air, but her lungs burned from the effort.

"Oh my God, I'm so sorry, Erin."

Why is she sorry? Oh right, I'm allergic to silver.

Erin panicked. The throbbing in her head escalated to a full-blown ache.

"Are you okay? Do you want me to help you up?"

Erin blinked a couple of times, hoping to clear her hazy vision. It slowly improved. She saw Pauline's lips tremble while she cast her eyes downward to where her fingers twisted nervously at the knife.

"So it's been confirmed," Erin said in a low voice. "I'm going to become a werewolf unless there are other creatures out there who respond this when they touch silver."

Pauline shook her head. Her face was set into a grim line. "I don't think so. I'm so sorry."

An irritated grunt followed. "Will you stop saying that you're sorry. It's freaking me out." Erin stood up then walked to the window. She looked down at her hand. It had healed.

Leopard genes or werewolf genes?

"I'd rather think of solutions. You said that you could help me."

Pauline nodded. "I have spells that should help you control it."

"Control it? What about a spell to get rid of it?"

Pauline glanced over at her, her eyes brimming with apology. "I don't think you can get rid of it with magic. Do you remember that when we first met in the hospital I talked about lycanthropy not being a spell? I think it's in your blood now."

"So people just stay that way, in movies too? What happened to Christina Ricci? Was she still a werewolf at the end of the movie?"

"Um no, s-she killed the other werewolf, I think."

Erin shivered. "Are you saying I should kill Billy?"

"No, of course not!" Pauline protested. "It was just a movie. We need to talk to other werewolves. Do you know any?"

"No, my werewolf neighbor Victor is gone. And I'm sure that if he knew, he'd just use it against me. I'd rather hide it than be forced to join Crispin's pack. I've just escaped one prison. I refuse to enter another," Erin vowed.

"Maybe you can ask Dane for help?"

Erin sighed. "Dane's been hounding me to quit my job and move in with him. I'm sure he'll use this to his advantage."

Pauline walked up to her and reassuringly squeezed her arm. "I'm honored you're asking me to help you. I'll do some investigating. I've seen some powerful magic, so it may be possible to undo."

"No black magic," Erin said quickly.

"Uh, okay. I'll see what I can do. How much time have we got?"

"A little over three weeks. December seventh. It will be the same week as that stupid team-building thing from work. Oh, what a nightmare."

"What, you've got to be kidding me! You can't go. Who knows how you'll act."

Erin frowned and opened her mouth. But then she shut it again, her lips forming a tight, mutinous line. "I thought you said you had a spell to control it."

"It's magic, not an exact science. There's no way to predict how you'll act. Look at how Billy behaved! You can forget about hiding from the werewolves if your first shift happens in front of all your colleagues. And what if you hurt them?"

"No need to get upset. I didn't even want to go to that stupid team-building week anyway. I'll get out of it."

I just hope that they'll let me get out of it.

SEVEN

Erin sat nervously in the reception area of Securistate. This was her fourth visit to the Securistate building. Her job didn't require her to see her manager often. But whenever she did, Nikko Vardalos had a talent for making her feel bad.

She didn't register at first when Sheila called out her name. She was still numb with shock, worried about the possible consequences of becoming a werewolf, and her thoughts were occupied with the task before her. A hand on her arm interrupted those thoughts.

"Nikko's ready for you now," Sheila said.

"*Don't worry, Erin,*" her mother said. "*You'll be fine.*"

Erin nodded, stood up and entered her manager's office.

He looked up when she came into the room, but he didn't rise to shake her hand.

She didn't mind not having to touch him, but she was concerned about what she expected his response to be once she made her request. He never hid his dislike from her. In fact, he would not have hired her had he not been ordered to do so. She knew this because he had told her, twice.

It was because of this dislike that she knew she had to make her request in person. Over the phone, he would just refuse.

She sat down in front of the desk. "Hi. How are you?"

Nikko frowned. "Busy. Why are you here?"

She drew in a deep breath. "I'd like to talk to you about the team-building event next month. I'm afraid I can't join you."

Faint amusement glittered in his eyes. "Everyone has to join, *ma chère*. Single parents with children, people with allergies, or people on jury duty must all attend. No exceptions allowed. Even I have to be there, and I hate the outdoors, especially in the winter."

"Well, uh. That's why I can't join you. I'll have my period then, so I would need to use the toilet at least every three hours. Not to mention that I always suffer from terrible cramps."

He winced and showed his disgust. "Just take a pill and use moist towels."

"I also suffer from winter toes."

He laughed. "Well, I have a solution for that. I've always known you were like an animal. I'm sure you can find a bear to cuddle up with or whatever animal it is you feel close to. Out in the wild, you can't hide the freak you are."

Annoyance fluttered in her gut. "A freak, am I?"

A flash of anger crossed Nikko's face. "Yes, don't think you can fool me. I saw the monster in you the last time you were here. I'll tell the performance review team to keep an extra eye on you."

"*Don't allow it,*" Altman said.

"I know. That's why I have you," Erin told Altman.

"You're not making any sense, as usual." Nikko nodded at the door. "Now if you don't mind…"

She sighed. "I do mind. I so didn't want to do this, but you leave me no choice."

"No choice?" He blinked in surprise, and then fury suffused his face, flushing it to near purple. "Don't you dare to threaten me, honey, I'll crush you!" He jumped up from his chair and pointed at the exit.

She ignored him and focused on her voice instead. She was ready. She stared up at her manager's face and felt a familiar sense of power arise, a power Altman had given her.

"You'll go to your computer and take my name off your list for the team-building event. It's very important to you that I don't attend the event. You'll check if there are other places where my name could be, and you won't rest until you know that my name won't be found."

Nikko's eyes had rounded in shock, and his hands hung limply at his sides while she used her ability to glamour him.

"So what will you do now?" she asked.

"I'll check my computer and take your name off the team-building event list," he said in a low and monotonous voice. "I'll ask Sheila to check if there are other places where your name could be, and I'll remove them."

She smiled and stood up. "Thank you, I'll let myself out." Her relief was so great that it made her light-headed. She even waved at Sheila as she passed her desk.

"Well, that wasn't so difficult," Erin said as soon as she left the Securistate building. She drew in a long breath and looked skyward. "Now if we could only find a way to stop me from becoming a werewolf that easily, then life would really be great."

"I have Mr. Vardalos on the phone for you," Stratton's secretary said.

"And why would I want to talk to him, Ms. Sloane?" Stratton asked.

"It's, um, it's about Erin Holland. I-I thought that you'd want me to put him through."

Stratton considered making another comment about him not paying her to think when he realized that his curiosity had indeed been piqued.

"Put him through," he ordered.

A second later, he heard, "Mr. Stratton! I'm so sorry. I didn't want to disturb you. I told your secretary not to disturb you!"

He scowled. "If you didn't want to disturb me, why did you then decide to call my office?"

"I just wanted to check that my employee would not be on any list of the team-building event in December. I assumed your secretary would be in charge of the invitations and any other arrangements."

"And who is this employee?" he asked, although

Ms. Sloane had already mentioned her name.

"Erin Holland."

"Hmm, and why would this Erin Holland not be on any lists of this event? Aren't you aware that it is mandatory for everyone to attend the team building? I expect all my managers to be well informed. Aren't you well informed, Mr. Vardalos?"

"It's very important that she isn't on any lists."

"And why is that important?"

"I won't rest until I have checked that she's off the list. It's very important that she isn't on any lists of the team-building event," Stratton's employee repeated.

What the fuck is wrong with this guy?

"Is she off the list, Mr. Stratton?" Mr. Vardalos asked vehemently.

Stratton sighed. "No, she isn't."

"But she must be," Mr. Vardalos cried out. "Please take her off the list. I won't rest—"

"Then you won't rest," Stratton said coolly. "Goodbye, Mr. Vardalos."

Stratton hung up.

What the hell was that?

He hoped that not all his employees were this irrational. If so, he had to seriously rethink his recruitment strategy.

It's as if he was possessed.

He narrowed his eyes as he realized just what it was that Erin had done. Mr. Vardalos *had* been possessed. Erin had used her vampiric power on his employee. If he weren't so annoyed, he might have been impressed by her cunning. Not that it mattered.

He picked up the phone. "Ms. Sloane?"

"Yes, sir?"

"Have you kept Ms. Holland on the invitation list?" he asked.

"Yes, Sir. You haven't asked me to take her off the list, unless you want me to? I haven't sent out the invitation yet. I, uh, I wanted to do that tomorrow."

"I have not changed my mind. Make sure that she gets her invitation."

He hung up the phone and smiled.

Good try, Erin. Better luck next time.

But why did she try to get out of the team building? Was she afraid she would expose herself?

He laughed.

You can fight all you want, but I will expose you, my dear.

"I thought you made sure that you would get out of the team-building week, right?" Pauline asked. Erin's roommate was standing in the doorway pointing at the large envelope in her hand.

Erin sat up on her bed. She lifted a brow, surprised that she'd even ask. "Yes, why? What is that?"

"It says invitation on the front."

"Oh fuck. It didn't work." She left the bed and rushed to Pauline, grabbing the envelope. A pounding on the door startled her.

She and Pauline opened the door to find her manager standing in the doorway.

TOUCHED BY DARKNESS

Nikko's eyes were haunted and fixed on her.

Pauline moved to stand by her side. "Who is he?"

Erin's hand covered her mouth, which was agape with shock. She had never considered her overweight and balding manager attractive, but she had never seen him look this haggard either. Lines etched deeply into his forehead, and wrinkles marred the corners of his eyes. He was pale, and it appeared as if he hadn't slept in days.

Oh fuck. That's because he hasn't *slept in days.*

"Erin. I've checked and checked, but you're still on the list. You're still on it!" Nikko's voice deepened to a hoarse, almost desperate tone.

Erin twisted her hands, guilt surging through her. She glanced at Pauline, who stared at them in confusion.

"I'd told him not to rest until he knew I was off the list for the team-building event. Well, it looks as though I'm still on the list," Erin said, waving the envelope. "So he hasn't been able to rest."

"You're on the list," he murmured.

"It's okay," Erin said to her manager. She closed her eyes and concentrated on her voice. As soon as she had summoned the power, she opened her eyes. "You will no longer check that I'm off the list for the team-building event. You will be able to rest again. You will go home now and sleep."

"Yes," he said calmly before turning around and walking down the stairs.

"Oh my God, I can't believe you just did that!" Pauline said.

"Yeah, me neither," Erin sighed. "I guess that's

it. I have no choice but to go."

"Yes, but I'll continue to look for spells to help you. Since you're a witch too, who knows what we can accomplish together."

"Can we accomplish that my colleagues won't notice that I'm about to turn into a werewolf?" Erin's voice cracked. "The idea of being forced to live with a pack of wolves doesn't really appeal to me."

"Are there any werewolves working at Securistate?"

"I don't think so, not anymore. Victor got fired, and I haven't heard anything about other werewolf colleagues."

Pauline put her hand on Erin's arm. "Then I'm sure you're okay. We'll do a spell to suppress the wolf, but at least humans don't have that keen sense of smell. It'll be easier to fool them."

Erin thought about Nikko telling the organization to keep an extra eye on her.

I doubt I can fool anyone much longer.

EIGHT

After their plane had landed in Edmonton, Erin and her colleagues had to travel an additional four hours by bus to reach their final destination.

During their road trip, Erin had watched snow falling densely, creating spiraling patterns in the headlights of the bus. Upon their arrival, the snow had stopped, and the roads were shiny in the reflected lights of the streetlamps.

A blast of cold air hit her as she got out of the bus, freezing her in her spot. She sucked in a sharp breath as the iciness seeped in through her jeans and jacket.

"Hey, move. You're blocking us," Sheila complained behind her.

Erin took a few steps forward so the bitchy redhead could pass. She took in the landscape around her. It looked like a winter wonderland. In the distance, mountains loomed against the sky, and moonlight reflected off the snow on the ground.

Moonlight, nearly full moon…

The moon was taunting her, encouraging her to give in. Of all the times to have a possible first shift as a werewolf, this had to be the worst timing in history.

She was terrified that her colleagues would find out, and that it would get back to the werewolf community. She pictured the werewolves she had previously run into showing up at the campsite, dragging her kicking and screaming to Crispin's pack. And who knew what happened there?

Billy knew, but she couldn't ask him without risking he would expose her to the others. They acted very secretive. She also had to keep in mind that a part of her was leopard.

Cats and dogs, who knows how werewolves will respond to my leopard?

Pauline had helped her with a spell to suppress the need to shift and to hide her werewolf from other werewolves. But so far, Erin had little faith her roommate's magic. Over the past weeks, she had discovered that as the moon became more and more illuminated, the intensity of her wolf pulling at her increased. Tonight seemed the worst. Her skin crawled and itched with the need to shift.

"*No.*"

"What no?" a voice behind her asked.

Erin turned to see her favorite tall, African-American colleague standing behind her.

"Hi, Frank. I'm sorry. I didn't realize I was talking aloud. I just said "no" to the cold and to this trip actually. Security guards from Louisiana in the cold, it's ridiculous!"

Frank shrugged. "Ah, don' worry 'bout it. It's only a game. You should enjoy the scenery."

She noticed the bus driver taking their bags out of

101

the bus. He had dropped her backpack to the ground. "I'd better get that before my clothes get wet."

As she returned to the bus, a big sign caught her eye with a smiling grizzly bear. It was welcoming her to Camp Happy.

She sighed. "Oh boy."

"I'm Mike, the camp leader. We're so excited that you're all here tonight, and I'm sure that everyone is going to have a wonderful week," a blond guy, wearing a training suit with a Camp Happy logo on it, said. He was standing next to a black TV screen.

Erin was sitting in a large meeting room of one of the Camp Happy lodges, wishing she didn't have to listen to this revoltingly fit young man anymore, even if it meant she had to return to the rustic cabin with seven other colleagues, where she had to share a bunk bed with Sheila.

She could not imagine having a wonderful week here. She missed Pauline. She realized that there were advantages to living with a compulsive cleaner. She had already used the community bathhouse once at Camp Happy. For her next trip to the bathroom, she would be better off hiding behind a tree or a bush.

"We want you to discover the magic of winter camping," Mike continued. "Winter is like a sea of extremes. It can be threateningly bleak or silently stunning. You've discovered the stunning part tonight, and tomorrow you'll experience the threateningly bleak part."

He laughed. "Did you know that winter is the best time for tracking? With its soft ground and snowy covers, who knows what we'll find, maybe a bear!"

Don't bears hibernate?

"Or maybe you'll find a wolf. Speaking of wolves, there are some people here I'd like you to meet." He nodded to his colleague, who was standing beside the main doors. The man opened the door.

A sense of unease passed over Erin. She could hear the sound of approaching footsteps and murmuring voices. As they became louder, she grew more on edge. She took a breath, suddenly bombarded by a familiar scent, a sublime fragrance that had reduced her to nothing but a dumb compulsion weeks before. Bile rose in her throat, and she swallowed convulsively as a hollow feeling settled in her chest. Her head jerked to the windows, the only direction of possible escape.

Too late.

Seven tall men in military gear entered the room.

No, not men, werewolves.

The discovery sent a jolt of panic through her. She felt Frank's hand on her arm. She saw him gazing at her with concern, a question in his eyes. She heard his words, but somehow couldn't make out what he said.

She tried to smile at him. She must have succeeded because he nodded before removing his hand and focusing his attention on the newcomers, *the intruders*.

They didn't act as if they wanted to be there either. Anger rolled off them so strong that she imagined she could taste it. One of them—a tall man with a military-style haircut and a thick scar on his left cheek—swept his gaze over the crowd, intimidating them all until he fixed his interest on her.

Sweat broke out on her forehead, and shock robbed her of breath. Only sheer will kept her glued in her chair.

"Quentin," the organizer said. He walked up to the man who was staring at her and held out his hand. "Welcome to Camp Happy."

The man called Quentin finally looked away from her, only to frown at the hand in front of him.

He growled, and the organizer immediately lowered it and took a step backwards.

He cleared his throat before he said. "Could you please take your seats while I explain your arrival to the others?"

"*Oh my God. Are those werewolves?*" Leila asked.

"*You're so fucked,*" Gideon said.

Is he enjoying this?

"*Don't worry,*" her mother said. "*Pauline's magic will protect you.*"

"You think?" she whispered. "Why was that guy staring at me then?"

"*Because you're cute, that's all,*" her mom said.

"What is it?" Frank asked.

Everything, my emotions are spinning like a roulette wheel.

"Nothing," Erin replied instead. She examined her hands. They shook, and she drew in deep breaths before letting them out slowly. Her hands steadied themselves.

"People from Securistate, we would like for you to meet the werewolves from Jonathan Stratton's private guard. We want you to feel properly challenged, and what would be more challenging than a competition between humans and werewolves?"

"B-but that's not fair," Nikko stammered. "We could never beat werewolves!"

"It's insulting that we even have to spend time doing this," one of the werewolves said.

"It's beneath us," another werewolf added.

"Don't you see what's happening here?" Mike said. "Two different species and you're already aligned. You'll find out you have more in common than you think."

Frank shook his head. "I don't believe it. What do we have in common with werewolves?"

"Don't worry guys! We'll have a fun time together with bonding exercises that will make you feel worthy of your company," Mike continued on his disgustingly positive note that made Erin want to puke.

"You'll all feel like you belong here. And you do! You'll leave here stronger, better human beings."

"Some of us are already stronger, better human beings!" a werewolf with long brown hair cried out. He was wearing a black t-shirt with his army trousers, obviously not bothered by the cold.

The blond man didn't seem to mind the interruption. He grinned. "This is exactly what I want. I want you to speak up, to participate. We're a team."

Erin raised an eyebrow at Frank who sat beside

her. "Shall we try to escape?" she whispered.

"Maybe it's not just physical," Frank said. "They can't really expect us to physically compete against these creatures."

Sheila, who was sitting in front of them, turned around and hushed them.

"You're all blessed because you work for Jonathan Stratton, the most successful businessman out there and a philanthropist. His generosity will be talked about years from now," Mike said.

"Good grief, is he in love with Jonathan Stratton?" Erin said to Frank.

Sheila glared at her again.

Under his breath Frank muttered, "I just hope Blondie here is not in charge of our group. That much enthusiasm will kill me."

Oblivious to their conversation, the man in front of them went on. "Everything Jonathan Stratton touches turns into gold. You're gold too, and he has a wonderful message he recorded just for us."

"Some manager," Erin mumbled. "He makes us go out in the cold, while he stays at his warm place in Las Vegas."

The blond man nodded at someone behind a laptop, and seconds later Jonathan Stratton appeared on the TV screen. "Good evening all," he said. The billionaire was sitting behind his desk, wearing a suit. He was an attractive man who appeared to be in his early forties. He had black hair with a hint of gray at his temples.

"Welcome to a week in hell. Who said that hell is supposed to be hot?" His eyes glimmered with amusement. "You may have thought that I had invited you to a relaxing team-building event, and I expect the gala on Friday will be relaxing—if you make it—but this part of the week will be about me testing you. I only want the best working for me. But don't worry. You won't have to go through this alone. This is about teamwork. I want my employees to work with me and not be here for individual gain. You're here for *my* gain. I may be the best at business and have successfully turned my name into a brand, but I need employees to continue this success. I need you, if you're good enough."

He smiled. "I'm not a believer of long speeches, and sometimes I prefer to let other people do the talking. I like to entertain, so tonight I'm showing you a scene from a movie where Robert De Niro puts into words my definition of teamwork. Sit back and relax."

The screen flickered, and Robert De Niro appeared. He was giving a speech at a dinner.

"Holy cow," Frank said.

Erin noticed other people started talking amongst themselves. Some were laughing. They were acting as if they had seen the movie before.

"What is it?" she whispered.

Frank shook his head. "It's *The Untouchables*. I know this scene. Jonathan Stratton sure has a funny sense of humor."

She watched as Robert De Niro's character talked about baseball while holding a baseball bat. He explained how people like Babe Ruth would be nothing without his team, and that he shouldn't decide to go off on his own. Robert De Niro then started whacking a guy repeatedly on the head with the baseball bat until blood from the guy's head spread out across the white tablecloth. Erin's brows lifted.

The screen flickered, and Jonathan Stratton reappeared. He flashed them a shark's grin. "I'm really looking forward to meeting you on Friday. I'll be watching your progress this week. Don't make me bring my bat!"

When the recording stopped, a roar of laughter and clapping followed. The blond guy, Erin noticed, was shaking with what appeared to be nervous laughter. She didn't know what to think. Apparently, Jonathan Stratton liked theatrics, and he probably intended to intimidate his employees with his little speech. She wasn't too worried about the tests he would make them endure. She was stronger than most people were, and she doubted that the well-known billionaire would risk his employees getting hurt. He wouldn't want bad publicity.

"What do you think?" she asked Frank. "Does this mean that if we decide to go off on our own, Jonathan Stratton will come after us with a baseball bat?"

He chuckled. "It's been a while since I've seen that movie. I should see it again. Have you seen it?"

She was about to answer when she noticed the back of her neck prickling, the hairs standing on end, warning Erin that someone was watching her. She turned around to see the scarred werewolf called Quentin observing her again from the doorway.

She sucked in her breath, and her body went on

high alert. There was no smile playing on his lips or in his intense green eyes.

His eyes trapped her gaze, holding her frozen. His jaw was set, demanding and hard. His body appeared coiled and ready to strike.

Werewolf, shit. Does he recognize what I am?

She could tell he was a warrior through and through. When his eyes released her, she almost fell backwards. Automatically, she searched the room, looking for an exit. But the only way out, other than escaping through a window, would be to pass him.

"Hey, you all right?" Frank asked.

She pointed at the werewolf who was still observing her. "He won't stop staring at me."

"Ha! So he's ready to compete with us. No worries, he's only challengin' you, *chère*. Just stare back. Watch me. I'll show you." He skewered the werewolf with a glare.

"Ooh, scary!" she said while pretending to shiver dramatically.

"Okay, guys," Mike cried out as he clapped his hands. "We're moving the chairs around so we can have a big circle."

She picked up her chair and sat down between Frank and Sheila while the werewolf who had been studying her sat down opposite her. She avoided his gaze but did notice a tall, dark-skinned man with raven-black hair walking up to the werewolf.

"Hey, Quentin, what's up?" she heard him say. She didn't catch his response because the annoying blond guy started clapping and shouting again.

"Okay everyone, take your seats. We're going to

introduce ourselves." Mike's mouth spread into a wide smile, showing perfectly straight, white teeth. "So now you know that this week is going to be about Securistate's humans versus Jonathan Stratton's werewolf guards. But tonight, we're all friends, so let's introduce ourselves with a fun fact."

Erin couldn't focus on what the other people were saying. She was trying to think of what she should say.

A fun fact: I hate public speaking. I have people in my head. I'll be turning into a werewolf soon and will be shifting teams.

She swallowed nervously and fidgeted when she saw that it was her turn to stand up and speak. She became even more uncomfortable when she noticed Quentin and his friend intently watching her.

"Uh, hi. I'm Erin Holland, and I've been working for Securistate for about eight months now. I, uh, I have a cat named Willow."

As soon as she finished speaking, she sat down. Heat bloomed across her cheeks. Relieved that was over, she could relax more and actually listen to what the others were saying. She tensed when it was Quentin's turn to speak. She glanced over to see him still watching her with suspicion. "My name is Quentin Scott." After a few seconds of silence, his voice took on an edge.

"A fun fact?" His eyes narrowed, and Erin felt pinned by the force of his stare. "I can smell shapeshifters a mile away."

Frank frowned. "What a weird guy."

"Right," Mike said. "Thanks everyone for

sharing these fascinating facts with us. Now you have some free time. We have an open bar, but I recommend that you don't stay up late since we'll be up early tomorrow morning. It will also be your last night in a comfortable bed, so enjoy that luxury while you can. Tomorrow our adventure begins."

"An adventure without a bed? Sign me up," Erin mumbled.

"I heard that, young lady!" he continued. "I'll have you know that constructing a shelter is a very serious business. It must exclude wind, water and cold. And it must have a ventilation hole."

She sighed. She hoped he would stop his lecture soon. When she saw that some people were already walking away, she decided to leave too.

"Thanks for your advice," she told Mike. "Great idea. I'm off to bed," she said.

"Don't you want a drink before going to bed?" Frank asked.

She shook her head and left the meeting room.

"*That's wise,*" her mother said.

"*Yes, you don't want to be around those werewolves more than necessary,*" Leila warned. "*I don't like the way that Quentin was looking at you.*"

"Maybe he could smell the leopard?"

"*I hope so. But just in case, you should try to avoid them,*" her mother agreed. "*I worry the spell wasn't strong enough.*"

"*Why didn't you use one of my spells? You're so dumb,*" Gideon complained.

"I'm not a warlock like you. I refuse to use black magic," she said defensively.

111

"*Well, that's very clever! As soon as they find out, they'll lock you up with the other wolves. Billy Blair complained that he was a prisoner. How do you think they would treat you, a female werewolf?*"

"Uh, I don't know. Why would it be different?"

Gideon sighed loudly. "*Think about it! Have you ever seen a female werewolf?*"

"Uh, no. So?"

"*But you have met quite a few male werewolves. So either there aren't many female werewolves, which would make you very rare, or they treat their women like second-class citizens, and they aren't allowed to leave.*"

"Hmm, I didn't want to say it, Gideon, but you're making sense. I'm fucked."

"Talking to yourself again, are you?" a familiar voice behind her said.

Erin gasped as soon as she realized who was behind her. He didn't have to say a word. She could recognize the coconut sunscreen smell of his skin.

Sunscreen in the middle of winter? No, that's not what I should ask myself! What the fuck is Victor doing at my team-building event?

She turned around to confront her enemy. "Victor, what the hell are you doing here?" Erin stared up at him, her throat working against the anger that twisted within her.

The last time she had seen him, he had betrayed her. With his help, a lunatic psychiatrist had kidnapped her. The psychiatrist had intended to torture her on camera. But instead, she had shifted into a leopard and ended up eating her kidnapper. She then had tried to find Victor to confront him with his betrayal, but the coward had disappeared.

Until now.

She eyed him coldly, allowing the full force of her hatred to bleed into her expression. "Give me one good reason of why I shouldn't kill you."

"*Yes, let's kill him,*" Leila said.

An expression of regret framed Victor's face. "I'm sorry. I was forced to turn you over to him. I'm a coward. If you like, you can hit my face. I deserve it."

"Your face!" She lashed out with her foot and kicked him squarely in the balls.

A loud curse split her ears as he hunched over in pain.

"I'm letting you off lightly. Get the hell out of here before I do something worse," she snarled.

"I-I can't leave," he groaned, still doubled over. "I'm the camp leader for the Securistate team."

"Did you know I was here?"

"I-I knew," Victor said as he straightened his back. "I used to work for Securistate, remember? When I got fired from the job at the hospital, they kept me on for other work. That's why I'm here."

"Well, not on my team. Stay the hell out of my way."

"I, uh, I can't," he said reluctantly. "I was assigned to your team because I used to work for Securistate. I know I have a lot to make up for. I'd like to use this opportunity to help you get through this week."

"I don't want your help. You're a werewolf. You should be on the werewolves' team."

"They wouldn't want me on there either. One of

them is my half-brother, but my mom and our dad were mates whereas he's a bastard. He resents me for that."

"I don't care."

"You should care. I saw him staring at you. As a bastard, Quentin's had it rough. He became so vicious that now he's Crispin's enforcer. But I have a high standing too in Crispin's pack. If he's interested in you, you could use my help."

He gave her an innocent smile that immediately made her suspicious. He didn't do innocent well. Besides, as a werewolf, she didn't want him to get too close to her.

"Please, Erin, let me make it up to you," he begged.

Throwing up her hands in disgust, she turned away. "You'd better not betray me again."

"I won't!" he promised.

"*I propose we still kill him,*" Gideon said.

"*I second that,*" Altman agreed.

She sighed as she reached the cabin. She had caught the eye of a werewolf, and now she had run into Victor.

Can this trip get any worse?

She needed to talk to Pauline. She could use a sympathetic ear. She switched on her new cell phone.

With this trip in mind, Dane had given her a smart phone to replace the cheap pre-paid phone she had been using. When he'd given it to her, Dane had demanded she keep him informed while she was at her team building. Otherwise, he wouldn't *allow* her to go. She had not been in the mood for a round of control-freak smackdown, especially because she found it so difficult to resist Dane when he used his stern, deep voice, so she'd quietly accepted the new phone. She intended to call him later that week, but first she had to speak with Pauline.

She couldn't call Dane to complain about Victor since he'd probably demand that she quit her job and live with him. He would turn her into his kept woman.

No, she'd just tell him that there was no signal where they took her.

I just hope that there won't be any consequences for keeping quiet.

NINE

"We're going to do a survival and treasure hunt exercise. You'll be challenged both mentally and physically," Mike said to the group. "Survival training is a character building exercise."

There's nothing wrong with my character, Erin thought rebelliously as she looked outside.

Through the window, she heard the wind howl as it blew snow to the ground in a great white sheet. The lodge groaned around them while the logs crackled in the fireplace causing flames to dance cheerfully on the wall.

"You want us to go out in this?" Nikko asked the organizer incredulously, waving his chubby fingers toward the window and the violent snowstorm beyond.

The man smiled. "There's no such thing as bad weather, only bad clothes. Fortunately, Jonathan Stratton has provided you with excellent material."

He was right. Erin was wearing snow boots, several layers of clothing and holding a pair of mittens in her hands. Actually today, the cold didn't seem to bother her as much. In fact, she could feel the sweat dripping from her body.

Maybe I'm sick.

"I don't understand why we have to do this. Some of us don't even have physical jobs. I'm a secretary," Sheila complained.

"But you're part of a team. As Mr. Stratton said, this is about teamwork. Your survival depends on everyone working together. You're allowed to sabotage the other group though."

Erin noticed Quentin and his friend staring at her again.

Great. Sabotage.

"The first exercise we'll do is going to be right outside our camp. That way we can also observe our opponents' strengths and weaknesses before we split up."

Okay, let's do this.

She opened the door, and a gust of wind blew in a dusting of snow. She thought it was quite refreshing as she inhaled freezing air into her lungs, foggy breath clouded before her when she exhaled.

She listened to the sound of footsteps crunching on the frozen grass as they walked behind the camp leader for a few minutes.

He stopped at a clearing with several large poplars. He pointed at two packages high up in the trees. On the ground were a helmet, harness, rope and some other climbing equipment.

The blond man lifted the helmet. "Safety first. And that is also what you must remember when we leave Camp Happy. I understand you might have to leave the group occasionally when nature calls. But if you get in trouble, you must remember to do six whistle blasts or torch flashes in quick succession."

"We don't have a whistle or a torch," Frank said.

The man put the helmet down. "Indeed, that's why you have to climb up this tree and get the equipment we put up on the top. You can't leave before you have them."

Victor appeared beside Erin. "Hi."

She frowned. "I don't see why they call this team building when they give us an exercise that only one of us can do."

"Maybe they expect us to stand on each other's shoulders, like a human ladder?" Frank suggested. He nodded at the werewolves. "Why aren't they shifting?"

"It isn't full moon," she said.

"We can shift when it isn't full moon, Erin. You know that," Victor said.

Right.

She had forgotten about the time she had used glamour on him to get him to leave her apartment. It had backfired. Victor had shifted into a werewolf instead.

Does this mean that I now also have to worry about my wolf emerging during the day? Great!

"Besides," Victor continued, "there isn't much use for them to shift into wolves for this exercise since wolves don't climb trees."

"But strong humans do. Look at them!" Frank said. He had been right about the human ladder idea. It seemed to be working for them.

"I'm not going to let Nikko stand on top of me," she said.

"Well, I'm not going to stand on the bottom and carry all of you!" Nikko protested.

Victor looked at Sheila. "How about you? Do you have any ideas?"

Erin had several ideas: a telekinesis spell or shifting into her leopard, but she didn't want Frank to see what she could do. She also wasn't sure if a shift into her leopard form would encourage the wolf to emerge too. Meanwhile, the werewolves reached the package.

In spite of her breath puffing while in the cold, she was so warm, she felt nauseous and faint.

Do I have the flu or is it something else?

If it was something else, she didn't want to draw anyone's attention, but she couldn't keep standing here. She narrowed her eyes on the package. She could get a gust of wind to make it fall.

"Go, Frank!" Sheila shouted. Frank had thrown the rope around one of the branches and was pulling himself up while Sheila, Nikko, Victor and three other colleagues were holding the rope on the other side.

"Hey, Holland," Frank cried out. "This is a team effort. Make sure that the others don't drop me."

She grinned and joined the others in holding the rope. She laughed when Frank arrived at the top of the tree and threw down the package, cheering as it landed on the snow-covered ground.

She turned to see if the werewolves had witnessed their success, but they had already left. The Securistate people continued to hold the rope while Frank lowered himself, and everyone applauded once he reached the ground.

"Well done, Frank. I didn't know you could be so resourceful," Nikko said.

Victor walked up to stand beside Erin. "It's funny. If I'd done a bet beforehand I would have said that you were the resourceful one."

She regarded Victor suspiciously. "Really, why's that?"

He shrugged. "No reason. Good job."

"It was Frank," she said. "I didn't do anything."

Victor winked at her, a teasing glint twinkled in his brown eyes. "I know. Well done."

She blinked in confusion as she saw him join the others, who were opening the package.

What does he mean, well done what?

She was relieved that they had managed to get the equipment without having to expose what she was capable of.

Victor had commented on her smelling different from humans before. Did he know she could have helped them with her powers, and had he just complemented her for her restraint by not helping her colleagues?

The resourceful one, did he expect me to use my powers? Did he want me to?

"*I still think we should kill him*," Gideon said.

"*I don't trust him. Be careful*," her mother warned.

"*I don't trust him either*," Altman said.

Erin's gaze skittered from her colleagues to Victor, looking down on all of them as they crouched to take out all the equipment. For a moment, their stares locked, but she couldn't read his expression.

Me neither.

Tilting her head back, Erin squinted up at the sky. Was this weather ever going to change? The snow was falling so fast she couldn't see more than thirty feet or so. The idea of hiking on steep, narrow trails in a snowstorm while carrying a heavy backpack did not appeal to her.

"Don't look so grumpy, Erin," Frank said. "It's an adventure."

She pulled a face. Snowflakes coated her cheeks. "You should see yourself. You even have snow sticking to your eyelashes."

"It's only for a couple of days. I bet they'll do the psychological part inside."

"I'm trembling," she complained.

Although, it's not from the cold.

"Maybe if we walk faster, we'll feel better," he suggested.

Picking up the pace, they trudged through the snow until they stopped in front of a river. A pile of tree trunks and a rope lay on the riverbank.

"Listen up, guys," Victor cried out. "We'll have to cross this nearly frozen river. You have ten minutes to think of as many alternatives as possible, no matter how absurd."

"Okay, anyone fancy a swim?" Erin joked.

"You first," Sheila said. "If you want, I can even hold your clothes."

"I think Sheila should go first. She shouldn't have any

difficulty staying afloat with those inflatable breasts as a life vest," Leila said.

Erin laughed while Sheila glared at her. "Hey, I just think you're funny."

"Oh, I forgot to mention," Victor added. "You're not allowed to comment on any suggestion during these ten minutes."

Frank pointed at the tree trunks. "It's obvious they expect us to make some kind of a bridge or maybe a raft. No paddles though."

"*Or you could freeze the river using an ice spell,*" Erin's mom said. "*I've done them before, so you and Leila could go ice skating. It's short and quick.*"

"*Yes, and then they'll put this in Erin's performance review,*" Gideon said.

"There are a couple of large rocks in the water and on shore. Maybe we could throw them all in the water in one line and step on them?" Nikko proposed.

"Yes, or maybe we could build wings out of the branches and then fly across," Erin said.

After that, nobody came up with any other solutions. In the end, they decided to build the bridge with the long rope. They cut it up and used it to tie two tree trunks together. After making three sets of doubled-up logs, they attached the top of each trunk to the other trunk. The trunks were about six feet wide and impossible to carry, so they pushed them until they rolled into the water.

Their bridge was long enough to reach the other shore, and thanks to the non-existent current, the bridge didn't move.

Sheila stared at the water and shivered. "I miss a railing."

"It looks pretty stable," Frank said. "I'll give it a try."

"Be careful, Frank," Erin warned. "You don't want to get hypothermia. Oh, I can't watch!"

She walked away from the group. "Mom, just in case, what was that spell?"

Her mother hesitated briefly before she said, "*Cool the breeze for the water to freeze. The water is no threat. We won't get wet. The ice won't shake. The ice won't break. The ice will hold me. As is my will so mote it—*"

"Frank!" Erin heard Sheila shout. She turned around, and a jolt of fear shot through her as she saw Frank lying on his stomach, clutching a tree trunk in the middle of the river. The other trunk had split and was drifting away. She took ragged breaths, trying to control her panic. They were at least three hours away from their camp.

"*Use the spell,*" Erin's mother shouted.

She swallowed against rising bile. Nobody was paying attention. But if she froze the water, her secret would be out.

Frank would be safe though.

Unless I use another spell, one that isn't so visible.

She closed her eyes to think, when inspiration struck.

"*As if the trunks were tied to the ground.*
In the water, the wood will be bound.
The trunks will be still.
As is my will."

TOUCHED BY DARKNESS

She heard the others still yelling, but when she opened her eyes she noticed that the trunk that had been drifting down the river had stopped moving. Of course, she couldn't tell the others what she had done, but she had to show them that Frank was relatively safe now.

"Erin, what are the hell you doing!" Nikko shouted as she stepped on the self-made bridge.

Ignoring him, she walked up to Frank. He gazed up at her and frowned. "It's bad enough if I fall in, but I can't have you fall in too."

She shook her head. "Teamwork, remember? Besides, I think you were right. It does look stable. Just watch the water. There isn't any current at all."

He looked down at the water. "Gee, you're right."

She held out her hand to him. "Let me help you up. But be careful! The wood is slippery." Together they walked to the other side of the river and waited for the others to walk across. In the end, everyone followed them, even Sheila.

Victor said nothing. He merely smirked at her, his teeth glinting. She waited for the others to pass, and then she returned to the water to undo her magic spell. She couldn't risk anyone else investigating why these trunks wouldn't move anymore.

She was about to say the words when she noticed the side where one of the trunks had split. It appeared to have been cut with a saw for the most part. Only the top looked rough, as if it had split naturally, but the rest was clearly a manufactured cut that was meant to break as soon as someone walked across it.

Sabotage.

"Should I show the others?"

"*I wouldn't,*" Erin's mother advised. "*Your colleagues might wonder why this one suddenly stopped moving too.*"

She agreed and broke the spell, watching the evidence float away.

"Hey, Erin," Frank called out. "You coming?"

"Yes, I—" Her throat closed, and her heart began to pound when she caught her reflection in the river. For a second, she could have sworn she saw the ripple of the face of a yellow gold wolf, its intense eyes staring back at her.

Startled she stepped back. She whirled around to see if any of the others had seen it too.

"Come on, Erin," Frank said. He was standing several feet away. He acted as if he hadn't witnessed anything out of the ordinary. "Hurry up."

After a moment's hesitation, she took a last glimpse at her reflection. Her human form looked back at her. She cleared her throat. "Yes, I'm coming."

She turned around and rushed to follow Frank, leaving the image in the water behind.

"We're going to sleep in snow holes tonight," Victor said. "But first we need to build a group shelter, so we can keep warm while we're having dinner."

"Snow holes? What are we, rabbits?" Erin muttered, although she did find the location impressive. She would probably enjoy the view of the snow-capped mountains before her more if she could stop scratching her skin.

Victor laughed. "I don't know, are you?"

"Ha ha, you're so funny. Please stop," she snapped.

"Hey, *chère*, will you please stop with hurtin' yourself like that," Frank said.

"What?" she asked.

"With them scratchin'," Frank explained. "Please don't tell me that the bunk beds gave you lice or fleas?"

She was hardly aware of her behavior. All she could focus on was a fiery itch and the urge to claw at her skin. "Or something," she muttered. The urge became so strong she had to cross her arms and tuck her hands beneath her elbows.

"Erin, you okay?" Frank touched her upper arm, his face creased with concern. "You look pale."

She felt twitchy and anxious, as if her skin was too tight. She could hear Sheila and Nikko stomping through the forest, searching for branches for their shelter. Maybe her ears were oversensitive, but it seemed as if every branch they stepped on cracked like a gunshot and that every leaf they brushed against squeaked in pain.

She gritted her teeth. "Could you please turn it down?" Her head swam as though she had walked through the bayou.

"What the hell is the matter with her?" she heard Sheila mumble.

"I bet it's that time of the month," Nikko

sneered.

"I can hear you!" Erin cried out.

"She's such a freak," Sheila whispered.

I can hear that too, Erin thought aggressively. *And maybe he's right about it being that time of the month.*

Agonizing cramps jolted through her belly, and she hissed in pain.

"Maybe you need to sit down," Frank said.

"*Or maybe you need to run as a leopard*," Leila suggested. "*It could be that your werewolf is emerging. My leopard might help you suppress these symptoms.*"

"*Or maybe you should call Pauline again. She promised she would continue to work on a cure*," Erin's mother said.

"*Only a witch would put that much faith in another witch*," Gideon whined.

"That's actually not a bad idea," Erin said.

"Great. Just sit and relax while we are making the shelter," Frank said.

"Uh, I want to try and call my roommate," Erin said.

Victor appeared and watched her through half-lidded eyes. "You don't have any reception here."

Her eyebrows rose, she wouldn't take his word for it. She shook as she took her cell phone from her pocket. Thanks to the input of some interesting horror movies, her roommate had tried to investigate possible cures with mariposa flowers and wolfsbane, but Pauline hadn't been able to find a lot of useful information before her departure. She'd refused to give up.

Please let Pauline have found a cure.

127

She turned on the phone, but quickly discovered that Victor had told her the truth.

Shit.

She hoped Dane wouldn't kill her, assuming these werewolf side effects didn't kill her first.

"Sitting still is probably not a good idea in this cold weather," Sheila said as she dropped the branches next to Erin.

Erin stared at Nikko's secretary in annoyance, feeling unease creep over her skin. Closing her eyes, she sucked in air as she tried to keep the predator inside. Frightening images flashed in her mind, wild monsters attacking big-chested secretaries...

"Your eyes," Sheila whispered.

Erin panted, and a groan worked itself from the depths of her chest. "What?" she growled.

"They're glowing," Sheila said.

Fuck.

She got up, her legs shaking. "I'll be right back," she said in a tight voice.

"Where are you going?" Frank asked.

"Looking for branches."

Erin had walked as far as she could before she collapsed. She couldn't stop the tremor in her hands and was racked by chills as her skin burned with fever.

"*Shift into the leopard,*" Leila repeated. "*Fight the werewolf.*"

Rolling onto her back, she peered up at the

cloudy sky. In spite of it being four o'clock in the afternoon, she could sense the moon's power. Her skin continued to crawl and itch with the need to shift.

"*Take your clothes off first!*" Leila shouted.

"*In the snow? She'll catch a cold,*" her mother said.

"It's okay, Mom. I'm burning up anyway." Erin's hands trembled as she got up and took off her clothes.

Okay, even if I'm burning up, it's never a good idea to wear nothing but socks while standing in a snow-covered landscape.

Leopard, she thought as she closed her eyes, breathing deeply. Her pulse increased as all of her senses went on alert. She could sense the wolf too, and a low snarl escaped her.

"*What the fuck was that?*" Gideon said. "*That sure didn't sound like any leopard I know.*"

She had never experienced such agony during her shift before. Heat exploded in her body, and she fell to the cold ground, her muscles contorting. The air around her seemed to shimmer. She felt the heat rise through her body as she let her animal out.

After the shift, she briefly experienced confusion.

What did I turn into?

She stood up and shook her fur. She glanced down at her familiar cream-colored legs covered with black spots. Triumphant that she had managed to resist her wolf, she took off.

Sprinting through the snow, her breathing came in shallow pants, and her heart pounded in this alien territory. It was starting to get dark, but in her leopard form, her night vision was far better, so the dense trees and snow-covered undergrowth did little to slow her.

She raced ahead. She had new smells to discover. The heady scent of the decay of winter filled her sensitive nostrils. She ran on uneven terrain. Several times she tripped, but she never fell down. She reached the edge of a small clearing when she heard a howl not far away from her. She froze and crouched close to the cold ground.

Enemy.

She examined the ground and caught a glimpse of something that seemed to be a depression in a small patch of muddy dirt. It was a print, the size of a werewolf paw.

She scouted the area for movement. She looked around the woods, half expecting to see werewolves emerging from behind the trees. Even though she was still in leopard form, she became conscious of the danger of her little escapade. She should have stayed at the camp, far away from the wolves. She should not have risked a repeat of her encounter with the werewolves.

She had heard that scent could be a powerful memory trigger, but could memory also evoke smell? She could swear that she smelled them again. It reached out to her, pulled at her, fur, temptation.

No. Enemy. Fight it.

She discovered Victor lurking in the shadows watching her in his werewolf shape. She charged forward, ears laid back and hissing. Victor's body rippled as fur and skin stretched out and faded as he shifted back to his human form.

Naked, solid muscle.

Evil.

A low snarl escaped her.

"Fucking hell, Erin!" Victor cried. "What are you doing shifting so close to camp?"

Her back arched, she moved closer.

Victor raised his hands and backed up. "I only want to help you. Don't you remember I'm one of the organizers? I had to find you when you ran off like that. It's dangerous out here!"

She growled.

"Okay, you look like you can defend yourself, but what if you'd run into the competition? How do you think a pack of wolves react when they smell a big cat? A cat that smells delicious by the way." A look of puzzlement crossed his face. "You smell different. What's wrong? Are you sick? Shift back so I can take a look."

No. I can't let him smell that I'm different.

This time she was the one moving backward.

"Oh come on. You don't have to worry about modesty. I have seen you naked before." A small smile twitched around the corners of his mouth. "I won't drool, I promise."

She hissed once more before she spun on her feet and stalked away.

"Don't be like that! Fuck. Please shift back. You don't want the others to see a leopard here. They might link it to you."

Shit. He's right.

She kept her back turned to his and focused on shifting back.

Nothing happened.

Okay, don't worry. It's just because he's watching. Ignore him.

Taking a deep breath, she stood in silence, waiting and picturing herself in human form, her golden eyes, her curly blond hair, her small breasts... The image became blurry, disappeared, and the leopard stared back at her.

She heard Victor approach her. "What's going on? Can't you shift back?"

I'm stuck!

She could taste panic, sour and nauseating, on the tip of her tongue. She was trapped as her leopard counterpart. Tears of frustration and weariness prickled behind her eyelids. She tried again to shift back, but the leopard held too much power over her.

Please let me shift back.

The feline must have sensed the lupine, and maybe she worried that if she allowed Erin to shift back, the wolf would take over. Maybe she felt threatened by having to share Erin's body with another animal.

Erin cried out and did what her instincts told her to do.

She ran.

TEN

Still in leopard form, Erin darted toward what she hoped was the direction of the camp. All the trees looked alike to her.

"*Stop freaking out,*" Leila said. "*Just relax, and you'll be able to shift back.*"

She won't let me.

Erin stopped running and took several deep breaths, trying to calm herself while looking at the sky. Ominous gray clouds gathered while gusts of wind drew snow from the rocky peaks.

Peaks.

She remembered those. She picked up her pace, hoping she could use the mountains as a reference point.

She had just enough time to wonder if the mountains had been right behind the camp or more to its left side when she heard laughter that reminded her of Nikko. Her recognition was cemented when she heard Frank's voice.

"I don't find this funny. I sure hope that Victor finds her quickly."

As she approached the camp, the scent of food hit her nostrils. Just as she reached the edge of trees, she saw Sheila piling up her plate with barbecue food. She crawled up to the clearing, hiding in the bushes. She remained entirely motionless and listened.

"I hope she wasn't attacked by some wild animal," Sheila said.

Nikko snorted. "Right, I think that wild animals have more to fear from her. She's nothing but a freak."

"I think it's very unprofessional to call your employee a freak," Frank said.

"I think it's very dumb to say to the person writing your performance reviews that he's unprofessional," Nikko countered.

Sheila got up and walked away.

"Hey, where are you going? We don't want another woman to disappear."

"To the toilet," Sheila whispered. "Geesh, Nikko, could you be any louder? I don't think the werewolves heard you."

Sheila walked in Erin's direction while sweeping the beam of her flashlight in front of her.

Please don't let her see me.

Erin pressed her body down into the snow but worried that the color of her fur would stand out too much compared to that of the fluffy white ground. She had even pushed her face into the snow. She realized that she couldn't hear the footsteps anymore. She hesitated, worried that if she took a peek, her movement would betray her. Her heartbeat accelerated when she lifted her head to find the beam of a flashlight blinding her.

She blinked and noticed that Sheila's eyes were

wide open. Nikko's secretary seemed frozen with terror.

Shit.

As Erin spun and took off, she heard Sheila scream with horror. The sound was so bloodcurdling that she flinched. Blind fear ruling her feet, she no longer paid any attention to her surroundings. The only thought in her mind was that she had to move away from the noise, and it didn't matter where to.

Branches cut into her as she ran through the forest. Cold wind ruffled her fur as she darted. The sounds and scents of the unfamiliar forest helped to distract her from her fear of her inability to shift back. She ran deeper into the woods, losing all sense of time and of direction, until she couldn't run anymore. Panting for breath, she collapsed.

She could hear the pounding of her heart, her heavy breathing and leaves rustling, but she couldn't detect anyone nearby. Her sense of smell also told her she was alone. She stretched out her muscles, trying to relax.

"I think she still can't shift back," Leila muttered.

"Maybe she can try to reach out to Dane," Altman suggested. *"They seem to be having some kind of connection."*

"He's only a vampire. What does he know about shapeshifters?" Leila sneered.

"Come on, honey," her mother said. *"Don't give up."*

Erin tried once more to focus on the image of herself as a human being, but kept seeing the leopard. Her throat was fast closing in, and despair swelled inside her.

Is Altman right? Can I reach out to Dane?

She tried to picture Dane this time, but again the leopard blocked the image. A low frustrated growl built in her throat.

Her mind whirling, she called out.

Dane! Dane!

But she was unable to speak and let out a snarl instead. She could feel tears gathering behind her eyes. She blinked them away.

Oh God, I'm going to stay this way forever. Until someone finds me and locks me up in a zoo somewhere.

She curled up into a ball, dread twisted in her stomach.

Please don't let me stay this way, especially not in this cold and barren place. How will I survive? Goodbye, Dane.

"Erin?" A man's voice. "Erin, is that you?"

Dane? Dane, can you hear me?

"*Erin, what is it? Call me!*"

It was definitely Dane's voice.

She tried to think of a response, but a mounting tension in her head made it hard to concentrate. She closed her eyes for a moment and took a deep breath.

I'm stuck.

The headache, which had begun as a faint pressure at her temples, was turning into something stronger.

There's no reception out here, wherever here is. But even if there was, I can't hold the phone.

"*What the hell is going on!*" he bellowed.

She shivered. His anger was pulsing through her now, pushing at her ribs, making the fur on her body feel as if it were electric with his fury.

I'm stuck in my leopard body.

"*Why the fuck are you shifting as a leopard around your colleagues in the first place?*"

She sighed. *Look, I can't have this discussion now, okay? I'm exhausted. Could you please help me shift back?*

"*How?*"

For some reason I'm not able to picture myself as a human. Whenever I try, I see the leopard instead. Can you think of me, the way you see me, and maybe then through you I can see me too?

"*I knew I shouldn't have let you go to this team-building event. Fucking Stratton,*" Dane said. "*Fine.*"

And then she saw herself as Dane saw her, long, curly blond hair, golden eyes, a smile on her face and not so tiny breasts, naked.

It helped. Thanks to the vampire, Erin was finally able to wrestle enough control from the leopard to shift back to her human form.

"It worked," she said with emotion thick in her voice.

"*Erin?*" he asked.

It worked, she repeated in silence this time.

Oh, fuck. It worked.

She was naked in the middle of a forest she didn't know. Meanwhile, the snow had changed over to sleet, which hit her like icy needles. She stood up, her bare feet slippery on the cold ground. She took a step when a wave of dizziness hit her. She managed to walk up to a large pine tree that seemed to be at least a hundred and fifty feet tall. She leaned against the trunk.

TOUCHED BY DARKNESS

"*What's going on? Talk to me,*" Dane demanded. "*Where are you? I'll get you back!*"

Her vision wavered, and blackness edged her consciousness before she finally fell down and passed out.

Victor stared at the unconscious woman lying underneath the tree. What the hell was she doing there, lying naked and vulnerable in the winter landscape? She had to be frozen solid. She was deathly pale with dark, smudged hollows below her eyes. Was this part of Stratton's plan? He bit back a growl. Had that bastard drugged her somehow? Victor's anger boiled but he kept a tight hold on it. He had been forced to cooperate with Stratton, but he hadn't signed up for murder. His nostrils flared and took in her scent. He couldn't smell any drugs in her system.

He had noticed her struggle when he had told her to shift back. Could it be that Stratton had used a witch to trap her in her leopard form? And why wasn't she in her leopard body now?

It doesn't make any sense.

So far, Stratton had told him what he wanted Victor to do and witness. If Stratton had arranged something without Victor's knowledge, how did he expect Victor to keep him informed of Erin's response to his twisted games?

And would Stratton have risked losing Erin when his sabotage had only just begun? What if he hadn't been able to track her down?

In her panic, Erin had run around in circles a couple of times. A less powerful werewolf wouldn't have been able to find her. Fortunately for him, it hadn't been hard to track down her scent at all, but that was because he knew her. She smelled like no one else.

He bent down to lift Erin in his arms. As he scooped her up, he gazed at her in shock. Erin should have been wet and chilled, but she was hot and feverish instead. He didn't know a lot about hypothermia, but this response seemed unnatural.

"Erin?" he whispered.

No response.

He sighed. He had hoped that she would wake up, so he could tell her to shift. Then he wouldn't have to carry her all the way to the camp. On the other hand, it had been a long time since he had been able to touch a woman, and touching Erin had been a recurring fantasy of his ever since he had found her naked and tied up to her bed, struggling with the handcuffs.

Holding her now as he was rushing back toward the camp, one arm under her bare legs, and the other supporting her back, made him feel like a groom carrying his bride to their wedding night. It wasn't his fault that she was naked, and that his hands were so large that his right hand covered a large part of her right breast.

He couldn't help but notice the silkiness of her skin. Damn it. She was passed out. He shouldn't be aware of her small but perfectly formed breast, her small waist and her nice, curvy hips. Those inviting curves begged to be touched. His thumb touched her rosy pink nipple. Though she was out cold, her body reacted, and a low moan parted her lips. He felt his cock hardening.

Fuck.

"Erin," he tried again.

Maybe it was the way he was carrying her. He stopped, squatted down, placed Erin's body over his shoulder and rose up.

Yes, much better.

This way he didn't really see her, and his hands only touched her waist and her creamy thighs. Only now, her hips were at the same level as his nose. Her scent wrapped around him. He tried hard to ignore the temptation to move her just a little bit so he could breathe in her feminine heat. He longed to lick every inch of her soft, creamy-pale, mouth-watering skin. His wolf was pushing at him to claim her.

But then he smelled something else, something new, something feral, fresh and sharp like a forest after the rain. He had smelled the leopard before, but this was different. This scent he knew.

She smells like a werewolf.

Was that why she had been stuck in her leopard form? Had a werewolf recently bitten her, and was she now trying to suppress her emerging wolf? He tried to picture Erin as a wolf. Would her fur be blond like her hair, or would she be gray like the three other female werewolves he knew from Crispin's pack?

His cousin's pack had twenty-eight members, so

the female werewolves were clearly outnumbered. The shift to werewolf was usually too brutal for a woman to survive. In fact, half the men that were bitten didn't make it either.

Poor Erin, to undergo that and Stratton.

And me.

Guilt pierced him like a blade. He had been responsible for the river incident, and he thought of the other equipment he had tampered with.

It's only going to get worse.

Stratton would love watching Erin become a werewolf, even if the long and painful shift tore her apart. Should he go to Crispin? Stratton might reward him financially if Victor told him what he knew.

But there may be a bigger gain for me here.

He could turn this around and create a win-win situation for both him and Erin. A satisfied smile curved his lips. If Erin survived the shift, she would need him to have a life with the pack. She would have little choice in the matter.

And she would survive. She was stronger than most men he knew. But if Stratton ever found out that he had known about Erin's wolf and had chosen not to inform him, he would kill him. And the bastard had the resources to succeed, after he played with him first.

He frowned. He shouldn't make any decision in the heat of the moment. He had to think about his discovery. But no matter what he decided to do with this knowledge, Victor knew that it would alter the course of his life—and hers.

TOUCHED BY DARKNESS

Large hands traveled down Erin's naked body, and it came alive under his touch. A mouth, hot and demanding covered hers. She offered no resistance as it plundered her own before trailing kisses down her throat to lick and suck at her neck. She cried out when she felt the sharp pleasure-pain of teeth.

His hands moved toward her breasts. A whimper escaped as her nipples pressed into his palms. Immediately, he rolled one of them between his thumb and forefinger while his other hand moved between her thighs. Tracing lightly, teasing her until she lifted her hips in an attempt to get his fingers where she needed them most.

"Please," Erin begged in a breathless whisper.

"Not yet," Dane murmured. He lifted his head and looked down at her. "Not until you promise me that you'll return to Hope Acres as soon as you wake up."

His words had the effect of a cold shower. A red haze distorted her vision, and her fists clenched at her sides.

"Get off of me. Now," she ordered. He smiled but the smile didn't touch his cool blue eyes. He also refused to budge.

"Let me go!" she demanded hoarsely.

"Never," he vowed, and it infuriated her. She pushed him away and rolled off the bed. When he followed her, she took a step back. She forced her chin up, glaring at him. His eyes narrowed, and his lips set into a fine line. She tried to ignore the sight of his erection jutting out from his body.

But she couldn't, damn it. She bit her lips to refrain from begging him to take her. She had to get her hormones under control.

Moving toward the doorway, she refused to turn her

back on him. She continued to watch him intently. But then she blinked.

He struck with incredible speed. A shiver of fear and desire ran through her. But when he pulled her arms over her head, she forgot everything but the need in her body.

He pushed her back into the bed, holding her captive, his mouth fused to hers. She gasped when he moved to kiss her neck.

"If you don't come back to me, I'll come and find you," he growled softly into her ear. She wanted to give in and moaned. His questing lips made surrender easy, and she opened her legs, offering herself to him without reservation.

But then the soft bed disappeared, and she found herself lying on a cold, hard surface. She tried to open her eyes, but her body refused to cooperate. It seemed frozen to the uncomfortable stone floor. Through her closed eyes, a shadow approached her. He bent down, and she sensed him observing her.

She recognized him. His intoxicating scent enveloped her before she felt his mouth on hers. His tongue caressed her lips. She wanted to lift her arms and return his gentle kiss. Why couldn't she respond? His mouth felt so good.

Sharp teeth sank into her lip.

Erin woke cradled in a man's arms. She felt the hard press of his naked body. Heat emanated from it, warming her. A muscular arm was wrapped around her waist. Disoriented for a moment, she opened her eyes a couple of times and blinked the sleep haze from her vision. She was surrounded by white. Her hand reached up and touched the cold ceiling.

Oh my God, I'm buried alive! She experienced a second of panic.

"Don't worry," a familiar voice behind her soothed.

Victor.

The previous night washed over her as she remembered.

"Good morning, sweetheart," Victor said as he nuzzled his face against her neck.

"Oh, bloody hell," she muttered. She pushed his head away, but he couldn't go far. She turned around. "What the hell am I doing in here with you?"

He flashed a mischievous grin. "What do you think you were doing? I'm naked. You're naked."

And his body has all the pent-up vigor of a wolf.

She shook her head to drive away the unwelcome thought when the realization of what had happened, hit her. "Of course, body heat, you must have found me nearly frozen."

He frowned.

"Oh, I'm sorry," she apologized. "Thank you for finding me and for warming me up. You saved my life. But now, I have to get out of here. I hate small spaces."

She saw the opening of the snow hole and sighed in relief. "I hope you haven't hidden my clothes somewhere. I would hate to shock my colleagues."

She tried to sneak past him when he grabbed her wrist. "Erin. We need to talk."

"No, we don't." She tried to pull free, but Victor tightened his grip.

"What happened to you?" he asked.

"Nothing, I just had to let out the leopard. That's all. Don't you sometimes need to let your wolf out?"

He gave a short bark of laughter. "Yes, sometimes I let my wolf out."

She managed to pull her arm from his grasp and found her clothes sticking out of the backpack next to their hole. It was still dark when she put on her clothes, but she saw on her watch that it was quarter past seven and expected the others to wake up soon. She hoped they wouldn't ask her any awkward questions.

"*I can't believe you slept with Victor*," Leila complained.

"*Don't tell Dane*," Altman warned.

She walked away from the snow hole, hoping that in spite of Victor's werewolf senses, she was out of his hearing distance. "Uh, but isn't it better if he hears it from me? I really believe nothing happened. Victor was just teasing me."

"*Believe me when I tell you that Dane doesn't want to hear this. If you forget about sleeping naked with surfer boy, there is that pesky little matter of you almost freezing to death*," Leila said. "*He will never allow you to go anywhere ever again.*"

"Great," she mumbled as she searched for a place to relieve herself. "More secrets that I have to hide."

I just hope I didn't reveal my werewolf secret to Victor last night.

ELEVEN

"**A**ccording to this map, we should be close to the treasure," Sheila said while looking inquisitively at Victor.

Victor lifted his hands defensively. "I'm sorry, but I'm not allowed to help you with the actual search."

"Then what *help* are you?" Erin whispered.

He growled at her, and she grinned sheepishly at him. It probably wasn't a good idea to antagonize him, especially since she couldn't stop shaking. If this turned out to be a symptom of her upcoming werewolf shift, she was better off not attracting his attention. No more than she already had with her adventure the previous night.

Meanwhile, her colleagues had continued their climb upwards. Erin and Victor followed them around the bend in silence. The path opened into a wide clearing, leading them to the edge of the earth. Some colleagues moaned as they dropped their backpacks and peered over the side of a cliff.

"Did we make a wrong turn somewhere?" Frank asked. She joined him, leaning over and staring straight down. Several feet below, a massive rock stuck out, offering them an area large enough to stand on and pick up the big wooden box that someone had left for them to find.

"Afraid not," she said. Below them, the powdery-soft looking snow-covered landscape was hiding the rocky terrain beneath. The flat surface could be covered in ice.

Please don't let anyone fall down.

Long, bare branches of poplar and birch trees fused with dark green pine needles surrounded them, closing them in. She drew in a deep breath of clean, pine-scented air. But it did not give her a sense of peace.

You're allowed to sabotage the other group.

The trunks they had used in their previous exercise had been visibly cut. What if the werewolves had decided to cut their rope too? She promised herself she would thoroughly inspect it.

"Okay, our next challenge," Victor said. "How are we going to collect our treasure box?"

"Not me," Sheila and Nikko said at the same time. Victor chuckled, and the sound ricocheted off the walls of vegetation surrounding them.

Erin noticed Frank's shrug, realizing that he was about to volunteer himself again. She vehemently shook her head. She would not allow him to get hurt, not after what had almost happened in the river. He caught her glare and closed his mouth.

"I don't think any of us wants to climb down there. Why don't we draw straws?" she proposed.

"People above a certain age should be excluded," Nikko said. He appeared to be in his early fifties and was clearly the oldest of the group.

TOUCHED BY DARKNESS

"*He wants to use his age as an argument? I would have picked his weight,*" Gideon sneered. "*There's no rope strong enough to carry him.*"

"*On the other hand, it wouldn't be such a big loss if he were to fall down a cliff,*" Leila said.

Silently, Erin agreed.

"I think Erin has a good idea. We can fold pieces of paper, and one of them will say something like 'treasure hunter'. I don't believe it's fair to exclude anyone though. Apart from myself, since I'm the organizer." Victor grinned as he took out a sheet of paper, tore it up and threw the pieces into a bag. After he had written something on one of them, he put it back.

When it was her turn to draw, Victor said, "Remember, no peeking!"

She drew a blank piece of paper. She sighed in relief when she heard Nikko curse. She turned around and saw that her manager's beady eyes were fixed in her direction. He twisted the piece of paper nervously in his fingers before throwing it on the ground.

"Fine, but if I die, it's *her* fault." Nikko pointed at her. He then walked up to Victor's backpack, taking out a long rope. He gave one end to Victor. "Tie it around that tree. I trust it more than I do my cowardly colleagues."

Victor did as he was told, while Nikko continued his ranting, his face red with rage. "You're nothing but a bunch of incompetents."

Holding the rope tightly, Nikko stood at edge of the cliff. The few graying hairs on his head blew wildly about in the wind as he got on his knees and let himself slide down.

"Are you paying attention? I'll show you how it's done."

Erin saw the rope pull taut and twitch, and she narrowed her eyes. Were some of its fibers coming loose? She ran to take a closer look when it broke apart. Seconds later, she heard Nikko's terror-filled scream as he fell. Her stomach lurched when she heard his crash. Reluctantly, Erin peered down the cliff.

Please don't let me see a smashed Nikko!

Victor walked up to stand beside her.

Nikko was in one piece. He was lying on his stomach on the boulder with the wooden box sticking out from under him, and he wasn't moving. His fall had caused the large rock to crack.

"Is he still alive?" Sheila asked hoarsely. The woman could barely be heard.

Erin understood. Her own throat felt closed off due to her heart that seemed to sit inside it. She nodded at Victor.

"You need to call for help," Erin told him.

"Fuck. I know. But I can't. There's no fucking reception here!"

"We can't just leave him down there!" Sheila shouted. "Who knows how long that rock can carry him? Have you seen that crack?"

And the crack in the bolder seemed to widen by the minute.

Shit, why didn't I warn them about the sabotaged trunk? Then we would have checked the ropes at least.

Guilt riddled her gut for what she hadn't done.

TOUCHED BY DARKNESS

Maybe I really did want him dead. Now, I may have gotten my wish.

"Do you have another rope, preferably one that hasn't been tampered with?" Erin asked.

Victor avoided her glare, but she noticed his flush. "There are no ropes," he mumbled. "I guess I can shift and run as fast as I can to the camp. It should take me six hours, tops. Maybe I can send a helicopter to pick him up. I just hope that rock can hold him long enough."

Sobs welled and tore from Sheila's throat. Erin saw that Frank had put his arm around the secretary's shoulder, hugging her.

She then noticed Victor staring at her intensely, almost as if he expected her to do something.

"What?" she snapped.

An eerie smile curved his lips. "I wondered if maybe you could do that thing you do to help him."

She bit the inside of her lip in anger. "What *thing*, and why aren't you doing that *thing* you do, like a partial shift? Why don't you use your claws and climb down?"

He shrugged. "I can't do partial shifts. I either become a full werewolf or stay human. Does that mean that you can shift partially? Could you climb down and carry him up?"

She lifted her eyebrow in suspicion. What was going on? First, he was involved in her kidnapping, and now he was present at another exercise that had been sabotaged, encouraging her to use her powers, pushing her to reveal herself to her colleagues. She remained silent for a long time while she considered her options.

"*If the rock breaks before the helicopter arrives, you'll never be able to forgive yourself,*" Erin's mother said.

"That's crazy! I can't reach him. Well, not without breaking my neck! But even if I did make it down there in one piece, I still couldn't carry him up. He's way too heavy," she protested.

"*Isn't there a spell you can use?*" Altman asked. "*Can't you levitate him?*"

She started to object, but then she remembered that she had used her magic to lift a pencil before. Could she lift him up with a spell after all? But what if her magic wasn't strong enough to keep his four-hundred-pound body afloat?

She shook her head. "He's not a pencil."

When she noticed Victor frowning at her, she turned around.

"*Can't you turn him into a pencil then?*" Leila suggested.

"*No, dear. You can't turn living things into objects,*" her mother answered.

"*I don't see why not,*" Gideon said.

She let out a deep sigh. "Because you'd kill them, duh!"

"*You're no fun. Oh well, I suppose you could turn him into a smaller animal,*" Gideon said.

"*That's not something I would have taught you,*" her mother murmured disapprovingly. "*We don't do black magic.*"

"*No, you don't, Ann. I do. And I think Nikko would rather be turned into a rat and be levitated off that rock alive than left to die.*"

TOUCHED BY DARKNESS

A rat?

"*But you could be lucky. He's so quiet. Maybe he's dead,*" Gideon drawled.

"Lucky!"

"*Well, yeah. If Nikko's dead, you don't have to worry about dropping him when you're trying to levitate him. You won't have to show your colleagues that you're a witch, a nasty one who could turn them into rats.*"

Is Gideon cackling with glee?

"You're enjoying this way too much," she muttered.

"*It'll be nice to finally get some action. You're always acting so paranoid about my magic. Although for the death of me, I can't figure out why you'd even consider exposing yourself for that jerk,*" Gideon grumbled. "*But maybe you don't have to.*"

She examined Nikko's body. "So how do I know he's dead?"

"*Just throw a rock at him. Try to hit him!*"

Erin saw several rocks on the ground but shook her head. "I'd only make it worse."

"*Don't do that, Erin. You're not making anything worse,*" her mother commanded. "*Just shut up, Gideon!*"

"*They'll hate her anyway*," Gideon said.

She heard a soft groan from below and let out a sigh of relief.

"Oh thank God! Nikko! Nikko!" Sheila cried out. "Can you get up? Please get up!"

He groaned again, but didn't move.

"Hey, guys," a deep voice behind her said. Frank touched Erin's back. "What a mess. I wish I could go down and get him, but there's no grip. Say, Victor, I suppose that as an organizer, you've had some trainin' about what to do when there's an emergency. Any thoughts?"

"I might," Victor replied. "Well, Erin, any thoughts?"

She thought of Gideon's suggestion. "A rat?" she said softly.

"Sorry, a what?" Victor asked.

She glanced at Frank and hesitated. Apart from Pauline, he was her only living friend. She thought about the "disgusting creatures" comment he had let slip a month ago. Was she going to lose him now?

Sheila walked up to them. The minute Erin saw Sheila's tearstained face she made up her mind. Erin nodded.

Please Frank, don't hate me for this.

She was going to have to risk it.

"Okay, Gideon. You'd better not blow this," she warned the warlock. She sat down on the edge of the cliff and closed her eyes.

"Blow what? Erin, what are you doin'? You'll get hurt if you go down there. Get up!" The fear in Frank's voice made her ache for him.

She heard Victor make soothing sounds as they moved away. She couldn't make out his words, but she didn't try to. She didn't raise her head to see if her colleagues were observing what she was doing but concentrated on clearing her mind and reaching down deep within herself.

"Don't expect me to kill anything for this spell," she warned.

TOUCHED BY DARKNESS

"*Nah, but you need to use blood*," Gideon said eagerly. "*I'm ready when you are.*"

"*Erin, you're not doing the rat spell,*" her mother said. "*I forbid it.*"

"*No fair,*" Gideon whined. "*You never let me have any fun.*"

"Don't worry, Gideon. You'll get your fun this time." She put her wrist between her teeth and bit down hard. A familiar tangy taste immediately filled her mouth. She looked down at her arm. A line of blood was dripping from the wound.

"Okay, Gideon. Hurry up before I heal again," she said.

"*Try to throw some of the blood on Nikko.*"

Erin leaned down and tried to squeeze out more blood while waving her arm over Nikko's body. Most drops fell on the boulder under him, and she wasn't sure if enough landed on him for the spell to work.

"*If it's too far, don't worry. He's probably wounded anyway. It's just a precaution. Now, repeat after me:*

With blood on my enemy's skin,
I accept to take on another sin,
With this blood curse,
To make things worse,
Without any remorse,
I call on you, Ramin Sceledorse,
And your unclean animal, the rat,
A smaller shape that,
I can easily kill,
And soon will,
My enemy's shift,
Will be painful and swift,

154

Hear my plea,
As is your will, so mote it be."

Erin had repeated the spell without thought. She realized as soon as she heard Nikko's piercing cry of pain, that Gideon had deliberately caused Nikko's shift to rat to hurt.

"Thanks, asshole," she grumbled.

"*You're very welcome,*" Gideon replied.

Nikko's transformation couldn't have taken more time than a minute, but his scream lasted forever, echoing in the abyss. She closed her eyes. When the scream turned into high squeaking and squealing, she opened her eyes to see that Nikko's large form had been replaced with that of a fat rat with pale little paws, big ears, oily black fur and a thick long tail.

It was the outcome she had hoped for, but she shuddered anyway. She could hear her colleagues yelling, but she was relieved that nobody tried to grab her. Maybe Victor held them back. She refused to turn around and acknowledge them and focused on her rat boss instead.

She found her center, letting her eyelids droop as she envisioned the rat floating above the ground within her mind's eye. She raised her hand, feeling the air crackle with electricity, diffusing around her. The energy building in her palms seared her fingertips as she pointed them at Nikko.

She used her telekinesis to call him to her. At first, he only twitched a bit, but slowly the visualization of a floating rat became a reality.

Her hand trembled slightly as she directed all her

power on keeping him up in the air and aiming him toward her. It worked. She let out a sigh of relief when she managed to land him safely on the snowy ground beside her. She put her hand on the ground to push herself up when Victor called out, "Get the treasure!"

"Oh. You've got to be kidding me," she whispered.

"You might as well take it," Gideon said.

"All right." She groaned as she turned to study the wooden box. It was large—probably too large for her to lift, so she pointed her hands once more at the box, imagining it open. It turned out to be surprisingly easy. Seconds after she had envisioned it, the box opened up. It appeared to be empty.

"Is this some kind of joke?" she asked.

"It looks like there's a USB stick inside," Victor said.

She glared at him. "I'm sure that you're really surprised."

"Hey, don't watch me. Just get it out."

She narrowed her eyes at the box, and sure enough, she saw something shiny inside. She directed the energy of her hand on the item and pictured it flying toward her. In less than a minute, the USB stick landed on the cold ground next to the rat.

Victor's brown eyes gleamed in amusement. "That was amazing!"

"Change him back, you bitch!" Sheila yelled at her.

"Hey, let her catch her breath," Victor said.

"Catch her breath. What about Nikko? He's—

he's a rat for God's sake!"

"*Can't we keep him in rat form?*" Gideon asked.

Holding Nikko by his neck, Erin sat up and examined the passed-out rat. "How to undo this?"

"W-what!" Sheila shrieked. "You turn a human being into a rat, and you don't even know how to turn him back?"

"*Turning him back is really easy,*" Gideon said.

"No more pain though," Erin ordered.

"What pain? What are you talking about?" Sheila asked. "Victor, why don't you say something?"

Erin saw Victor shrug. She wondered why she felt the same. So what if her colleagues knew what she was capable off? But then she saw Frank. He looked quickly away, but Erin had caught the expression in his eyes, equal parts hurt and confusion.

Shit. Did I just lose my friend?

"*You're going to need blood again though,*" Gideon went on. Erin touched her wrist, but the wound had already closed.

"*It doesn't matter. The blood needs to be fresh anyway,*" Gideon explained.

Without any hesitation, Erin bit through the skin on her wrist once more. Sheila wouldn't stop screaming. "What are you doing? What do you need that blood for? Frank, why don't you say something?"

"Let's just see what she's going to do with it," Frank said hoarsely. He still avoided Erin's gaze. "She has a lot of witnesses who saw her—"

His voice trailed off, and Erin closed her eyes.

I hurt him.

"*What a bunch of whiners. You saved a life. Next*

time you shouldn't do anything. Let's just get on with it! You must put the blood on Nikko's body again," Gideon said.

She nodded, dripped the blood from the cut on the rat and put her hand on its greasy, bloodstained fur.

"*Repeat after me,*" Gideon continued.
"*My blood curse shall be lifted,*
This man will no longer be shifted,
Instead of a rat, a human we'll see,
As I command, so mote it be."

It took Nikko less than a minute to shift back to his human form. He had a cut on his forehead, a bruise covered his left eye, and blood trickled down his face. He remained unconscious, but his soft, even breathing indicated that he was getting better. As she got up, Erin noticed Sheila staring down at the boulder. She then turned to glare at her, her green eyes filled with anger and disgust. "It's still there. So you didn't have to humiliate our boss like that. He was fine. You should have waited for the helicopter."

Erin heard Frank expel a long, deflated sigh. Before he could say anything, Nikko opened his eyes. Groaning, her manager lifted one of his hands to rub his forehead. She got up, walked to a tree and leaned against it. She was tired of all the reproaches and didn't want to hear what he would say when he found out that he'd been a rat a few minutes ago.

"*Ungrateful lot,*" Altman said. "*Gideon's right. Next time, don't help out.*"

"Thanks for saving Nikko," Victor said, startling Erin.

"Sure," she said automatically. "No, wait, what the hell is going on here? First the cut tree trunk and now the cut rope."

Victor watched Nikko. "You noticed the trunk, did you?"

She clenched her teeth. A snarl tore from her throat with her rising anger. "So you knew about it! You could have warned us! Nikko could have been killed just now."

Victor turned to look at Erin. Regret showed on his features. "I was told not to interfere."

"Just so these stupid werewolves can win? Who cares? Oh, right. You do, because you're a bloody werewolf!"

Victor didn't contradict her.

"Well, at least we have the treasure, and nobody's dead," she said. "Does this mean the physical part is over now?"

"I'm, uh, I'm not aware of any additional sabotage," Victor replied carefully. "We will travel back to the camp and should arrive there sometime tomorrow afternoon unless Nikko is unable to walk. Oh, at least he's standing up again."

"And he can walk," Erin mumbled as she saw her manager stagger toward them.

"Erin. Thank you very much for turning me into a rodent!" Nikko spat out the words, so angry he vibrated.

"Uh, you're welcome?" she said.

"I'll put this in your performance review!" Nikko threatened, before marching off.

"Great team–building week," she said. "I've

never felt more like a team."

Victor snickered.

She picked up the USB stick. "I wonder what's on here. Maybe it has to do with the psychological part. Could the werewolves have sabotaged this too?"

He shook his head. "I doubt it. But if they have, then I haven't been told. Seems like a lot of work to climb down to put a USB stick into a treasure box."

She grinned. "Well, with the werewolves sabotaging us, we'll need to get even."

Victor narrowed his eyes at her. "You don't want to draw their attention, especially not *now*."

She froze. But before she could question him, he walked toward the rest of the group.

Does he know about my werewolf? Is he going to tell the others?

Oh God. Please don't let me be forced to live with them.

TWELVE

Victor waited for everyone to be in their snow holes before he turned on his tablet and connected the "treasure" into the USB port. It had been relatively easy to steal it from Erin once she had put it back in her pocket.

He saw the files appear on his tablet and swore. He wasn't surprised to discover that the USB stick contained files with everybody's names, but he hadn't expected to find his name among them.

Stupid, I was a Securistate employee once as well. Of course I'm not safe.

In spite of his curiosity over what his own file would contain, he decided to open Erin's file first since she was the one under investigation. He stared at the screen in shock when he saw the film of Erin on his tablet. In it, she was wearing a pair of panties—only a pair of panties—panties so big that it was a miracle that they weren't falling off. A familiar figure appeared on screen, and he swallowed down the rising nausea.

Doctor Quirkhart. The man he'd been forced to assist when the psychiatrist had kidnapped Erin. Victor had never heard what had happened and never

161

wanted to know. Now, he couldn't help but have a morbid curiosity about what had happened. Obviously, Erin had escaped him. Was he about to see how?

He watched Doctor Quirkhart raise his arm, pointing a gun at Erin. He shot at her, and she leapt at him, shifting into her leopard form. The psychiatrist didn't stand a chance.

Good.

Then she started to eat him. Victor's guts wrenched. He didn't want to watch *that*, and he was convinced that Erin didn't want her colleagues to watch that either.

How long is this film?

He moved his finger over the screen and saw there were three minutes remaining. He skipped through till the ending. Great, this made her seem like a monster, even though she never would have eaten her kidnapper if he hadn't abducted her in the first place.

Reluctant to see what the film would be if he clicked on his name, Victor decided to click on Sheila's name instead. She was shown sitting behind her desk in her office, staring at her screen.

Is she watching porn?

She looked around briefly before she started to pick her nose, and then she ate the mucus. The image went black for a second, and then Sheila appeared again, sitting behind her desk as usual, this time wearing a different outfit. Victor expected her to pick her nose again, but this time Sheila's fingers were rubbing the inside of her eyes before entering her mouth. The image sent a shiver of pure revulsion up Victor's spine.

"Okay. I'm not sure I want to see this but knowledge is power," he whispered. He clicked on Nikko's name. He wrinkled his nose in disgust. This time, he saw what he had expected to see, Nikko binge eating while he was at home.

A sense of dread filled him as he finally double-clicked on his own name. Even though he had switched off the security cameras when he and Doctor Quirkhart had abducted Erin, there had been hidden cameras to record him luring her to the fourth floor, Doctor Quirkhart drugging her, and Victor carrying an unconscious Erin outside.

He had been set up. Stratton had forced him to kidnap Erin, and then he had taped him doing so.

Sick bastard. God, I want him dead.

Shaking with a thunder of anger, he managed to regain control of his raging thoughts.

His first instinct was to destroy the film. Of course, Erin was already aware that he had been involved with her kidnapping. But knowing it and seeing it could hurt his case with her when he took her to Crispin's pack. If he removed the film, Stratton would know he was responsible and would not be amused. Crispin would protect Victor against Stratton's wrath once he had brought a new female to the pack, but he wouldn't be safe to leave the pack again. He liked his freedom. Then again, Erin wouldn't be allowed to leave either.

Do I really want to risk gaining such a formidable enemy?

TOUCHED BY DARKNESS

The fever had returned. Erin couldn't stop shaking, but maybe burying herself in a snow hole was the reason behind her discomfort. It was cold, small and dark. She wrapped her arms around herself, feeling her skin break out into an outburst of chill bumps. She took deep breaths, hoping to control herself. Control the leopard. Control the wolf. She struggled. She longed to feel the moonlight on her bare shoulders. The fact that there weren't any clouds blocking the energy of the moon that night only seemed to increase the desire.

If only her phone would work, so she could ask Pauline if she had found a way to suppress the wolf. Erin needed to find a way to distract herself from these urges. Seeing what was on the USB stick she had found might be a good distraction. She wondered what the werewolves' treasure was. She assumed they had found a USB stick too, but probably with different files. Could she destroy their "treasure"? She pictured the anger of the werewolves when they discovered they had been beaten, and a delighted smile curved her lips.

She closed her eyes, yanked the sleeping bag over her head and huddled her knees to her chest. "Think happy thoughts," she mumbled. "Or maybe start counting sheep."

"Hey, you alright in there?" Victor's voice.

She stuck her head out of the sleeping bag and opened her eyes. "Yes, I'm great. Fuck off," she growled.

Victor stuck his head in her little snow cave. "Really? You don't sound so great. Feel like running?" His shoulders were naked.

Why won't he go away?

"You look like shit. You're shaking for fuck's sake. Why are you resisting it?"

She rubbed at her skin to douse the internal burn. "It hurts."

"That's because you're fighting it. The wolf is going to come out whether or not you're fighting it. Come up here. I'll help you."

She sucked in a deep breath and joined him. "So you knew."

He grinned. "Of course. Oh, you managed to fool me at first, but when I held your naked body last night after I found you, I sensed your emerging wolf. I'm actually surprised you managed to hide it for so long."

As soon as she got out of the snow hole, her eyes went heavenward, squinting against the rays of light that wanted to twist her, change her. She saw that Victor was watching her. He was only wearing his jeans. His grin got on her nerves.

"I don't see what's so funny. What if I end up attacking someone?"

"Is that what happened to you? Who attacked you?"

She narrowed her eyes at him. She didn't want to get Billy in trouble even if he was the one responsible for a lot of trouble now. She shrugged. "It doesn't matter."

TOUCHED BY DARKNESS

She gazed up at the sky again. The energy of the moon above her was so intense. Once she gave in, there would be no going back. The wolf would be out and not be contained. Victor led her away from the camp. She gasped for air as she followed him, feeling as though she had just run a marathon through the forest. They reached a clearing when Victor stopped.

"You don't need to worry." He turned to reassure her. "Tonight you can let the beast out. I'll keep an eye on you." His eyes danced merrily.

"Why are so you happy?" She peered suspiciously back at him.

"Because I found you first. If you and I mate, the others won't be able to claim you." He touched her arm, and she recoiled in shock.

"*That jerk!*" Leila shouted.

"Fuck you! I'm already 'mated' to Dane." She winced when a sudden pain seared through her stomach.

"That doesn't count. As long as you're not mated to a werewolf, you will get passed around the pack. It's the lesser of two evils, Erin. And my position in the pack is quite high because I'm related to the alpha. I only have to see him once a month. I'm free. You won't be." He smirked at her, his teeth glinting in the bright moonlight.

"Fuck you," she snarled again. She doubled over as agony washed over her.

"Okay," he conceded. "No mating for now, just running." He took off his jeans. With quaking hands, she followed suit.

"B-but what will happen to my leopard if I shift?"

"I don't know, but I don't think you can resist the wolf much longer. Let go."

Need clawed its way ruthlessly to the surface. Her naked skin felt stretched, and she couldn't stop the shivers racing through her limbs. She fell to her knees in the snow and screamed. She roared in pain as her limbs elongated. It was as if she was being turned inside out, and a heavy sweat bathed her entire body, stinging her eyes.

Nothing like my leopard shift.

She fought to get up and collapsed to the fluffy white ground again. Lucid thoughts disappeared, and then something ruptured. There was a sharp burning pain in her temples. She gagged and coughed. Her brain was like a mass of thick cotton.

I'm going to die.

She was sliding. She got a brief, blurred impression of a dog.

No, wolf.

The animal wavered in her vision and then died away to blackness.

Erin jerked awake. For a long while she couldn't move. She stared, trying to make sense of what had happened. Something warm covered her. She inhaled deeply.

Fur.

A growl erupted from her throat as she turned to

167

face the brown wolf touching her body. It didn't appreciate her growling and bit her nose. A pain-filled yelp escaped from her mouth, and her paw lashed out. The wolf jumped to its feet and shook its head. It barked several times, racing in circles around her before running off.

She could sense it wanted her to follow him, but she was in no rush. Instead she stretched, brushing away the snow. She felt stiff and looked down at her yellow-golden fur.

She heard a howling, and it called out to her like a cry of triumph. But the call for food was stronger. Raising her nose to the air, an alluring scent caught her attention. Her nostrils flared as she took a deep breath. She recognized the smell of an animal.

Prey.

She took off, digging her claws into the snow as she ran, hurling herself faster and faster into the forest. She tracked the smell through the trees, following it to a grouping of bushes. She stopped, her heart pounding wildly against her ribs, gulping in breaths of the cold night air. In the light of the moon, she scanned the ground and noticed small prints in the snow.

Out of the corner of her eye something moved. She ducked when a rabbit skittered past her. The sight made her mouth water. It didn't seem to have detected her or perhaps it had, but didn't consider her a threat.

In silence, she snuck up on it and pounced. She bit down hard and tasted blood. Greedily she suckled while shaking the rabbit's head, breaking its neck without even a second's pause. She had become so engrossed with her meal she didn't realize that she had company. A dark blur darted past her, and she dropped her dinner, ready to attack. With her ears laid back and lips curled over her teeth, she snarled at the intruder.

In the distance, she heard another howl fill the night. The urge to join was so overpowering that she forgot all about the brown wolf standing in front of her. She took off, but a hard nip to her flank made her stumble. She glanced at the wolf that made a wailing sound in the back of its throat. She continued in the direction of the sound when the brown wolf dove through the air, its paws catching her on her back, pushing her face down into the icy snow.

She growled deep in her chest and tried to dislodge the heavy wolf on top of her. She was unable to dislodge it, and it clamped its jaws on her neck. It seemed as though the wolf was waiting for her to calm down but when she felt its desire on her back, of all the different emotions she experienced, calm wasn't one of them.

Dane was sitting behind his computer when panic kicked him in the gut. It engulfed him, swelling his throat.

Erin.

He got up, wavering on unsteady legs as despair crawled up his chest, the pressure so intense as if it was going to explode.

TOUCHED BY DARKNESS

What the fuck is going on?

He closed his eyes, and the image of a yellow-golden wolf came to his mind. A chill danced down his spine. He concentrated in order to reach Erin's thoughts and briefly sensed her confusion, a mixture or fear, anger and...*sexual stimulation*? He mentally roared in frustration, and his body tensed, ready to lash out, kill anyone who would dare to take from him what was his.

Erin, talk to me. Talk to me now.

Their link was gone. He picked up the phone and swore when once more he got the generic message that her phone had been disconnected. He left his room and ran up the stairs, entering Brock's room after a single knock on his second-in-command's door.

He peered up from his laptop and frowned. "What is it?"

Agitated, Dane started pacing. "Have you found out yet where Stratton has taken his employees?"

"No, not yet. I managed to break in into Securistate's computers and found the letter Stratton had sent them about the team-building event. It just stated at what time they had to be at the airport and that everything would be explained to them there. It also mentioned a gala at the end of the event in Las Vegas, so maybe they're near Sin City. I'm now trying to look at flight information to see if I can find Erin's name on one of the flights."

Dane took a deep breath and blew it out in a frustrated sound that was a combination between a grumble and a sigh. "Thanks. But it's not enough.

Even if we find the city she flew to, they wouldn't have stayed at the airport. We need to know their final destination."

Brock shrugged. "There's not much else I can do."

Panic abated the moment inspiration stuck. "But there is something I can do."

Dane's sense of impatience and urgency made him leave the room before Brock could ask him to explain. He didn't have time to waste. He wanted answers *now*.

And he knew just the right witch to provide them.

THIRTEEN

"*Erin, you have to fight him,*" a female voice said.

She had no idea how long the brown wolf had been straddling her. She had lost all sense of time and place. It used pressure to keep her down on the frozen ground while it sat on top of her and held her with its weight and teeth. It let out soft growls and purring sounds, and it was wearing her down. It would be so easy to stop fighting and give in.

"*Don't you dare lift that tail!*" the female shrieked.

Confused, she looked around, taking in her surroundings. She couldn't find the source of the voice.

"*Erin! I know I tried to set you up with Victor before but that was obviously a mistake. You're a cat! Cats and dogs don't mix. Are you in there? Please tell me you're in there.*" The desperation in Leila's voice broke through to Erin's foggy wolf brain.

What am I doing?

She turned her head and saw the brown paws covering her yellow-golden paws.

Oh God, Dane!

She whined.

She felt a long tongue licking her neck, its saliva seeping into her fur, and her stomach quivered in disgust. She realized that it was determined to get her to yield and would not let go until it got what it wanted, which was why she had to pretend she was going to surrender, and she hoped that she didn't have to go too far.

Sorry, Dane.

She forced her body to loosen her muscles and lowered her muzzle to lick the wolf's leg. It started to rub its lower body against hers as it grunted in her ear.

Oh God, I'm getting dry humped by a wolf. Although... It could also penetrate me for real. Yuck!

She struggled not to let out a disgusted grunt.

At least it let go of my neck.

She knew that if she moved too quickly, its first instinct would be to bite down again. On her stomach, she didn't have a lot of options. She could bite its legs or try to get up and throw its heavy body off her. But if it responded by biting down on her neck, she would be here until the morning, and she shifted back.

What if I lie on my back? I'll have more freedom of movement then.

She continued to lick its leg, moving up her tongue until her muzzle reached the wolf's shoulder. Its grunts and moans filled the night as she slowly turned to lick its neck. She saw its eyes peering down at her, and she sensed its distrust.

Too late, asshole!

She opened her jaw and bit down on its neck with all her strength. It howled in agony as dark blood splattered all over its brown fur.

Desperate to get the heavy animal off of her she shoved it away with her forelegs.

It staggered backward and snarled at her. Teeth flashing, it foamed with rage.

She jumped to her feet, barking at him to stop. She knew she wouldn't be able to win a fight with a more practiced, larger wolf. She might if she could shift into her leopard form. If only she could have control over her body right now.

Keeping her eyes locked on the werewolf, she backed away. The blood dripped from its body to mar the white ground. The possible implications of the rich, coppery smell terrified her. The animal raged, and she needed it to calm down. Of course, her biting its neck open wouldn't have helped its temper.

"*Shift back,*" Leila said.

What? I'll be defenseless when it attacks me…

But then the realization hit her.

As defenseless as I am now.

She didn't want to close her eyes, but she didn't know how to shift back other than picturing herself in human form, and she found it hard to concentrate while a bloody werewolf kept snarling at her. She hoped she wouldn't need Dane again to shift back, because she sure as hell didn't want to explain her latest predicament to him.

If only Pauline could find some kind of cure.

She focused on a spot behind the werewolf's head so it would think she would still be able to defend herself if it struck. The tree trunk distracted her less, and she could finally concentrate on the shift. She shook, using all the energy she had. Her muscles rippled and twitched but finally she managed to shift back to her human self.

Head held high, she stood naked in front of the wolf. It snapped at her, but it didn't charge forward. She blinked a couple of times and took a deep, shuddering breath.

"Victor," she croaked. All the growling and snarling must have hurt her throat. "Please, Victor. I'm sorry I bit you. But you scared me. You're still scaring me."

Her voice had started to tremble. Tears filled her eyes until her vision went wet and blurry, and she no longer managed to see the wolf's face.

Am I getting through to him?

She bowed her head and let her hands cover her face as she started to cry.

Please don't attack me, she repeated silently in her mind like a mantra.

She didn't know how long she was standing there, crying her heart out. All she knew was that if something didn't happen quickly, she wasn't going to die because of a wolf attack, but for freezing her naked butt off.

A calloused hand touched her shaking shoulders, and she froze.

Victor?

Slowly, she lowered her hands from her eyes and opened them. Victor was standing in human form in front of her. She could barely breathe for the relief beating in her chest. She noticed a slight cut on his neck, a dark blush on his cheeks, and that he looked down, seemingly to avoid her gaze.

Guilty conscience? Good.

"I, eh, shall we walk back to camp now?" he asked, his voice hoarse.

She looked down at the snow covered ground and her bare feet.

"I-I can c-carry you, if you like," he stammered.

She turned away from him and ran toward the camp in silence. She could still smell him on her body, and disgust knotted in her chest.

What would Dane do if he knew?

She didn't think he would blame her for Victor's behavior but he might resent her keeping secrets from him and could decide to never let her out of his sight again.

That may not be a bad thing, judging by the way I keep getting into trouble.

She found her clothes lying next to Victor's and put them on while she was shaking from the cold. She then walked to the camp and was relieved that no one was there to witness her arrival. She must look a mess. Tears welled in her eyes again, and she sniffed. She touched her wet cheeks and wiped away the trails of tears.

She saw the snow hole she had built and entered it. She hoped he would leave her alone from now on. She just wanted to forget it. The first thing she would do when they returned to Camp Happy was call Pauline. She must have found something to help her get rid of the wolf.

She thought about her witchy roommate, the only friend who accepted her, warts and all, unlike

Frank.

She crawled into her sleeping bag and buried her head in the fabric so no one would hear her sobs.

Stratton watched the footage of Erin walking up to her snow hole and zoomed in on her face.

Are there tears glistening on her cheeks?

Was he finally breaking her? But why now? What had happened? He stared at the screen but after she had entered the little cave, she stayed inside. He got up and froze when he saw Victor arrive at the camp, wearing nothing but his jeans. Victor stopped walking and stared at Erin's sleeping place.

What the hell is going on?

Stratton sat down once more.

He used the hidden camera to zero in on the werewolf but Victor stood too far from it for Stratton to read his face. He narrowed his eyes when he noticed a dark smudge on Victor's neck.

Blood? Had he fought with Erin? Was it because of his involvement in her kidnapping last October?

Victor's bare chest glowed in the pale moonlight. Was something going on between the two of them that Dane didn't know about?

He hated having all these questions and no answers.

Victor returned to his snow hole.

How long had they been gone?

Stratton rewound the film until he saw an image of a bare-chested Victor standing in front of Erin's snow hole, talking. Whatever it was he said he convinced her to leave her cave. After she got out, Erin was frowning, whereas Victor had a big grin on his face. He appeared ravenous whereas she acted fidgety, rubbing her arms and trembling as she watched the sky.

In fact, Stratton noticed her looking up several times while she was speaking with Victor.

Is she deliberately avoiding Victor's taunting gaze? But why would she be talking to him at all if she didn't want to? Or is she expecting Dane in his eagle form?

Anger surged while he glared at the screen. If Dane were to show up now and take her away after all his efforts, he would be forced to reveal Dane's blood exchange to Erin early. He hated it when people interfered with his plans. Whenever that happened, someone paid. This time Dane Lynch would pay, and it had better hurt.

His rage was short-lived. Dane didn't appear. Instead, he watched Victor lead her away from the camp. So she hadn't been searching the sky for Dane.

He calmed and let out his pent-up breath in a long sigh of relief. He turned off his computer and grabbed his phone. He still needed to find out what had happened between her and Victor.

A good thing the guy is working for me.

His call was diverted straight to voice mail. He clenched his hand around the cell phone.

Unacceptable. Perhaps I need to teach Victor a lesson too.

FOURTEEN

Pauline leaned over the table, desperate for an answer and irritated because she didn't have one that would help Erin get rid of the wolf forever. She grunted with frustration. She wanted a permanent solution, not just a potion Erin would have to take three days each month. And what if her roommate became emotional? Even without the full moon, Erin wouldn't be safe since extreme reactions could also trigger a shift.

She grabbed the bottle with the concoction she had brewed the previous evening. The witch at the magic shop in New Orleans she had once been forced to visit on a regular basis had stared at her with open curiosity when she had bought all the ingredients. The essence of eucalyptus, myrrh and spearmint were common in magic, but the most important one, aconite, better known as wolfsbane, wasn't.

"Aconite is extremely poisonous. What are you doing messing with werewolves, *petite fille*?" the witch had asked.

When Pauline had begged the shopkeeper not to tell anyone, the woman had laughed. "Of course I won't tell! Who'd want to attract the attention of Crispin? But he'd better not find out that you came to see me. I would be very unhappy."

Pauline had paid in cash and wished she'd had a spell to make the woman forget her purchase, but that would be bad. She eyed the dark, forbidden notebook that was filled with black magic spells and lying on the table in front of her. It was tempting her. Magic was a lot more efficient than simply praying the woman would keep her mouth shut.

Next to the notebook were notes of her online research and the copies she had made at the library. The more she read about werewolf curses, the more worried she had gotten about Erin's first shift at the team-building event. She knew now that the weak spell she'd cast prior to Erin's departure would never stop her from shifting. She should at least have combined it with wolfsbane, even if the herb was known for its deadly side effects.

Thinking about deadly things turned her mind back to the dark magic notebook. In spite of Erin telling her not to touch it, she had looked for werewolf cures in there. There wasn't anything in the notebook about werewolves, but there had been spells about turning people into animals. Perhaps she could create some kind of reverse spell. But she had to try it out on someone else first to make sure it wouldn't harm her new roommate. A tiny smile curved her lips. Maybe she could get even with Eartha and Aislin for helping Selena try to kill her last month.

A loud pounding on the door caused it to rattle in its frame. Startled, she whirled around to stare at the closed door.

"Pauline, open the door. We need to talk," a man said.

Who knew she was here? There weren't many men she was acquainted with, apart from... She froze, afraid to move. Her heart raced frantically when she realized who was standing on the other side.

What have I done to piss off Dane Lynch, and how can I undo it? Maybe if I remain quiet he'll go away. Please go away.

"Pauline, I can hear you breathing." He sighed. "I understand if you're nervous about talking to me, but it's important." He sounded almost compassionate. She moved toward the door as though without her own volition.

The sound of his voice had been misleading. As soon as she opened the door, she discovered that anger rolled off Dane Lynch's shoulders in thunderous waves. The darkness of his expression unnerved her.

"Where is Erin?" He all but snarled his question at her.

Swallowing a lump in her throat, she lifted her chin. "Didn't she tell you? She has a team building this week."

"I'm fucking aware of that. Do you know where they took her?"

"Oh, uh... They flew to Edmonton, and then they took the bus somewhere, a-a camp?" Her belly lurched, and her hands shook. She forced them to stillness, pushing them against her stomach until they grew steady. "But w-why do you need to s-see her?"

"I can't reach her."

TOUCHED BY DARKNESS

"Uh, okay. That's probably because she has no reception out in the wild."

A scowl drew his eyes together. "No, *that's* not it. What I meant to say is that I can't reach her mind anymore."

"You can read her mind?" Shocked, she cast her gaze to his face. "Can you read my mind too?"

"Why? Is there something you're keeping from me?"

"N-no. Of course not!"

"There's something weird going on. Erin was acting all animal-like. Almost as if the leopard took over, but the energy I sensed didn't seem feline."

Anxiously, she glanced at the papers on the table behind her.

Why hadn't Erin told him?

"It sounds crazy, but I detected a lycan spirit inside her," he continued.

She looked up and moved slightly to block Dane's view of the table. She must not have done that inconspicuously enough since he frowned at her and tried to see what was lying on the table behind her.

"What is it?" he asked.

She pretended to examine the floor. "Er... I, uh…"

He pushed her aside easily enough. "What the hell is this? Werewolf spells?" He picked up the copies from the library and her notes. "Aconite?" he read. "Has she been bit? That's it, isn't it?"

He threw them on the floor. "It happened last month at the hospital, right?" Only he wasn't waiting for her to respond. "She must have known she would shift. Her first shift at Jonathan Stratton's team-building event, brilliant planning! That's why she's making you find some kind of cure, right?" This time he did make eye contact.

She nodded reluctantly. "Uh, yes, I'm trying to."

He narrowed his eyes. "I can't believe she didn't tell me."

"Uh, maybe because she was worried you'd lock her up?"

"Damn right I would! Didn't that guy's first shift at the hospital teach her anything?" He pointed at the potion on the table. "Is that your cure? Is that what she's using right now?"

"I created that last night using wolfsbane. I think this should help her suppress the wolf at least temporarily. It hasn't been tested though."

"So Erin is not doing anything to suppress the wolf at this moment?"

"A s-spell," she whispered. "We tried a spell."

"A spell!" he sneered. "She's at some mystery camp going feral, and you let her?" He bent over and grabbed Pauline by the top of her arms, hauling her up against the wall.

Her eyes filled with tears. "P-please," she begged. "L-let go. It's n-not a mystery camp."

He dropped her. "What do you mean?"

She fell on her knees, heaving as she struggled not to cry.

"Where the fuck is she?" he roared.

"C-Camp Happy," she replied hoarsely. "Erin said the place was called C-Camp Happy."

"Fine." He took hold of her potion, put it in his

183

pocket and walked to the door. "I'll take this to her and escort her back home, even if I have to drag her away kicking and screaming."

"Mr. Lynch!" He opened the door, pausing and turning around to frown at her. "Just don't make her take the entire bottle. Uh, a spoon should be enough!"

He didn't nod or say anything. He moved out into the hallway and closed the door behind him.

She shut her eyes, drew a deep breath, but it caught in her throat. She hadn't had the courage to tell him that Erin probably wouldn't be at Camp Happy anymore, or he would have been able to reach her on her phone unless Erin had deliberately turned off her phone. Witnessing the master vampire's anger first hand, Pauline couldn't blame her. Dane Lynch was terrifying.

Please don't let him blame me if he's not able to find her.

As soon as Erin's team left their camping ground, it began to snow again. It filled the air like a powdery-soft cloud. Victor pointed out the deer prints on the snowy path, but Erin was not in the mood to enjoy the scenery. She was not in the mood for anything he said. After her crying fit the previous night, she'd had trouble falling asleep. She kept thinking about his threats.

Do they really pass around female werewolves if they aren't mated, or was he just using that excuse to get me to mate with him?

She thought about the pack of werewolves that had followed her in the woods a couple of weeks ago. The comments she had overheard indicated that he hadn't been lying to her.

She studied Victor.

Frank was walking beside him, talking.

She narrowed her eyes at the colleague she had once considered to be her best friend.

So werewolves are acceptable to you, but I'm not?

As if Frank had heard her thoughts, he peered in her direction and walked up to her. She stared at the ground in front of her while continuing to move forward.

"Hi," Frank said.

"I thought you'd continue to avoid me," she said without meeting his gaze.

He sighed. "It seems to me like you're the one doing the avoidin'. Aren't you even goin' to look at me?"

She did for a brief moment, knowing that her red-rimmed eyes had to reveal to him that she'd been crying. She hated feeling vulnerable, even if it was in front of Frank. She thought she could read regret in his dark eyes. But maybe she was projecting her own emotions onto him. She also noticed dark hairs had begun to sprout onto his face. She realized she'd never seen him with a beard before.

"I'm sorry you've been upset," he said. "You're always so tough. I've never seen you cryin' before."

A slight smile twisted her lips. "And you still haven't." She made a show of blinking slowly. "See.

No tears."

Faint amusement glittered briefly in his eyes before his expression turned more serious. "What you did yesterday with Nikko... It—it surprised me, okay?"

She swallowed and couldn't quite answer.

"I thought I knew you," he continued. "We talked about things, personal things. We–we're friends. And then I find out you've been hiding somethin' about yourself, somethin' so huge from me. I was hurt. I'm still hurtin'."

Sadness tugged at her heart. "I'm sorry. I was afraid that if I told you, I'd lose you. And then when you didn't talk to me after I had revealed what I could do, I did lose you."

"No you didn't. I just needed some time to myself. I didn't mean to make you feel like I rejected you." His voice was heavy with regret.

"The way you were talking about Dane, how you wished I would date a normal person. But I'm not normal either. I have vampire in me too, and leopard, and witch, and warlock."

And wolf...

Although, the last part she didn't want to say aloud.

Pauline will find a cure.

"I even hear their voices sometimes."

"You hear voices? Do you think they're real? What are they sayin'?" There was a note of incredulity in his voice.

She grinned. "Now, they're remarkably silent. But yesterday, one of them taught me how to turn

Nikko into a rat."

His laughter rang out over the forest. He laughed so long and hard that he had to wipe away the tears streaming down his cheeks. "Nikko the rat. I wouldn't mind a voice like that. Oh look." He pointed at his wet face. "Now you're making me cry."

She giggled, and his eyes widened. "I'm shocked! You giggle too. I've never heard you laugh like a little girl before. I don't know if I can be friends with someone who giggles. The other stuff, I might be able to handle but a guy's got to draw the line somewhere."

And in that moment, she knew that they would be okay.

When Erin returned to Camp Happy, it was nearly dark. She couldn't wait to leave the hulking dark mountains behind, hidden by the large skeletal trees.

"Think you'll miss the snow?" Frank asked.

She merely arched an eyebrow in disbelief. "Will you?"

He laughed. "Right, see you later. I'm gonna call Janice and Daphne."

"*And you're going to call Pauline*," Erin's mother said.

"*And Dane!*" Leila shouted. "*You must want to talk to him too, right?*"

Erin briefly checked if anybody could see her talking to herself and concluded that her colleagues had already gone inside.

"I would like to hear his voice, but I'm not sure what to tell him about this trip so far. I'd rather make sure that we've tried everything possible before revealing to other people that I'm a werewolf. Unless you think he could help me."

"*I doubt Dane knows of a cure,*" Altman said. "*I think he'd be bound in his role of master vampire of Hope Acres to inform Crispin about the new addition to his pack. If Crispin finds out he knew and kept it from him, he'll have a war on his hands. Vampires and werewolves have a bit of a history, you know.*"

She sighed. "No, I didn't know. Well, that settles it. I won't call him then, but I am gonna call Pauline."

A lot depended on this call.

Has Pauline found a cure?

She took out her cell phone. Her heart began to pound, and she could feel her throat close in as she opened up the name of contacts and tapped on Pauline's name.

Pauline answered immediately. "Oh Erin, I'm so glad you're calling me! What the hell happened last night? Is Dane Lynch there yet?"

"W-what? Dane's c-coming?"

"Yes, and he's very angry with you. I can't believe you never told him you got bit."

"He knows?" Erin's stomach knotted, and she swallowed, trying desperately not to panic.

"I-I'm sorry. He barged in last night, demanding to know where you were, and then he saw my notes on the table. But he told me he could sense the wolf in you before he discovered my research, so I think he'd deducted it all without my help. It's not because I told him. Did you know he could read your mind?"

"Hold on. You said that he's on his way, on his way to do what?"

"Oh right, the potion, I created a potion with wolfsbane in it. It should help you at least suppress the werewolf on the nights of the full moon. I doubt it's going to cure you forever, though. If only you had a werewolf you could talk to about it without having to worry about exposing yourself."

"Actually, I do know a werewolf I could talk to about it." Erin checked her surroundings to see if the man in question wasn't eavesdropping on her conversation, but she couldn't see him.

Doesn't mean he's not there.

"Unfortunately, it may not be in his best interest to help me."

"What do you mean?"

"He wants me to mate with him."

"What!" Pauline shrieked. "He wants to what?"

"Mate. Apparently, female werewolves are so rare that if they have no mate, they are passed around by the pack." Erin sighed in disgust. "So according to him, I have no choice but to accept his generous offer. As if I'd rather be raped by one monster instead of many. Wait, that does seem like the lesser of two evils."

While she was talking, she thought she heard Pauline gasp in shock on the other side of the phone. "Good grief! We need a plan B."

"Maybe Victor lied. God, I hope so. I wouldn't

put it past him. He's been sabotaging me, again."

"But if it's true then you must find a way to get rid of it. I think you should kill the werewolf that bit you after all."

"Kill Billy? For God's sake, have you gone completely bananas?"

"Think of it like you're putting him out of his misery," Pauline suggested.

"Forget it! I don't want to hear another word. You know, you're not sounding so Wiccan right now. You haven't been reading my notebook have you?"

"I told you I wouldn't." Erin noticed that Pauline didn't deny it though.

Oh well, I have other things to worry about now.

"I've got to go. I'm going to sabotage the werewolves too, and I'd better do that before Dane shows up. You wouldn't believe the crap they put us through!"

"That sounds like a terrible idea! Are you sure you want to risk drawing their attention?"

Erin shook her head. "I'm just so tired of being pushed around. They're making me feel like a victim."

Again.

"Promise me you won't get caught," Pauline urged.

"I promise." She said her goodbyes before breaking the connection. She put the phone in her pocket and turned to enter the building when Victor walked out of it.

His grin almost swallowed his face. "Ah, just the

person I wanted to see." He touched her arm, and she recoiled in revulsion. His joy at her misery turned her stomach. "You really shouldn't flinch when I put my hands on you, sweetheart. Crispin might not believe that we are true mates."

She cleared her throat. "I really don't see we have anything to talk about."

"*He might know of a way to get rid of the werewolf curse,*" Leila said.

Actually, that's not a bad idea.

"Unless you know how to get rid of the werewolf curse?" Erin asked.

Victor lifted his hands up in the air. "Ah. Don't be like that! It's not a curse. Werewolves have a lot of fun too. You'll find out soon enough. But I've got to go now."

She narrowed her eyes at him. "Go where? There's another full moon tonight, isn't there?"

He shrugged. "Don't worry 'bout it. You've survived your first shift, and the good thing is that we're in the middle of nowhere, so you can go for a run undetected, unlike Hope Acres. I could ask one of the other werewolves to keep an eye on you, but to be honest I'd rather not share you, and I don't think you'd want that either. Just try to avoid them for now. I'll take you to meet Crispin soon. At least before the next full moon, to make sure that nobody else is bitten. Speaking of which, how did you get bit?"

"Why?"

"To make sure that doesn't happen again. We have rules to prevent this."

"What rules? Would you kill him? Wouldn't that undo the curse?"

"*Are you complaining right now?*" Leila asked.

Agitated, he wrung his hands in front of him. "What is it with you and undoing 'the curse'? Get it through your thick skull that there is no undoing of anything. You're becoming tiresome. You're a werewolf now. Accept it."

"Accept to get gang raped if I don't accept getting raped by you? I would rather fight you all and die than accept this! Fuck you, asshole!" Tears of frustration bit angrily at her eyes, and she stormed off. She could feel his eyes on her as she fled.

Fuck it. I never cry, and now it's all I do. No more, I'm going to get even with these werewolves even if it kills me.

Her jaw tight, she entered the main building.

I'll never accept this.

The ache in Erin's voice had made Victor's gut twist. He watched her slam the door in frustration, and he knew that she was going to fight him and fight Crispin every step of the way. Crispin would never allow her disobedience, and he hoped that the alpha wouldn't break her spirit in the process.

The buzzing of his cell phone interrupted his thoughts. He looked down at the name appearing on the screen and sighed. Should he let it ring? He didn't want the tycoon to find out that Erin was about to join his pack, only not answering might convince the

Las Vegas vampire that indeed something was going on and could even cause him to take action. Reluctantly, he pressed answer.

"Mr. Stratton."

"Finally! I haven't talked to you for so long that I thought you perhaps wanted me to come over, Mr. Nichols!"

"I'm sorry, sir. We, uh, we had no reception where we were."

"Let's not discuss it now. I want to know what happened with our Ms. Holland. How did she cope?"

Victor cleared his throat. "Uh, she knows about the sabotage, just not the reason behind it."

Stratton chuckled. "Of course she knows. I would have been very disappointed if she hadn't discovered it. But I want to know the details. How did it go? As expected, the downside of doing this in the wilderness is not being able to place cameras everywhere. I did catch her having a little bit of a cry at the campsite last night. What was that about? Did you have some kind of lover's tiff?"

Victor swallowed nervously. "Of course not, s-she's with Dane Lynch after all. I wouldn't want to trespass on his territory."

"No. We wouldn't want to do that," Stratton said, although the tone of his voice indicated to him that he would want nothing more.

"But you haven't answered my question, Victor. Why was she crying last night?"

"I-it's about an argument she had with Frank, her colleague," Victor improvised. "He found out what she could do, and I believe he resented her for hiding

193

it from him. I think they used to be friends."

"I don't understand why she's so intent on hiding who she is. I'm happy that she's been exposed."

Victor wondered why Stratton pretended not to understand. He wasn't exactly telling the world that he was a vampire either, not that Victor would dare point that out. "And now that she's been exposed, is it over?"

Stratton laughed. "What makes you say that? Tonight is the start of the psychological game."

Victor was so horrified he nearly dropped the phone. "Tonight? But tonight is the full moon. We'll need to run. If not, you'll create a blood bath!"

"I'm sure you can all suppress your urges," Stratton said. "And I'm not going to explain myself to you. Goodbye, Mr. Nichols."

Stratton hung up before Victor could respond. He uttered several profanities and threw his phone on the floor. He doubted any of the werewolves would be able to suppress the wolf during the full moon, especially if they were being provoked with one of Stratton's twisted games.

But he worried about Erin most of all. In her case, he *knew* she wouldn't be able to suppress the werewolf. Having to leave her at this point was the worst timing. On the other hand, he had to arrange many things, so he could go into hiding at Crispin's pack. He couldn't have any reason to leave the pack again or Stratton would be waiting.

But what will happen if Erin's wolf emerges? What will the other werewolves do?

FIFTEEN

Erin had been searching endless lodges and had even tried tracking prints in the snow but to no avail. All were dead ends. Victor had truly left.

"*I don't understand why you're trying to find that* putain *anyway, Erin,*" Leila said. "*I think your confrontation with him should have scared him off, and a good thing it is too.*"

"*What's this, Leila? I thought you wanted Erin to sleep with him,*" Gideon taunted.

"*That was a long time ago. He hadn't shown his true colors then. I think we're better off with the vampire. Don't you think so, Altman?*"

"*Leave me out of it,*" Altman said. "*But I do agree with Leila about Victor. You shouldn't look for him, and I think you shouldn't put too much faith in what he said about the werewolves either. He obviously has his own agenda.*"

"Well, those werewolves I ran into at the forest a couple of weeks ago made some disturbing comments that might prove him right, but I'd rather not think about it. I'm not gonna give him what he wants. I only want to use him. I lost that USB stick, and I

195

know just the person who's responsible. And I'm sure he can get me the other one too."

"*Oh, I wish you'd listened to Pauline. If you sabotage the werewolves, they'll notice you. That's the last thing you want,*" Erin's mother said.

"Maybe I won't need to sabotage them. Like with the physical part, it could be that the USB sticks have been tampered with. If I could just see what's on them, at least I'll be prepared if something goes wrong. I'll see if I can find Frank."

She found him in the large meeting room. The organizers were busy putting all the chairs in rows in front of the same large television screen they had looked at when they'd arrived.

"They said it'll start 'bout thirty minutes from now. Aren't they even gonna feed us?" he asked.

"Perhaps they're hoping that the werewolves will get so upset with the psychological games that they'll end up eating the Securistate employees. It might be cheaper than firing us."

He glared at her.

"Oh, don't worry, Frank. I have an idea."

He frowned. "I'm not gonna like this idea of yours, am I?"

She grinned. "You know me so well. See, this team-building week isn't so bad after all. You finally get to comprehend who it really is you're working with."

"Quit stallin', Erin. What's the idea?"

"I thought it might be fun if we get to see what's on those 'treasures' we got. We can prepare ourselves in case the werewolves have done something to it, or we can arrange a little payback after what all the werewolves have done to us. Do you know where we can find them?"

"No, no, no! I'm not gonna let you drag me into this."

"Oh, come on, Frank. You almost fell into that river because of them. Don't you want revenge?"

"Gandhi said that 'An eye for an eye makes the whole world blind.' I agree."

She sighed. "Fine, can you at least tell me if you know where they are?"

"I probably shouldn't tell you this, but yes. I overheard someone say they put it in the safe, so nobody would be able to touch it until the big moment. But there are probably cameras in that room. So if you don't want to end up on this TV screen yourself, you'd better forget about it. I'm sure we've got nothing to worry about." He looked around briefly before leaning forward and whispering, "Those dumb werewolves wouldn't know how to open a safe anyway, but you might. Maybe you can ask that voice who told you how to turn Nikko into a rat."

"*Finally some recognition!*" Gideon said.

She took a deep breath. "Alrighty then, wish me luck."

"You don't need luck. You need an intervention."

She ignored his last comment and entered the corridor. While she had been searching for Victor, she had discovered a tiny room with someone staring at monitors. She found it surprising that a camping ground had all this security, although it could have been arranged because of the werewolves and their volatile nature.

She walked past the guard's office again and noticed that he was still staring at the monitors. She needed him out of there.

"Want another cup?" she heard a raspy voice say from the same room.

Shit, where did that guy come from? Great, now I have two security guards to get rid of.

"*A spell perhaps?*" Erin's mother suggested.

She moved away from the door and whispered, "I can't. My colleagues have seen me use magic on Nikko and will know it's me."

She was about to give up when she noticed the smoke detector on the ceiling. She smiled and hurried to her cabin where Sheila was lying on top of the bunk bed.

"Is it starting already?" she asked.

Erin shook her head while she went through her bag. "You still have about twenty-five minutes to mentally prepare yourself." She saw that Sheila's eyes were closed. She put the matches in her pocket.

The secretary moaned. "Can't they give us a break? I'm exhausted!"

"Yeah, me too. See you later." Erin ran off.

When Erin arrived at the main lodge, she noticed that a group of ten had already gathered at the meeting room. Worried that she would get caught if she tried to set off the fire alarm in the hallway, she moved to the toilet instead.

She let out a sigh of relief when not only did she find the bathroom empty, but she also spotted a smoke detector in there. She opened the large window as a means of escape once the alarm went off. She lit the match and held it under the device. Seconds later, an extremely loud and shrill sound resonated in the bathroom, and she quickly blew out the match before jumping through the open window.

The snow-covered ground broke her fall. She immediately got up and walked around the building to enter it again from the entrance. As she walked in several people left the lodge while keeping their ears covered.

"If this is going to damage my ears, I'm going to sue them. Stupid humans with their stupid alarms."

She didn't waste time listening to further comments by disgruntled werewolves and moved to the security office that had now been left unattended.

After locating the security footage for the main office, which was displayed on the central monitor, she rewound the recording before she stopped and set it to loop. After ensuring that the camera was no longer recording, she pressed play, leaving the screen to display old, looped footage instead.

Glancing briefly at the screen, she noticed that the office was home to a large desk with the head of a deer mounted on the wall above it.

Happy that the security team would be watching an older recording of the room, and the security cameras would not capture her invasion of it, she left the room and hurried past the bathroom where she found both security guards switching off the alarm.

She couldn't help but smirk as she passed them.

She made her way to the main office, breathing a sigh when she found no cameras in the corridor.

Her breathing was shallow as she knocked on the door. She hoped that nobody would answer. If they did, she intended to ask them where to find Victor. She waited for a few seconds, but there was no reply. She pictured Jonathan Stratton standing behind the door, ready to swing his baseball bat, and she swallowed back the nausea that rose in her throat. After she had checked that nobody was there to witness her entrance to the room, she went inside. Her heart raced, and her palms felt clammy. Fortunately for her, the office was empty. She noticed the camera straight away. It was pointing at a painting behind the desk.

In case the security guards discovered that they were watching a recording instead of live footage, she needed to cover it up immediately. She saw a garbage bag in the bin, removed it, threw the rubbish back in the container, and put the dirty bag over the camera.

She turned to the painting.

The safe has to be behind it.

"*Any ideas on how you're going to open it?*" Gideon asked. "*You need my help with a spell?*"

"I can think of one myself, thank you very much." She took the painting off the wall, put it against the floor and stared at the large gray safe underneath.

"Bingo," she muttered.

Heavy footsteps rushing down the hall outside caused her pulse to race. She dropped to the ground on instinct, pushing aside the chair and crawling underneath the desk as she heard someone turning the door handle behind her.

Shit. Shit. Shit.

"*Now you're in a lot of trouble,*" Gideon said in a mocking voice.

"*I'll use the invisibility spell again,*" Erin's mother said, and she rushed through the words of the incantation.

"I knew something was up as soon as the alarm went off," a man said. From under the desk, she watched as two men entered the office, and she heard the rustling sound of a plastic bag. "See. I was right."

"Yes, well done, Otto. I'm not sure I would have noticed the monitor showing a recording since I'm obviously not as observant as you." Brown shoes with dark blue trousers moved behind the desk. If she stuck out her hand, she could touch the guard's legs.

She pressed herself against the wooden surface and covered her mouth to silence her frightened gasps.

She watched as the painting rose from the ground, imagining it covering up the safe once more.

"No need to be sarcastic, Eddie. I'm just sayin' that I noticed the clock in the office being behind on the monitor. I'm not sayin' anything about you."

The shoes of the guard that had put up the painting turned to point in Erin's direction. A head popped under the desk, staring straight at her. Her belly lurched in fear, and she wanted to scream, but pushed down harder on her mouth instead.

"Nothing here," the man said, staring straight at her.

No, she realized. *He's not staring straight at me, but right through me.*

Her mother's spell had worked. The man rested his right hand on the desk and pushed himself up. "Whoever it was, he's gone. There's no place to hide in here."

"So are you going to call Ms. Sloane, or shall I?"

"Well, Otto, since you were the observant one, I think you should be the one to take the credit for this and call Mr. Stratton's secretary."

"But, we weren't successful. I'm not sure I want to let him know that we weren't able to catch the guy."

"Well, the safe alarm hasn't gone off, so the USB sticks must still be in there. Whoever it was must have left unsuccessfully. I don't mind keeping this from Mr. Stratton if you want to keep this quiet."

Safe alarm, my actions were doomed right from the start.

As soon as the security guards left the room, she squeezed herself past the chair without touching it. She couldn't have a chair moving of its own appear on camera. Standing up, she blew out a resigned breath before she silently followed them.

She saw several people in the hallway going to the meeting room and wondered where she could undo the invisibility spell. The door to the bathroom was open. She snuck in and recited the spell before she appeared in front of the mirror. She was unnaturally pale, and lines etched deeply into her forehead. She studied her eyes and arms. But so far, there was no sign of the wolf.

Looking out the window and gazing up at the sky, she could sense the energy of the moon calling out to her in spite of the cloudy weather.

"*You'll be fine,*" Erin's mother said. "*At least you know the werewolves won't have sabotaged the USB sticks either.*"

Erin could feel a headache coming on, and she rubbed her temples. "Putting them in a safe doesn't mean anything if Victor did something to ours before handing it over to the organizers."

"*Right, I'd forgotten about that,*" her mother said.

"I can't wait for this night to be over. But whatever happens, I'm not going to let these werewolves push me around or anyone else for that matter. This time I'm pushing back. If Dane is pissed off about me keeping things from him, then too bad for him. I had valid reasons. So if he or those werewolves want to fight, then bring it on."

She opened the door to find Dane in front of it, leaning against the wall. The pose seemed casual, but she wouldn't be able to pass him without touching his body.

He had yet to speak, but there was something in his eyes, something feral, that made her glad her colleagues were less than ten feet away. She shivered under the intensity of his gaze.

"U*h oh,*" Gideon said.

"I don't s-suppose you heard that, did you?" Erin whispered as she swallowed back the nausea that rose in her throat.

"Which part, about you wanting to fight the werewolves, or where you said you wanted to fight me?"

Dane frowned as Erin settled into a fighting stance. He considered his next move while taking in her defiant pose. In spite of the blackened holes visible below her eyes and the disheveled state of her golden hair, she radiated pride.

Why did I think she would be sorry, afraid to face my anger? I have been too lenient with her, too kind.

People feared him. When he ordered something, they obeyed and set out to please him.

But she seemed determined to infuriate him. Her fierce nature fascinated him, but he couldn't allow it to interfere in their relationship.

He worried that it was already too late. He kept reliving the feeling of panic he had experienced the moment the wolf had taken over. He refused to let her bite break their connection, a connection he didn't regret having forced on her and would make sure to keep no matter what.

Crispin would not want to have a female werewolf to be with a vampire, but Dane wouldn't allow anyone to take her from him.

Including her.

He injected ice into his tone. "I was expecting you to get on your knees and apologize, hoping I would forgive you for lying to me."

"I d-didn't lie to you," she stammered.

He leaned over her, wanting to savor the closeness, but he didn't care for it to interfere with his demonstration. He breathed in deeply, catching the intoxicating perfume that was all Erin, and the deeper, muskier scent of both leopard and werewolf.

"Oh no, you didn't lie?" His tone sharpened. "What is this smell on you then?"

"I'm s-sorry. I have been out in the woods for several days, and I haven't been able to t-take a shower."

Enraged, he lashed out. "You know what I mean!"

He put his hand in his pocket and took out the potion Pauline had created. "You should have told me about this. Are you really that arrogant that you think a tiny spell can break a curse that is centuries old? Here, take it." He pushed it into her hands. "Take a spoon of this, and then take your bags because we're going home.

She flinched. "I w-wish I c-could, but I have to do this psychological test now. We all do."

Stratton's job. This is all Stratton's fault. That werewolf never would have attacked her if it weren't for him. It's another reason why I'll have to kill him tomorrow.

He clenched his jaw and spoke through gritted teeth. "Tell them you're leaving."

"*What are you waiting for?*" he heard one of the male voices say. Was it the warlock? "*So far, this week has been nothing but a nightmare. You should jump at the chance to leave.*"

"I do. I do want to leave." Obstinate, she raised

her chin. "But I have a job, and I can't just abandon my colleagues. This potion should help me get through the night without any incidents. So, thank you."

An icy, dead rage, strong enough to choke him took over. "I. Am. Not. Your. Errand. Boy."

He wouldn't have thought it possible, but her face paled even further. "I-I know. I'm s-sorry. I know I should have told you I was bitten, but Altman told me that in your role as m-master vampire of Hope Acres you'd be forced to tell the alpha of the Hope Acres' pack about it. I didn't want to put you in that position. I hoped that Pauline and I would be able to find a cure before we had to tell others."

"*Clever*," he heard Altman say, and he narrowed his eyes.

Is she lying to me again?

"I-I just hope this potion is strong enough," she continued.

"A spoon a day keeps the werewolf at bay," he said. "What is the name of the werewolf that bit you?"

She shrugged. "That's not relevant."

"Unless killing the werewolf that made you means that you'll be human again."

"As if I ever was human! Besides, I thought that was a myth. Isn't it like an infection, that the wolf is now part of my blood?"

"No, I heard that part of it is magic. As long as you haven't killed anyone yourself in werewolf form, you could be free from the curse if you kill your maker. That's why there is so much suspicion and hostility in packs. Alphas need to reign in fear."

She glanced up at him. "*You* reign in fear."

He scowled. "It doesn't seem to be working on you."

"It doesn't matter. I won't let you kill him."

"Do you want to stay a werewolf now? Is that why you didn't tell me?"

She audibly swallowed. "I-I wanted to call you but I was afraid you'd be furious about me getting bit. I didn't want to keep it from you. When Victor told me how they treat female werewolves, I wanted to run to you."

"Victor?" He glared at her. "Are you telling me that the werewolf I told Stratton to send away last month is here, and he *knows*?"

"What do you mean you had told Stratton to send Victor away? Are you talking about Jonathan Stratton, *the* Jonathan Stratton?"

"Don't try to distract me, Erin. If Victor knows, then he will inform Crispin, assuming he hasn't done so already. Where is he?" Overcome by a strong need, he grabbed her. "We have to stop him."

"It's t-too late. He's already left."

He released her and stepped away. "Then you're doomed. The biting with the transformation usually kills humans, especially women. That's why you're so rare as a werewolf. If you gave birth to a werewolf, it will survive the first shift."

"They'll never let me go," she whispered.

"I'm not letting them keep you."

Erin stared at something behind him and stiffened. He turned around to see her bald black colleague walk up to them.

"Hey, uh, Erin, they're about to start. Are you coming? Please don't leave me alone with them."

Dane saw her hesitation and shook his head.

"It's just one night. Tomorrow is the big party," her colleague went on. "We might even shake hands with Jonathan Stratton."

"I'm sorry, Dane, but Frank's right. And I must say that this trip has brought us closer together. I don't want to abandon him now, and you should trust me to do my job."

"I let you do your job!" he bellowed, his hands clenching into fists at his side. "And you got—" He stopped before he realized he was about to scream what she'd been trying so hard to hide.

"I-I love you," she said. "But I can't be with someone who won't let me be free."

She loves me!

He felt something inside him release and evolve.

She really is mine.

She had given him a wonderful gift, and he didn't want to ruin that by forcing her to leave with him.

He studied her colleague. "If I let her join this, make sure that she's safe." He then looked at her and gently cupped her cheek before capturing her lips in a long kiss.

Reluctantly, he released her. "Promise me you won't get hurt," he murmured.

"If you promise me you won't go after that, uh—you know. I want to fight my own battles."

"It's not weak to ask for help, Erin. I'll let you stay tonight, but you must let me handle the other matter."

He saw the flash of anger cross her face. "You'll *let*! Fuck you, Dane!" She turned around and stomped away.

Dane noticed her colleague's shocked expression before he rushed to follow her.

She'd just insulted him in front of someone else, but he didn't care.

She loves me.

He smiled in great satisfaction.

I'll get her to change her mind because she loves me.

SIXTEEN

Stratton sat in the dark at his desk and closed his eyes in anticipation when his phone rang. He frowned when he saw Ms. Sloane's name on the screen. He would have thought his secretary would have known better than to disturb him tonight, but the psychological test hadn't yet begun, so he could spare her a moment.

She couldn't have known that though.

"Ms. Sloane. I'm surprised by your interruption. I thought you were properly trained. I see that you require more education."

"N-no, please!" The terror in her voice pleased him. "It's urgent."

"Yes, I'm sure it is." His voice took on a cool edge. "I realize now that my skills as your manager have been lacking. I should have paid more attention to you."

"T-the police are here," she said.

"Never mind, ma'am," he heard a man say as he saw someone opening his door. "We'll find our way."

What had started out as an amusing distraction, as fun as it was to terrorize one's secretary, quickly became an infuriating interruption. He swallowed at the rage knotting his throat as he turned off his computer.

"Mr. Stratton. Thank you for seeing us," a chubby, gray-haired cop said. "My name—"

"No, I'm not seeing you. Get out," he ordered.

"We would like to ask you some questions," the fat cop's younger colleague said.

Stratton ground his teeth together so hard he feared breaking them. "I'm busy. Come back... never. Get the fuck out of my office."

While the younger cop inspected his bookcase, the other one sat down on the chair in front of his desk. "Now Mr. Stratton, it would be wise if you gave us a moment of your time. We just need you to clear up a few matters, and I'm sure that can be done in a pleasant manner."

"Don't touch that book," Stratton snapped at the younger cop. The man immediately dropped it.

"Stevens, stop moving around. Sit down before you break something." The older cop smiled at Stratton while lifting his hands as if he wanted to say, "The younger generation."

He wasn't amused. "I don't have time."

"Make time," the older cop said, letting his mask drop. "We need to ask you some questions about a writer you've had dealings with."

He made sure he kept his expression blank and impassive with no indication of what he was thinking.

"No, that doesn't ring a bell? How about if we give you a name? John Tennant?"

When he didn't respond, the man continued,

TOUCHED BY DARKNESS

"Are you telling me that you don't know John Tennant?"

Tired of not being able to watch what was happening at Camp Happy, Stratton said, "Stop beating around the bush. I haven't told you anything, and I'm not going to either, not without a lawyer."

"If you're sure, Mr. Stratton. We thought it would be more pleasant for you if we talked here, but if you like, we could ask you to come to our station."

"I'm not going anywhere with you." He dropped his voice a notch. "Unless you're going to arrest me?"

"Arrest you?" The old cop laughed, low and deep. "Whatever for?"

"Indeed, officer, whatever for?" They had nothing, and he knew it.

The cop frowned. "It's detective, Detective Hill."

"Good," Stratton taunted. "It's always good to have a name when you're going to someone's supervisor to complain about harassment."

"Fine," the detective said, and he stood up. "If you want to meet my supervisor, I'll make it easy on you. Please turn around, sir. Jonathan Stratton, you're und—"

"It's alright," Stratton said. "You people have no sense of humor. I'll go with you. Just let me call my lawyer."

"You can do that from our station too. Will you please follow me?" Detective Hill said.

Stratton sighed, and after casting one last glance at his PC, he left his office with the two cops.

"Okay, are we all here?" Mike asked. He was wearing an identical training suit to the one she'd seen him in a few days ago. He also radiated the same disgusting cheerful optimism as before.

"I hope you had a great time these past couple of days, getting to know your colleagues a little better."

At that comment, Erin peeked at Frank sitting beside her. He noticed it and reassuringly tapped her hand. They were fine.

"And the fun doesn't end here because tonight comes the hard part."

She raised her eyebrows and mouthed at Frank, "The hard part?"

Frank chuckled. "Don't worry about it."

No, she wasn't anxious. Five minutes earlier, she'd taken a large sip from Pauline's sour potion, and now she couldn't sense the wolf anymore. She wanted to celebrate.

"When are we going to get something to eat? Is this about starving us?" one of the werewolves growled.

"Yeah, if you don't serve us quickly we'll just have to hunt for food ourselves."

"And we'll start with you, Blondie" another werewolf cried out.

The camp leader's smile slid right off his face. "Now guys, please, bear with me. Dinner will be ready at eight thirty, so we still have a little over two hours left to have some of you finish the test before dinner."

"I'll give you a test on survival!"

Frank's face twisted into a worried frown. "I think we're about to have a revolution on our hands."

Another organizer joined the not-so-cheerful blond organizer. "Guys, it's only for a couple of hours. You need to cooperate." He nodded at the camera aimed at them. "Your attitude tonight will be taken into consideration for your next performance evaluation."

The werewolves calmed down after that threat.

As Erin watched the crowd, she caught the attention of Quentin Scott again. His intense green eyes lit up, and he tilted his head back, baring his teeth at her in a frightening grin. Her heart skipped a beat, and she looked away. She could still feel him staring at her though, and her hands balled into tight fists of anger.

"Okay, good, great," Mike babbled. "I now leave the stage to the wonderful Doctor Meredith Jones. Will you please join me in welcoming her?" He started to clap his hands as an attractive redhead wearing a suit with a short skirt and low cleavage walked up and stopped beside the television screen. Except for the other organizers, nobody had applauded.

The doctor frowned.

Are all these psychiatrists miserable? Maybe her expression is sour because of the lack of applause.

"Good evening. As Mike told you, these last couple of days helped you bond with your colleagues a little better. Tonight you'll find out even more about them…" The woman seemed to pause for dramatic effect, meeting everybody's eye "…and more about yourselves. Everybody has weaknesses. Tonight, we will reveal them, so you can conquer them."

Weaknesses, which one? I have so many. Did they know about the werewolf, about my stay at the asylum, the voices in my head, Doctor Quirkhart?

Trying to control the fear that was threatening to fill her mind, she forced herself to breathe slowly.

Whatever it was that they had on her, she hoped they wouldn't keep her waiting until the last minute. If what they revealed didn't kill her, the suspense would.

"The treasures that you collected—and congratulations to both groups for finding them—contain information about each and every one of you. Since we only have two hours now, we will regroup after dinner, so we can all have our turn."

"I wish I had left that horrible USB stick behind," Erin muttered.

"Both USB sticks look alike, so I don't know which person will go first. After the film, I'll switch the USBs, so the other group won't get too comfortable."

Too comfortable, that woman is crazy!

"Mike, if you'll do me the honor of bringing them over?" Erin saw the blond guy carry the despised sticks to the doctor as she fought off insistent waves of nausea. A hand on her arm nearly made her jump off her chair.

"Are you okay?" Frank asked softly. "You look

like you're about ready to bolt."

"How come you're not worried?"

"My life's an open book," he replied.

The woman had picked one of the USB sticks and put it into the port. On the screen appeared a file marked "werewolves". The doctor double-clicked on it, and although Erin had hoped that she would be able to get it over with quickly, she still let out a sigh of relief.

"First one up: Hugo Callahan," Doctor Jones said. "Could you please come up and sit here?"

The werewolf in question smirked, strolled up to the chair that was beside the television as if he didn't have a care in the world and sat down. "Sure, baby."

The woman smiled, but it didn't reach her eyes. She double-clicked on a film that was named "Callahan", and the first image that appeared on the screen was someone's hairy back.

"Wooow, that's your secret! You're in need of a shave!" one of the werewolves yelled.

The camera zoomed out, and she saw Hugo Callahan leaning over a chair. A woman sat on it, crying, struggling to move, but he had her wrists trapped.

"Please!" she begged. "Help me. Someone help me!"

Hugo Callahan's head turned slightly, so she was able to see his leering face. "Scream all you like, baby. Nobody here will rescue you. Nobody cares. See, if I do this." He let go of one wrist to hit the woman in the face. "Nothing happens."

"Oh my God," Erin whispered. "I think I'm

going to be sick."

"Me too," Frank said. "Are they really gonna show this to us?"

The film lasted several minutes. The images chilled her to the bone. Meanwhile, the werewolf in question was making eye contact with Quentin, almost as if he was waiting for instructions. She saw the warrior wolf shake his head at Hugo.

What's going on?

When the film stopped, Erin swore she could still hear the desperate screams of that poor girl.

"So, Mr. Callahan, is there something you'd like to tell us about this?" the doctor asked.

The sneer on the werewolf's face had returned. "No."

Doctor Jones laughed, moved to stand behind his chair and put her hands on his shoulder. "Oh, Hugo," she moaned. "I think you can do better than that. I thought werewolves were so virile." She rubbed the side of her right breast against his face.

"Does this mean you can only get it up if you have to fight some weak girl? Have you ever been with someone like me before?"

"A n-nut job?" The werewolf's voice shook as the woman sat down on his lap and started moving her hips around.

She chuckled. "Nuts? Oh, yes. I can feel them. You're all nuts."

Twin spots of red burned high on his cheeks, and he laughed a short bark of a sound that fell flat in the large meeting room.

"Oh, no." The woman stopped moving. "I do

feel something coming alive down there. Aw, I'm so sorry. That's so tiny. I can hardly feel it. I understand now why you have to force women."

She left his lap and peered down at him with a snide snigger. Then she looked at her audience. For a few seconds there was a dead silence, broken only by the sound of the wind outside.

Then she heard the growling, and her gaze shot to the werewolf, still sitting in his chair.

Oh my God, taunting a werewolf during the full moon. He's going to tear her apart!

Hugo's pupils started to dilate, and his jaw shifted slowly until it had become a muzzle.

Sheila screamed, but the doctor didn't even flinch. It surprised Erin until she noticed that Mike was now pointing a gun at Hugo. She saw that Quentin had detected it too. "Get out, Hugo. Right now," he ordered.

A werewolf pulled the meeting room door open wide and rushed into the hallway. Hugo ran after him.

"Now it's the humans' turn," Quentin said. "One more humiliation before we call it a night." She could see the muscles in his jaw clench as he spoke.

"Now, wait a minute," Doctor Jones protested. "You're not in charge here."

Quentin's showed the woman his teeth with a white predatory grin. "Oh no, are you? Do you want to fight me, Red?"

Her eyes widened, and she gave an audible gulp. She didn't answer but grabbed the other USB. After a double-click on the "humans" file, no films appeared.

Erin blinked, hardly able to believe what was happening.

"Are you not seeing what I'm not seeing?" Frank mumbled.

"Thank God," she said.

"What the hell kind of show is this?" Quentin roared. "I want to see the humans humiliated too. Right now."

"Mike, find me a copy." Doctor Jones raised her voice. "Hurry." The woman didn't act so composed anymore.

Mike walked up to the doctor, and thanks to Erin's excellent hearing, she could overhear his whisper, "There are no copies. Mr. Stratton didn't want to risk anyone finding the material before tonight."

"Well someone obviously did," the woman shrieked.

One of the other organizers walked up to them, muttering, "We've been trying to reach Mr. Stratton for the past couple of minutes, but his phone has been switched off."

"What should we tell them?" Mike asked in a low voice, pointing at the crowd.

"Why don't you tell *them* that if the USB can't provide us with entertainment, *you* will entertain us instead?" Quentin jeered. "Oh Mikey, didn't you know that werewolves have super hearing? And you Doctor Jones, you seek to take down werewolves a peg or two and would like to record what happens, well, this is what happens!"

Around them, the werewolves started to tear at

their clothes. Doctor Jones scanned the room in panic as if waiting for someone to rescue her.

"Stop this," the woman gasped, but it came out as a breathless whisper.

Erin realized that they had to get out of there, *now*!

"Let's go," Frank said, grabbing Erin's arm, and everyone ran out of the room while the werewolves continued to shift.

The first werewolf who had completed his transformation was about to follow them in the corridor when she threw the door shut. Everybody ran out of the building while Erin used her body to keep the door closed. The heavy creature threw itself against it.

"*Dépêche-toi*, Erin," Frank called out as he ran outside.

As she let go of the door, she heard glass breaking. She followed Frank, and the cold slapped her face as soon as she got out of the building. Like most of her colleagues, she had left her coat inside, and the iciness crept all the way to her bones.

Behind her the door burst open, slamming back against the wall, and four growling werewolves followed her out into the open. Her colleagues had spread out, seemingly running around in circles while the werewolves that had escaped through the windows were in pursuit.

She ran toward the parking lot, where the bus had dropped them off when they had first arrived, but it was empty.

She saw Mike running toward one of the cabins,

and she called out at him. When he turned around, she pointed at the empty parking lot.

"I called the bus driver," he shouted. "He's on his way, but it'll take at least an hour. Hide!"

She followed him. But before she could reach the cabin, a large brown werewolf blocked her path. Panic jolted through her. Rage slanted the wolf's features into those of the devil, made more demonic by the scar on its cheek.

Quentin.

Crouched low with its upper lip curled over its teeth, it waited.

She shivered and tried not to allow her fear to overwhelm her. "D–don't you want to go after Doctor Jones instead?" she suggested.

His roar hurt her ears, and he lunged at her. With a cry, she jumped aside and ran. As she fled, she inwardly chanted *shit, shit, shit…*

She could hear him chasing her, and she tried to speed up, moving away from the growling noise and toward a dark wall of pines.

The crunch of snow beneath her feet was too loud. Bushes caught at her jeans, the icy wind tugged at her hair, and it hurt to breathe, but she refused to let any of it slow her down and continued her escape.

She ran out of strength. Gasping for air, she turned around, expecting Quentin to be right behind her. He wasn't. Instead, she could only hear herself breathing.

Heart racing, she took in her surroundings. The moonlight cast a ghostlike luminescence over the snow-covered landscape.

"*Erin, what's going on? Are you okay?*"

She stood in shock for a minute when she thought she recognized the deep masculine voice.

Dane?

"*Yes, it's me. I'm not interrupting anything this time, am I?*"

Oh, well. You kinda are.

"*I'm coming back, one hour tops.*"

A howl in the night sent chills down her spine. She lifted her head to capture the faint sound as the resonance died in the distance. Sweat gathered on her brow, and her gut lurched.

Too late…

"*What do you mean 'too late'?*"

Irritation flashed.

I don't need this right now. Do you remember the last time you distracted me? We'll see each other at the party. We'll talk then."

"*Fine, but if I see one mark on you, there'll be consequences.*"

She tried not to laugh hysterically. She wished she could worry about what he might do. But right now, she had other pressing matters.

Get out of my head.

He didn't respond this time. She hoped he really was gone.

She wondered if Frank had found a safe place to hide. If she tried, she could probably track him down. She took a breath, hoping to detect the scent that was Frank's. Instead, as she inhaled deeply, another exquisite scent overwhelmed her senses.

Wolf.

But instead of being lured by it, this time she was aware of the danger. She no longer had to fight her instincts.

Pauline's potion must be working.

"Why are you in human form?" Leila asked. *"You should shift right now."*

"I don't know. Quentin's really big and aggressive. He's probably stronger than my leopard."

"Well, he's definitively stronger than your human self. He was right behind you. Maybe he's playing with you."

Erin started taking her clothes off. "Yeah, you're right, Leila. He's had it in for me right from the start. Why couldn't he go after that horrible doctor instead?"

"Why are you bothering with your clothes? Who cares about that? Shift now!" Leila shouted.

She could sense the wolf approaching. He was stalking her, a silent predator chasing beneath the cover of night.

She stepped out of her underwear and turned her thoughts inward, focusing on the image of her leopard. She could feel her shoving against her from the inside. Her arms shook as her claws started to slip from her fingertips and toes. Every muscle in her body rose within her, like a stinging of a hundred small claws trying to escape from her skin all at once. Erin let the heat rise through her naked body and watched the familiar yellow, orange brown fur grow out of her pores. Throwing her hands on the ground, she let her leopard run free.

"Why are you running around? Hide, for God's sake!" Leila said.

TOUCHED BY DARKNESS

Cold blasts of air kept hitting her as she searched for a good tree to climb up.

She found one.

She was about to jump up, when something from behind took her down, smacking her nose into the hard trunk. Pain splintered her face as she fell to the cold ground. For a second her vision blurred, and she struggled to stay conscious. She blinked a couple of times and saw tiny red droplets lying sprinkled across the snow, her droplets.

No.

For a second anger clouded her mind. She tried to kick off the wolf, but its heavy weight held her down, and the smell of fur flooded her nostrils. She turned her head and recognized the scar on the face of the snarling wolf. Its fangs were dripping with saliva. She snapped at its snout, and when her teeth touched its skin, it yelped, withdrawing its head.

She used the opportunity of its distraction to crawl away before she whirled around. Fury had transformed its features. She jumped and took an instinctive step backwards as it lashed out at her. Its paw backhanded her across her face, and warm drops of liquid spurted from her mouth. She winced at the sharp sting, but the taste of her own blood galvanized her.

With her heart galloping in terror, she lunged forward, scratching and biting, her claws slashing at the animal.

As their bodies connected, she felt sharp, dagger-like nails penetrating her flesh. She fell on her back and found the werewolf crouching on all fours over her body with its face a looming shadow over hers. It snarled, lips curving and teeth glittering in the darkness.

Her claws had mauled its chest, and dark red stains smeared its fur. The wolf didn't act as if it was about to collapse though. It looked furious.

I'm going to die.

A wave of panic swept over her.

Stay calm, she ordered herself.

He sliced her through her right side, and she let out a snarl.

"*We can't just let him kill her,*" Leila said. "*Erin, what about if you call out the wolf and confuse him?*"

"*I don't think she can do that,*" her mother answered for her. "*Pauline's potion must have gotten rid of any trace of the wolf.*"

"*Can't you confuse him another way? Like with that invisibility spell?*" Altman suggested.

"*Of course, why didn't I think of that?*" her mother said and began to recite the spell.

Erin struggled to make out her mother's words. The wolf towered over her, and it opened its mouth over her face.

In the background, she heard the words, "*So none may smell her or hear her speak…*"

Confusion momentarily swept over Quentin's face. The wolf leaned forward and inhaled deeply as if it was sniffing her.

This is it.

She used that moment to bite down on its neck. She tasted the coppery flavor of blood and heard a howl as she refused to let go. Her killer instincts took over. A garbled noise caught in its throat, and it exhaled a deep, shuddering breath.

"*... So none can touch her, so none can see*
As is my will so mote it be."

As soon as her mother had finished the spell, Erin stopped biting on Quentin's neck.

That it couldn't touch her had to mean that she couldn't touch it either. She rose on unsteady limbs to step away from the werewolf. She waited for it to jump up and reach for her, but it didn't even stir. She could still taste its blood.

Choking down a wave of bile, she forced herself to take a closer look at the wolf. Its throat didn't just have a bite mark. It looked as though it had been torn out.

"*It's dead. Oh my God, she killed it!*" Leila said.

It has to be a nightmare, some kind of crazy dream. But dreams don't taste like blood. Dreams aren't icy cold.

She stared down at her bloodstained fur.

Dreams shouldn't hurt.

In the distance, she could hear howling.

"*Oh fuck. What if the others find him? Her blood is all over him. They'll tear her apart!*" Leila said.

"*Ann, you just did a spell to make her smell disappear. Can't you do that with the blood? And she needs to get rid of the clothes too. You need to make sure to include anything else that could be used to track her down, like hair or sweat,*" Altman said.

"*Oh, yes. Wait, let me think,*" her mother said.

"*You'd better hurry. They could show up any time,*" Altman warned.

"*Maybe I can help. The guy's dead anyway. We*

226

might as well be using this as a blood sacrifice to cover up his murder," Gideon said.

"It wasn't murder. It was self-defense," her mother protested.

"We don't have time for semantics. Yes, Gideon. Please do your thing," Altman said.

Gideon didn't need more prodding, satisfaction was clear in his voice when he began reciting his black magic spell:

"I call on Ramin Sceledorse,
Your will Erin Holland shall enforce,
In your name she has killed,
For you this blood has been spilled,
This creature has bled,
So your power will be fed,
In return, I ask for her sacrifice to not be detected,
From prosecution, she will be protected,
Any trace of hers must disappear,
It will be as if she was never here,
No blood, hair, fiber, tears, footprint or sweat,
Not even screams heard tonight will have a lasting effect,
Help her live, so she continues to honor thee,
As is your will, so mote it be."

As soon as Gideon finished with the spell, the muscles in Erin's chest and abdomen cramped and went rigid. Agony rushed through her body with pressure building up in her forehead, causing a throbbing headache. It felt as though someone—no some*thing*—was pushing his way forcibly into her mind. It succeeded.

TOUCHED BY DARKNESS

For a few seconds, a horrible evil presence was looking at the carnage she had caused through her eyes. Their mental connection taught her the creature was satisfied with what she had done.

She opened her mouth and let out a scream. She staggered as bones cracked, and her fur retracted into her skin. Soon her human body replaced the leopard's.

She sensed its curiosity, as if it had never entered a shapeshifter's body before. Then the intruder left her body, and she lost her last hold on consciousness. The last thing she saw was her legs becoming transparent before the white ground rushed up to meet her.

The wet cold awoke her. Her brow wrinkled at the force it took her to open her eyes, tears distorting her vision. She lay there a moment as she assessed her surroundings. Right in front of her lay the dead body of the werewolf. For a moment, she thought that Gideon's spell hadn't helped, but as she rose, she noticed that her pile of clothes had vanished.

With excruciating slowness, she walked up to the tree where Quentin had earlier shoved her face into the trunk. With each step, she noticed that she couldn't hear the crunch of snow under her feet anymore.

She peered down at her feet. She couldn't see them anymore.

Oh my God, I'm a fucking ghost!

The drops of blood were gone, but so was she! She wanted to yell at Gideon, but discovered no sound left her mouth.

"*That spell came way too easy,*" Erin's mother

accused. *"You've used that before. Who'd you kill?"*

"What the fuck's your problem? Aren't you happy I'm helping your daughter?"

Helping? I'm a ghost! How's that helping? Don't they realize I'm dead? I'm a naked ghost freezing my butt off! Although, if I'm dead, would the cold still be a problem? I've never heard Leila complain about being cold, and she always complains about everything. Maybe I'm not dead?

"Ramin who? Who is this guy?" Altman asked. *"And did you have to name her? Won't he be pissed off if he found out it was an accident and not a real sacrifice?"*

"Of course he needs to know her name. He needs to know who to protect. And don't worry. I'm sure he won't mind. He's not that popular anymore. He'll take what he can get," Gideon answered.

She heard them bickering. Maybe she was see-through because the creature was still protecting her, even if it didn't seem the nurturing, protecting type.

Maybe I'll get my body back once I return to Camp Happy.

She moved away from the body when three snarling werewolves sprinted past her toward their dead enforcer. The sight sent chills chasing down her spine.

One of them put its face against Quentin's neck and let out a sound that was a disturbing combination of a howl and a whine in one. She wondered if he was sad.

They all shifted into their human forms. The one who had touched his body with his nose had a smear of blood on his face reminding her of war paint. He rose up, his eyes blazing. She shivered, recognizing him. He was the tall, tanned guy with black hair who had sat next to Quentin during their short fun fact introduction.

"Who the fuck did this? I want to know now," he growled with piercing black eyes.

"Don't worry, Carter. We'll track him down and tear him apart. Nobody gets away with killing Crispin's enforcer! Crispin and his pack will be furious if we don't catch this guy."

"They'll blame us if we can't track him down but I can't smell him! What creature can do this without leaving a trace? A warlock?" Carter suggested.

"I can't smell him either. Should we move him?"

"Not now. Call our best trackers and see if they can find the murderer. On the other hand, we don't want the humans to find his body either. Hmm, we'd better get rid of it. Maybe we can smell everyone at Camp Happy before they drive off. We should be able to find someone without a smell. Maybe Victor can help."

"You think he'll help? You know that Victor and Quentin weren't exactly friends, right?"

Carter frowned. "He'd better help. This *thing* killed his brother. I'll stay here and watch Quentin's body while you two inform the others."

Oh shit, I forgot about that, another reason for me to avoid Victor.

She ran back to the camp, praying that she would get her body back as soon as she returned. She arrived at the cabin and reached out to open the door when Sheila walked out. She shrieked as soon as she laid eyes on Erin.

"What the hell happened to you? You're all cuts and bruises. Where are your clothes?" When Erin opened her mouth, Sheila raised her hand, saying, "Oh my God, did the werewolves—? Uh, should I get a doctor? The bus is leaving in about five minutes, but I can ask them to wait."

Erin shook her head. "Thanks but I don't need a doctor," she said hoarsely. She had never expected Sheila to act with kindness toward her, but she could see pity filling the eyes of Nikko's secretary, and Erin had to force back the tears that threatened.

Sheila reached out to her and placed a hand on her shoulder. Erin winced, and the hand was removed. "You don't have to go to a doctor if you don't want to. It's okay, Erin. Do you want me to help you?"

For some mysterious reason, Erin nodded. She let Sheila help her get dressed while she sensed a bottomless, numbing cold within her.

"It's okay," Sheila repeated a couple of times.

After she had her clothes back on, Sheila gave Erin a moment to use the bathroom. Erin looked at her pale reflection in the mirror above the sink. "Thank God. I'm solid again," she murmured. She wiped the blood from her mouth and was relieved that her clothes covered up most of the bruises. There was only a small cut on her lip, but hopefully not too visible.

She sighed. "Couldn't he make the cuts on my body disappear too, and the blood?"

"Who cares, as long as it's not on that werewolf?"

"Just so you know, Gideon, I'm never letting you

do black magic again!"

"*Why not, it worked, didn't it?*"

"I suppose. But now I feel dirty, as if I was possessed. What the hell happened?" she hissed. "Didn't you use the same name when we turned Nikko into a rat? I sure as hell didn't sense him then!"

"*Well, we did call on him twice. He must have got curious.*"

"Erin, are you ready?" Sheila called out. "The bus should leave now."

They left the cabin. Sheila carried both their bags as they walked to the bus. Erin recognized one of the werewolves standing by the door and froze.

"You don't have to worry," Sheila said pulling her along with her. "They've got their emotions back under control. They won't hurt you anymore."

Her stomach rose up in her throat as she watched him sniffing everyone as they climbed inside the bus. As she entered the bus, she met the werewolf's gaze. She took a shaky breath, and the werewolf had the grace to look contrite.

"I'm sorry we lost control, ma'am," he said without recognition.

"*Oh my God!*" Gideon laughed. "*They think you're afraid of them, that you need help because you're weak. They'll never think you killed their enforcer. It's brilliant!*"

Sheila led her inside, and they sat at the back of the bus. She noted Frank staring at her when she passed him, a question in his eyes. Sheila's shaking of the head was barely noticeable, but both Erin and Frank spotted it.

Grateful, Erin smiled at her. Sheila tapped her hand. "It's okay. You're okay," she said.

Erin glanced at the werewolf standing by the bus while he continued to smell everyone who passed him. She was safe, but then she remembered what Dane had told her just a few hours ago.

"*As long as you haven't killed anyone yourself in werewolf form, you could be free from the curse if you kill your maker.*"

I killed someone tonight. Does that mean I'm going to remain a werewolf now?

Stratton entered his office, slamming the door behind him. He marched to his computer and turned it on, wanting to see the fiasco of the psych evaluation with his own eyes.

As soon as the cops had finished fishing, they had allowed him to turn on his mobile. When he'd listened to the messages on his voicemail, the red-hot rage had been so vivid it had been fortunate for Detectives Hill and Stevens that they had already left the interview room.

Not so fortunate for his lawyer, but the man would survive. He should have stopped the interview as soon as it had become apparent that they weren't getting anywhere with the interrogation, but the incompetent man probably wanted to make most of his billable hours.

He couldn't believe his misfortune. If the cops hadn't interrupted him, he could have sent his people

TOUCHED BY DARKNESS

the footage of Erin eating Doctor Quirkhart. Who cared about watching how a werewolf responded when he was confronted with footage of him raping some girl?

I sure as hell don't.

He rewound the film of the test and watched Erin's disbelief when the USB turned out to be empty.

So it wasn't her, then who?

Stratton scrutinized the images again and again, but all the humans spared had acted shocked when they discovered there was nothing to be used against them. The werewolves wouldn't have tampered with the USB. It wouldn't have been in their interest. Unless…

Victor had that USB all to himself.

If there had been something going on between him and Erin, he probably would not want her to see the way he had aided in her abduction.

Stratton rewound the film and searched the audience for the werewolf's face.

You should be here. Where did you go?

His next move was to call the werewolf. When he got Victor's voicemail, he disconnected and dialed his second-in-command's number. Edward answered immediately.

At least some of my employees can be trusted.

"Edward, you're the one who provided that werewolf, Victor, with a cell phone, right? I want you to track it."

"And once we find it?"

"If you find Victor with that phone, I want you

234

to bring him to me, alive."

After he hung up, he pondered over the werewolf's actions. They made no sense to him. Victor had to have known he would be caught and put on his list. Why would he risk that just to avoid looking bad for a potential girlfriend?

And although he liked the idea of Erin cheating on Dane, he doubted she was the type. He doubted even more that Dane wouldn't notice it, and once he did, he would never let her get away with it.

It didn't matter. The werewolf had interfered and would be punished. He suspected that Victor had already disposed of the cell phone, but he liked to be thorough.

For now, Victor was alive and probably hiding from him somewhere. He didn't want to think about it anymore.

Think happier thoughts…

Tomorrow, I'll finally meet my enemy's daughter.

Tomorrow, I'll finally expose Dane for the weakling he is.

SEVENTEEN

It took Erin less than three seconds to open her hotel room door after Dane had knocked on it.

He scanned her red dress, and his desire for her rose as he remembered the last time she had worn it. But he ignored the compulsion to take her in his arms. He needed to check she wasn't hurt. The dress showed quite a lot of skin, and he couldn't see any evidence of a fight.

She chuckled. "My face is up here, you know?"

"I was checking you for signs of violence. Against my better judgment, I left you alone last night, just as you asked. Don't you think I'm a considerate boyfriend?"

She blushed, self-consciously slipping a strand of hair behind her ear. He couldn't stop himself from drawing her tight against him. "So what happened, Goldilocks? It seemed like your heart was pounding right out of your chest when I talked to you."

She cleared her throat. "The werewolves shifted and started chasing everyone." When his grip tightened, she added, "But nobody got hurt."

"No one?" He narrowed his eyes on her.

She swallowed. "No one."

He inhaled deeply. Control was becoming more and more difficult, especially now that she had revealed her love for him. What started as a seduction, had changed into a want so intense, it dazed him. He turned his head and lowered his mouth to hers, breathing in her very essence before kissing her long and deep.

What if I lose her tonight?

He let his cheek rest against the side of her head, closing his eyes as fear swept over him before he stepped back.

Her smile lit up the entire hallway. "You're looking very handsome tonight in your suit. I thought that you only owned jeans."

"Tonight is special."

It's not every day that I set out to kill Jonathan Stratton. I just hope that if I fail, he won't punish me by killing you. I can't fail. I won't.

"I really appreciate you being here for me tonight. We'd better hurry though. Frank is waiting for us downstairs."

They walked to the elevator. "How did it go last night?" he asked.

Her eyes narrowed in suspicion. "Why? Did you have something to do with that USB?"

"What are you talking about? I meant the potion. Did it work?"

"Ah, right. Of course, yes, it worked perfectly unlike our USB stick. That was such a relief. You wouldn't believe what was on the one about the werewolves. Unless you would believe…"

He didn't say anything and waited for her to continue.

"I knew it! You did do it!" She wrapped her arms around him and kissed him, squeezing him tight.

The high-pitched sound of the elevator's arrival interrupted them.

She stepped away, her chest heaving as she tried to catch her breath. "I know I told you I wanted to fight my own battles. But in this case, I'm very grateful for your help."

He frowned as they entered the elevator. "You were quite adamant about your desire not to let me interfere."

A blush worked over her cheeks. "Well, I'm glad you didn't listen to me. When they showed us what they had on one of the werewolves, I was terrified to find out what they would have on me. You didn't happen to have seen what was on there, did you?"

Dane opened his mouth to say he hadn't done anything with the damn USB when she raised her hands. "No, stop. I don't want to know, should I? No, never mind. Don't tell me."

He couldn't tell her anything if he tried. She grabbed his hand as they left the elevator and entered the hotel's reception area. Her eyes gleaming with excitement, she turned to him and kissed him again. "Thanks for saving me last night."

"Ah, there you are," he heard a deep voice say from behind them. He saw Erin's colleague walk up to them arm in arm with a pretty, petite woman.

"Hi Frank, Janice, you're looking great. I'd like you to meet Dane Lynch."

As his eyes met the woman's, she took a hasty step backward. He saw Erin's displeasure and tried to smile in a non-threatening matter. He knew he tended to overwhelm and make people nervous. But after more than twenty years as a master vampire, he didn't know how not to intimidate.

"Shall we go?" Frank suggested.

The party was being held at the same hotel where Erin had spent the night. Before entering the ballroom, everyone went through security. Handbags were searched, and guests were told to walk through a body scanner. Dane wasn't carrying a bag, and he was asked to put all metallic objects on a tray. He shivered involuntarily. He had known this was going to happen and had taken these objects, keeping in mind that he might be frisked, but a lot of his plan succeeding depended on this.

He caught Erin's frown when she noticed the cigarettes and a lighter.

"You smoke?" she asked.

He shrugged. "Hey, unlike you I don't have to worry about cancer."

He then took out the flask with alcohol, pure alcohol. The security guard lifted it from his tray.

"You think you're not going to get enough to drink tonight?" the guard asked.

Dane grinned, hoping he succeeded in hiding the tension he felt. "Yes, wine probably but not the strong stuff."

The very strong stuff.

When the security guard held the flask hesitantly, Dane offered. "If you like, you can take a sip."

Erin glared at him. "Are you crazy? This man is not allowed to drink alcohol while he's at work, and what are you doing, carrying liquor around? You're not only a smoker but an alcoholic too?"

The guard's expression creased in sympathy, and he held out the tray to him. "Here you go, sir. I think you'll need it."

This comment caused Erin to aim her scowl at the guard instead. Dane quickly removed the items from the tray before she convinced the guard to change his mind.

"I hope you're not going to smoke around me," she said as they entered the ballroom.

"I didn't know you felt so strongly about it," Dane said.

"I don't like the smell."

He sighed. "I tell you what. I promise you I won't smoke tonight."

But if I'm lucky, someone else will…

Jonathan Stratton had spared no expense to entertain his guests and had even arranged a Grammy winning artist to perform at the gala. In spite of Erin's lack of knowledge when it came to music, she recognized it.

"Do you know who he is?" she asked Dane.

He smiled, grasped her hand and coaxed her to the dance floor. He caught her around her waist and started moving, and she found herself following with ease.

"It wasn't a hint to get you to dance with me,"

she said, even though it was nice being held by him again. She recalled the last time they danced together and how that evening had ended.

She allowed the music to embrace her as he held her close, his arms securely around her as she was enveloped by his strong, masculine scent.

"Erin, I need to tell you something," he said in a low voice, his breath warm against her ear. "Stratton and I have a history together."

"What?" she murmured.

"It might not be safe for you here," he continued.

"*Especially not after I have tried to set your boss on fire.*"

"What!" she hissed. She stopped dancing and glared at him. "Did you just say that you're going to set Nikko on fire?"

"No, I did not *say* that," he said through clenched teeth. "And I did not *think* that either."

"Then what was it that I heard then?"

He grabbed her arm, dragging her off the dance floor until he had reached what appeared to be a quiet corner. He glanced around, probably checking that nobody could eavesdrop on their conversation before he whispered, "I just told you that Stratton and I have a history together."

"You want to set *Jonathan Stratton* on fire? You must be out of your mind! Is that why you brought a lighter with you?"

But a lighter alone wouldn't be enough…

Suddenly the realization hit her. "The flask, what's in the flask?"

"You don't want to know, and stop asking me all these questions. You're going to ruin this."

"Is that why you wanted to join me tonight?"

She thought she could read a glimpse of guilt in his expression. But a second later, determination sparkled in his blue eyes.

"So *it is* why you joined me. Was it also part of your plan to get me to tell you that I loved you?" Hurt squeezed her chest.

"Erin, no, I joined you because I wanted to join you and will continue to join you."

Betrayal was a bad taste in her mouth. She turned away from him. "Don't. I don't want you to."

She heard people clapping and glanced in the direction of the sound. Jonathan Stratton had entered the room, and a spotlight followed him as he made his way through the crowd. Oblivious that someone intended to set him on fire. Someone *she* had invited. "Oh my God, they're going to blame me."

"No, Stratton's people know I would never involve you. If the police link me to his death, I'll make sure that you won't be implicated."

"But you did involve me just by being here as my date. Please," she pleaded as she put her hand on his arm. "Don't do this."

"I must, but you should go. Go up to your hotel room and feign a headache."

"The headache won't need to be faked." Exasperation beat painfully at her temples. "I can't leave because it will only make me look guilty if I go and something happens. No, if you want to have your little bonfire, you're gonna have to do it with me present."

She hoped he cared enough about her to break off his assassination attempt if it meant that she would have to be there, but his brief nod taught her that he didn't care about her at all.

He never said he did, did he?

"Erin. You must not tell a soul," he said. "Check with Altman if you want to know what kind of man he is."

She blinked back tears and left in search of the bathroom. She needed to get rid of any signs of distress and pretend to have a good time, or she could inform Jonathan Stratton of Dane's intentions that evening.

"*Stratton did seem to have a bit of a creepy reputation when I was part of the vampire community,*" Altman said. "*Something about making sure that you never owe him anything, and there were also rumors about his pranks that were never funny.*"

"Just because someone has a different sense of humor, doesn't mean you have to kill them," she muttered.

"*Depends on the joke,*" Altman said.

She found the bathroom, and she was about to enter when a cheerful and somewhat familiar voice behind her froze her in her steps.

"Erin Holland, how wonderful it is to finally meet face-to-face!"

She reluctantly turned around and found herself staring up at Jonathan Stratton.

Jonathan Stratton! How does he recognize me? Why is he talking to me? Does he know about Dane's plans? Does he consider me an accomplice?

"You look positively horrified, my dear." He laughed. "I assure you that whatever Dane has told you about me, has been greatly exaggerated."

"Y-you know who I am?" Her voice cracked. In spite of his friendly demeanor, she felt a dark chill whisper through her. There was something about the way the immaculately dressed man glanced at her that reminded her of the way a predator considered potential prey. In fact, the power he exuded reminded her of Dane.

Altman mentioned his reputation within the vampire community. He has to be a vampire.

She took in his slightly receding hairline with a touch of gray on his sideburns.

He must have been sired at an older age.

"Yes, of course. I'm interested in all my employees but especially the ones who show such promise like you did at the team building these past couple of days. I'm delighted to have you as part of my team."

"Oh, uh, thank you."

"And where is our friend Dane Lynch? I understand that he's your plus one."

Reluctantly, she nodded. "We, uh, we had a fight."

"Oh no, I'm so sorry." He narrowed his eyes at her face. "I see, arguing at my party… Would you mind giving us a little privacy?" he told the six men in uniform behind him. He put his hand on her back and guided her to a separate room. He shut the door behind them.

What is going on?

"I wanted to tell you something that I think you should know about Dane Lynch. You see, Dane and I, we've had a couple of disagreements too. He's tried to interfere with some of my activities. Because of that, I had him watched." He took out his smart phone and tapped in a code.

She peered at the door, wishing she could be on the other side. In the background, she could hear the music pounding. "I d-don't see how this concerns me."

"You will. Ah, here we are." He handed her his phone. "I suppose I could just tell you what he's done but pictures speak louder than words."

She swallowed down the lump in her throat as she stared at the film on the screen. The images were quite dark, but she was able to recognize the Devereaux church.

The night we tried to get rid of the voices.

She saw herself lying on the ground, passed out, while Dane got down on his knees and held her tenderly.

Yes, I had passed out that night because of the magic blast of Pauline's spell.

She saw Dane kiss her, fondling her while she was unconscious.

What's he doing?

Goosebumps pricked her skin. She glanced at Stratton, who seemed to be watching her response.

"Okay. I've seen enough," she said. "That's too disturbing." She held out the phone, but he wouldn't take it.

"There's more," he said.

More?

Her mind whirling she stared down at her phone again, and on the screen she saw Dane lifting his head, something dark was glistening on his mouth. For a moment, she was able to look at the face of her passed out self and discovered the blood on her lips.

"W-what?" she whispered. She shook her head in denial.

This can't be happening. It's not real. It must be fake.

In the film, Dane leaned over her once more and put his mouth on hers before he began forcibly rubbing her throat as he continued to kiss her.

The images on the phone shocked her so much she stood immobile, watching Dane finish whatever he had been doing before holding her in his arms, waiting for her to wake up. There was a roaring in her ears.

"… a blood bond," a deep voice said beside her. It faded in and out. Her brain refused to work properly, like the rest of her body. She dropped the phone.

"Careful there," Stratton said as he picked it up. "Ah, it's fine. But you're not, are you? I'm sorry, but I felt that you should know."

She found her way to a wall and leaned against it as numbness spread through her limbs. "He forced his blood into me?" She gazed at the veins in her arm. "I have his blood under my skin?"

She dropped, bracing her hands on her knees, trying to suck back a wave of nausea but failing. She retched.

"Haven't you felt a change in your relationship with him?" he asked. "I've had a couple of humans I shared a blood bond with. We became closer, more involved. When someone tried to hurt them, I felt it and was able to stop it. With the right vampire, a blood bond can be a good thing. It's all about protection."

"Protection... Right." She remembered the werewolf attack at the hospital. While she had managed to subdue Billy, Dane had started ordering her around telepathically. His distracting her had caused her to be bitten.

Anger rose in her. His *forced upon* blood bond had caused her werewolf bite.

She opened her mouth when the door slammed open, and Dane stormed in. She saw him staring at her, and she knew he had to see the hurt and betrayal in her expression because his face turned grim as he screamed, "You fucker!" at Stratton. Dane moved so fast, his speed made him a blur.

She couldn't actually see him remove the flask from his pocket. But from one second to the next, the metal container appeared in his left hand, and he doused Stratton in his face with the spirits. Some drops reached her too, and she jumped away when the liquid hit her arm. The strong smell of alcohol filled her nose.

She blinked and saw Dane holding the lighter next. She gasped in fear. But before he could flicker the flame to life, Stratton's six bodyguards tackled him with the force of a hurricane, slamming him against the marble floor.

247

The shock of the blow caused Dane to drop the lighter. Erin knelt and snatched the weapon from the ground—out of Dane's reach—while the men piled up on top of him, pinning him down. Fingers on her shoulder made her jerk in surprise.

"Shall I take that from you, hmm?" Stratton asked. He took away his hand and held it out, a cool smile forming on his lips. She rose, glad to let go of the reviled lighter. But as she stuck out her hand, an agonized wail made her look down. Dane was watching them, his mouth twisted in a snarl, fangs gleaming. One of the bodyguards put his fist in Dane's hair and smashed his face against the cold hard floor. Stratton grabbed the lighter before she could change her mind and bent down to pick up the flask too.

"Empty, aren't you lucky?" he asked, his voice laced with sarcasm.

The bodyguard still holding Dane's hair drew a stiletto switchblade from his back pocket. He flicked the blade open as Dane began to thrash wildly, growling like a wild beast. The knife glinted in his hand as he poised it over Dane's heart. Erin yelled.

"No!" Stratton ordered. Relieved, she glanced at Stratton. He walked up to the desk in front of Dane, and in spite of the fire accelerant on his face, he leaned against it in a seemingly relaxed pose. When he caught her stare, he winked at her.

"Don't worry, dear. I'm in a good mood tonight. I don't want him dead."

"But we can still wound him, right?" the bodyguard said before pushing the sharp point against Dane's back, forcing it through muscle and tissue while blood spurted from Dane like a fountain. Dane screamed with pain.

Stratton seized the bodyguard by his throat, his fingers digging into his neck as he pulled him off Dane's body. The man let out a high-pitched sound as he was thrown against the wall.

"Did I tell you to cut him?" Stratton asked.

"No, sir. But I thought—"

"I don't pay you to think." Stratton nodded at the other bodyguards. "Just throw him out. I'll deal with you later."

Dane coughed as the men pulled him up. He stumbled, but they managed to support his weight and kept him from falling down again.

Erin sucked in her breath when she noticed Dane was leaving a trail of blood behind.

Her legs trembling, she stared at the puddle of blood in front of the closed door.

Please be okay.

The silence in the room seemed even thicker after all the commotion.

"Have a seat, dear," Stratton said. "You're so pale. Can I get you anything to drink, a glass of water perhaps?"

She let him lead her to the sofa and sat down. She shook her head. "No."

"He's fine, you know. Vampires don't die that easily."

She swallowed. "Yes, I hate this. I hate that I'm upset because he got hurt. I should be angry. It's that blood exchange, right?" She glared at her left wrist and rubbed the blue veins with her right thumb. "It's because he's still here, under my skin. I'll never be free of him as long as I have his blood flowing through me, will I?"

Panic flared within her. She heard herself whimper while she continued to rub at her skin, harder and harder with movements becoming more frantic, more anxious.

I'll never get him out. He turned me into this weak, needy girl.

She closed her eyes, not wanting to see the veins anymore.

"Careful, Erin," Stratton warned. "You're cutting yourself open."

"Maybe cutting myself open isn't a bad thing." She laughed with a bitter edge. Her chest tight, she let out a sob. "If I bleed out, I'll get rid of his blood too, right?"

His hand grabbed hers, stopping it from causing more damage. She opened her eyes, the tears made her vision blur. She blinked, staring down at her arm. A thin trickle of her blood welled between their fingers.

"But you bleeding out would be such a waste, don't you think? There's another way. A blood bond can be broken if a newer bond is created. You just have to make sure a lot of blood is exchanged, so it can suppress the previous connection."

"And who would be willing to have this newer bond with me?" she asked, pulling her hand from his grasp.

He grinned. "That would be me, at your service, my lady."

"*Oh, you mustn't, Erin,*" Altman warned. "*You don't want to do that. You don't even know him.*"

"*Listen to Altman,*" her mother said. "*Before doing anything rash, you should talk to Dane. Let him tell you he's sorry.*"

"If I were you, I'd stop listening to what those voices are telling you and make your own decisions from now on," Stratton said.

"W–what, you know about the voices?"

"Know of them? I can hear them loud and clear. I would assume Dane should have been able to hear them too."

She remembered Dane telling her his touch had helped silence the voices in her head.

Her mind was spinning.

Could all vampires hear the voices?

Stratton tapped her on her knee. "It's okay. If you like having these feelings for someone who's been lying to you, I won't push. I just thought I'd be doing you a favor."

He got up. "Well, it was lovely getting to know you a little bit—"

"Wait. I'll do it."

Quick before I change my mind.

He looked down at her with a satisfied grin covering his face. He sat down again. "Let's do it then. Maybe it's best if you close your eyes and try to relax a bit. Or I can glamour you if you like. But then, you must keep your eyes open."

In response, she closed her eyes. No mind control. This time it was going to be a conscious decision.

"*You might end up regretting this, Erin,*" Altman tried again.

She felt lips sliding over her throat. "Tell him to shut up, Erin," Stratton murmured, his breath warm against her neck.

"Shut up, Altman," she whispered.

She heard Stratton's brief chuckle before he bit down, and pain shot through her. Very much unlike Dane's bite, Stratton's bite burned as if his teeth had been covered in acid.

Wanting it to stop, but unable to speak, she struggled against a body hard as steel. He'd put his hands on her arms, and she felt his nails cutting in her flesh. She screamed as agony sucked her into its jaws.

Vaguely, she thought she heard Dane screaming in her head.

"*He's worse.*"

Stratton removed his mouth and released her.

Weakened by the loss of blood, she didn't even have the energy to open her eyes. She felt him lift her up and put her on his lap. He must have removed his shirt since her face landed on a warm, hairy chest. In spite of the strong smell of blood, she was still able to detect cologne.

"Here you go," she heard Stratton say before he pressed her mouth against the wound on his chest.

"*Don't swallow,*" Altman ordered.

Stratton chuckled again. "Be a good girl and swallow, Erin." He pushed her face down so deep that she was unable to breathe. Automatically, she opened her mouth to inhale and swallowed a large amount of blood instead.

"That's my girl."

EIGHTEEN

Erin woke when the bed beneath her started to move. She struggled to open her eyes and blinked when everything remained blurry.

"So, was it as good for you as it was for me?" Stratton asked as he slipped out from beneath her.

Drawing on a reserve of strength she didn't know she possessed, she forced herself to sit up. Insistent waves of nausea hit her. She started to heave and covered her mouth to keep it in.

Stratton put a bin on her lap. "Here you go. Please try not to throw up all the blood," he said. "I don't want my sacrifice to be for nothing."

She vomited blood while he laughed. She looked up from the bin and watched him close his shirt. The wound on his chest had already healed.

"Okay, I've got to go out and mingle."

She put the bin down. "Do you—?" Her throat was sore and swollen, making it painful to talk. She swallowed. "Do you think Dane is still out there?"

"Waiting for you?" He shrugged. "Probably. Don't you worry your pretty, little head. I'll have my secretary arrange a flight back to Louisiana with my private plane."

"W-why?"

"Why what? Why I'm offering you my private plane, or why did I create a blood bond between us?"

"All," she said hoarsely.

"Maybe it's because I'm a good guy."

She expected one of the voices to make a comment now, but they were all remarkably silent.

He grinned. "Nope, you don't believe me. Very wise. Oh well, I'm a vampire, so I enjoy tasting blood, and you were very tasty."

She frowned. "It h-hurt."

"Ah yes. But that's because you didn't want me to glamour you. Bites always hurt without glamour."

Do they? When Dane bit me during sex, his bite was pleasurable. I didn't sense him using glamour.

It was almost as if Stratton had enjoyed making it painful.

"Altman?" she whispered.

"I also like the idea of taking something that belongs to Dane," Stratton continued. "He wants you, used trickery to get you, and I took you away from him." His eyes lighted in triumph. "I find that immensely satisfying."

He moved to the door. "Stay here while I get my secretary. Unless you want to boogie…?" When she shook her head, he laughed. "I didn't think so."

When he shut the door behind him, she tried again. "Altman, Mom, are any of you out there?"

It reminded her of what had happened at the Devereaux church. At the time, she had believed it had been because the ritual to get rid of the voices had worked temporarily. Now, it appeared that it had been a side effect to the blood exchange.

She hung her head and sighed. "Oh Altman, you were right. I'm already regretting it."

She closed her eyes and thought she could use another nap when the door opened, and a brunette in her forties walked in. The woman was wearing a dress suit, stiletto-heeled shoes and her hair was in a tight bun. The bun seemed to be so tight that it looked painful. Her face was grim.

"I'm so sorry to be taking you away from the party," Erin said.

The woman frowned. "The party is work. I'm working."

"Oh well, thank you very much for helping me. Uh, my name is Erin Holland."

"Yes, I know who you are. I needed to know your name, so I could cancel your plane ticket for tomorrow morning."

Is she deliberately being obtuse?

"So what's your name?"

"I'm Margot Sloane. Mr. Stratton has asked me to give you my number in case you need to talk to him." The secretary handed over a business card.

Erin pushed the corners of her lips up into a smile as she accepted it. "Thank you." She was curious about the woman's experience with Stratton, but the woman acted so miserable that Erin doubted she would even understand her if she asked her if she enjoyed working for him.

"If you get up now, I'll take you to the airport. Mr. Stratton has asked us to leave through the back entrance. I have asked one of the people of the hotel to pack your bags."

"Wow, having someone to fill my suitcase. I'm starting to feel like royalty here."

Not even a smile.

She groaned.

This is going to be a long journey.

The plane had just taken off, when Erin heard Gideon say, *"We're on a private plane? When did that happen?"*

She peeked at Ms. Sloane, who was sitting in a large seat near the cockpit, as far away as possible from her. The secretary was busy working on her laptop.

"Stratton offered me his plane, so I could avoid Dane," she answered softly. "How about you, were you in the dark place again?"

"We were away again, yes. But about avoiding Dane, isn't that only prolonging the inevitable?" Altman replied. *"He knows where you live. It's not like he needs an invitation to get in."*

"I know. I just didn't have the energy for a confrontation right now," she whispered.

"Stratton drained you," Altman said.

"Yes. About that—I wanted to ask you—Stratton claimed that bites from vampires always hurt unless you use glamour, is that true? I remember you telling me that a bite was harmless. In fact, you warned me it could become addictive."

"Oh yes. We had discussed that after you let Dane bite you during sex," Leila giggled. *"That bite was orgasmic,*

right?"

"Shut up, Leila," Erin hissed. "Let Altman answer."

"*You already know the answer, Erin,*" Altman said. "*If the bite caused you pain, it's because he wanted it to hurt.*"

Dread curled in her stomach. "I've just made a deal with the devil, haven't I?"

Erin had killed Quentin.

Victor would not have thought it possible. But when the others had told him about a mysterious creature tearing open Quentin's throat without leaving any scent behind, he knew it had to be her.

He owed it to his pack to tell them who had killed their enforcer.

Hell, I owe it to my brother, even if he was always such an asshole.

It didn't matter. His first loyalty lay with himself, and there was little gain in telling the others what he knew. There was more to gain if he kept quiet.

He grinned.

It's one more way to tie her to me.

Driving up to the werewolf pack always felt like coming home to Victor. They were located a fifteen-minute drive from Hope Acres and surrounded by a thick forest. Unlike the woods in Canada, these trees spoke to him. They brought back memories of his first shift, of the time he lost his virginity and of his first werewolf fight.

In spite of his love for the land, he never stayed with the pack for more than a day each month. That was probably another reason why he didn't feel obligated to tell them about Quentin's murder.

He didn't care for all the politics, nor did he appreciate the way Crispin's mate kept looking at him. A little over twenty years ago, Roxanna and he had been involved in the mating dance. When she'd discovered his lack of ambition, she had left him for Crispin, who had rewarded her by making her the highest-ranking female in the pack as mate to the pack alpha.

He never blamed Roxanna for choosing his cousin over him, and Crispin had never expressed any displeasure over Roxanna's history with his cousin. But over the years, Victor had noticed her becoming more and more interested in his sex life, especially in the fact that he was still without a mate. He'd even overheard her bragging to another female that he was still pining for her. If Crispin had heard her say that, Victor would have been sentenced to death. One did not covet the alpha's mate.

That's why he believed that Crispin would gladly let him mate with Erin. In fact, he was counting on his cousin's support on winning her.

As Victor stepped out of his car, he noticed Roxanna staring at him from the kitchen window. He ignored her and greeted Crispin instead who was waiting for him in the doorway.

TOUCHED BY DARKNESS

They shared the same coloring, but unlike Victor, Crispin had his brown hair military-short. With his seven feet height, Crispin towered over him. Even his body appeared to be more muscular. Of course, if Crispin wanted to remain pack alpha, he had to be in excellent shape. As Victor walked up to his cousin, he noticed his intense brown eyes assessing him.

"Victor, I'm glad to see you. Are you here about your brother? What the hell happened in Canada? I heard that something tore out Quentin's throat."

"You mean my *half*-brother. I had already left before Quentin was killed. I had other things to worry about, and that's what I wanted to talk to you about."

"I know you two weren't exactly close, but I'm sure you'd want to find whoever—or whatever—is responsible. How am I supposed to find another enforcer? You don't happen to know anyone, do you?" Crispin sighed. "What a mess. Never mind. What was it you wanted to talk to me about?"

"There's something else that happened while I was in Canada. I had a conflict of interest."

"A conflict of interest, you?" Crispin raised an eyebrow. "I thought you only had one interest—your own."

He followed Crispin into the house. "You know me too well. No, this time it was the client's needs versus werewolf business."

They entered his office. Crispin closed the door and turned to him, viewing him with curiosity.

"My client had asked me to keep an eye on a woman that he was...evaluating. When I discovered that she had recently been bitten by one of us, it put me in a difficult position."

"How did it happen?"

Victor shrugged. "She works in security. Maybe she was bitten at one of Star Knight's parties. She's had to subdue one of us there before."

"I just hope it wasn't one of ours. How did her first shift go?"

Victor smiled. "Perfectly. She's perfect. In fact, I want us to mate."

"Ah, that makes sense. You were looking out for your own interest after all. And how does she feel about you?"

He scowled at the wooden floor. "She wasn't exactly jumping for joy when I mentioned it. She's dating someone else at the moment. A vampire. Dane Lynch."

"Dane Lynch? Dating? Seriously?" Crispin snorted. "Don't worry about him. I'll have a chat with him, but I doubt he'll put up much of a fight to keep her."

"You obviously haven't seen him with her, but I hope you're right. I do have another concern though- my client. I haven't informed him of her werewolf status, and he'd set up some nasty situations for her that I ended up sabotaging, so she wouldn't get hurt."

Crispin nodded. "That's understandable, but your client probably won't agree. What's his name?"

"Jonathan Stratton."

"Damn. Dane Lynch and Jonathan Stratton? You sure do pick 'em. Well, I can't wait to meet her. I hope she's worth it though."

Victor grinned. "Oh, she's worth it."

TOUCHED BY DARKNESS

She was in an office, sitting behind a fancy, mahogany desk. A skinny man who appeared to be in his late thirties was sitting in front of her in a dark gray suit. The man was writing something on a notepad.

"Mr. Stratton, I'm so honored that you're willing to see me," the man gushed.

"The honor is mine, Mr. Tennant," she heard herself say in a deep masculine voice. "I'm familiar with your work. I found it surprising that a horror writer would be interested in switching to non-fiction."

Sweat gathered on Mr. Tennant's brow. "Well, uh. I used to write books about vampires, and now I'm writing a b-book about you. That doesn't s-seem like such a b-big leap."

"Hmm. Doesn't it?"

"A-as I mentioned in my letter, I'm c-currently working on your biography and have several facts that I would like to check with you."

"You're a careful man," she said. "I can appreciate that. So am I. As you can imagine, I can never be too careful as a man in my position."

The writer forced a smile. "Of course. A careful man."
She saw him write it down in red ink with a silver pen.

"Oh, what a lovely pen," she said. "I see it's engraved."

"It says 'blood writer'. It was a g-gift from my kids. They saw a si-similar text at an attraction once and thought of me."

"Ah, yes. How charming, a horror writer writing in

blood." She laughed. "But wouldn't you rather record our conversation?"

"I-uh, I thought that y-you w-wouldn't let me."

"You thought right, Mr. Tennant. But it does make me wonder why you thought I wouldn't allow you to tape our conversation but that I would allow you to write a book about my life, my private life."

She noticed that Mr. Tennant's hands started to shake. When he caught her staring at them, he put them onto his lap. She could see his nervousness, but she sensed a strong determination to overcome that emotion. Rather than retreat, he moved closer. "Mr. Stratton, you are a public figure."

She leaned back, fiddling with a glass of scotch. "Do you enjoy writing horror stories because you like to be frightened or because you like scaring people?"

He cast a fearful glance her way. "J-just scaring p-people I guess."

She smiled. "Well, how about that. We have even more in common than I thought. I also enjoy scaring people. I especially enjoy scaring people who are meddling in my affairs."

Mr. Tennant dropped his gaze, and his body went rigid. "I won't write lies. I w-will check them first."

"You don't seem to understand, Mr. Tennant, that I don't want to check your 'facts'." She sighed. "You seem determined to write this book. I guess we have nothing to say."

She stood up from her desk, and the writer did the same. "Goodbye," Mr. Tennant said.

"I prefer what the French say. 'Au revoir, monsieur Tennant.' I'm sure we'll see each other again soon."

She waited for him to leave before returning to the desk

and picking up the phone. On the other side, she could hear someone say, "Mr. Stratton."

"He just left," she said. "I want you to set everything in motion. No warning this time. Oh, don't forget to check my schedule with Ms. Sloane to see when I'm free. I want to join in on the fun."

The fasten-your-seatbelt sound of the airplane jerked her awake. Erin pried open her eyes to find the flight attendant standing beside her, holding out a tray with champagne glasses.

"Would you like some champagne before we land?" she asked.

"Uh no. No thank you. Maybe water?"

The woman left after she had given her a glass of water. She caught Jonathan Stratton's secretary staring at her. When Erin raised one brow, the woman turned around.

She wondered about the dream she'd just had. Had that been something that had really happened or merely a dream that her overactive mind had created?

It has to be just a regular dream.

She looked at the back of Ms. Sloane's head. The woman seemed rather formidable. She couldn't imagine her aiding her manager to hurt some writer.

It's nothing, nothing but my busy imagination.

NINETEEN

areful not to wake Pauline, Erin slowly opened the door to her studio apartment. To her surprise, the lights had been switched on.

"Hi roommate," Pauline said cheerfully.

Erin took a peek at her watch. It was nearly two o'clock in the morning. "Hi. What are you still doing up?"

"Are you kidding me? When all you told me on the phone was 'can't talk now, but I'm coming home tonight'? Of course, I had to stay up and hear what happened. I couldn't fall asleep after that."

Erin grimaced. "It's not a pretty story."

"The potion didn't work, and you ended up attacking someone. No wait, the potion didn't work, and you ended up eating Dane."

For a second, she saw herself tearing open Quentin's neck, and she swallowed down the nausea.

The less people know, the better.

"No, no eating anyone, not this time," she mumbled.

"Are you okay? You look kinda pale. The potion?"

"No, the potion worked perfectly. Thank you

very much for that by the way. And about Dane, I didn't eat him even though he does deserve to be eaten."

"So what happened?"

"At the party, I first had an argument with Dane because... Well, it doesn't matter. I then ran into Jonathan Stratton, who showed me a recording of what had happened at the Devereaux church last Halloween. He'd been watching Dane because they're enemies or something like that. On that film, you see me passed out, and Dane, he... Well, he took advantage of that."

"He *raped* you?" Pauline's eyes rounded in shock.

"No! He, uh, he bit me, and then he made me swallow his blood too."

"Gross! Why would he do that?"

"I-I'm not sure. Stratton mentioned that it creates a blood bond, and then when you're in danger, he senses it and can help you."

Pauline frowned. "So it's a good thing? He did it because he wanted to protect you?"

"No! If it's a good thing, then why did he do it while I was passed out? No, it's because he's a control freak."

"So you didn't want to stay at the party anymore, and Jonathan Stratton let you take an earlier flight?"

Erin sat down on her bed and rubbed her temples. "Uh, not quite. You see, when I saw that film, I was so angry at Dane. And then Dane barged in and tried to kill Jonathan Stratton."

Pauline gasped. "*Kill* him?"

"Uh, yes, but he didn't succeed. Then I said I

would do anything to get rid of that connection between us. Mr. Stratton kindly offered to help me by getting a blood bond with him instead."

"Probably to get even with Dane for trying to *murder* him."

"Well, I guess. So I—"

When a knock sounded, they jumped and turned to watch the door.

"Who could it be?" Pauline whispered.

"It's me." It was Dane's voice. "Erin, open the door. We need to talk."

"I don't want to talk to you. Go away."

"I'm not leaving until I see you," he said. "I need to see that you're okay."

Reluctantly, she got up and sucked in her breath before unlocking the door. He'd changed into his usual dark jeans and shirt. Of course, the other clothes had been covered in blood, and there would have been a hole in the shirt where that guard had stabbed him. Worry lines were stamped all over his face.

"Please, Erin, hear me out." His voice deepened to a hoarse, almost desperate tone. "I know I shouldn't have pushed the blood exchange on you, but you need to think about the timing. I created the blood bond just after your abduction. I could have lost you then. If we'd been bonded, I would have found you and saved you."

She shook her head. "I don't need to think about anything. It's over. Those feelings I had were just part of that blood bond you forced on me, and that's gone now. Go away."

He reached out, but she took a defensive step

back before he could touch her. "Your feelings are gone? I don't believe you. My feelings are still here."

"What feelings?" she snapped. "You never told me you loved me. You were just using me."

"No," he said through clenched teeth. "Erin, I-I love you too."

She felt the tiniest sliver of hope, but then she recalled the image of him making her drink his blood, and her flare of hope quickly died. "It's too late. And I'm exhausted. Just go."

"Yes, just go," Pauline called out from the bathroom.

"Alright, I'm leaving, but this is not over. *We're* not over," he said coldly, his expression grim but determined. "You also have no idea what you've gotten into with Stratton. That man has plans for you, and you're giving him exactly what he wants."

She closed the door in his face.

Pauline got out of the bathroom and walked up to her. "Are you okay? Do you know what he was talking about?"

"No, but I'm too tired to think straight. Let's go to bed. I'm sure that tomorrow morning is early enough for me to start worrying about what Dane said."

They said goodnight, and Erin went to the bathroom to get ready for bed. She felt so drained that she struggled to keep her eyes from closing as she brushed her teeth.

Even though she had expected to fall asleep in a matter of minutes, thoughts of Stratton's plans kept her awake.

What plans does Jonathan Stratton have for me?

"Come on, Erin," Pauline said as she held out the silver knife.

Suspicion narrowed Erin's eyes. "Forget it. I'm not holding it."

"The spell didn't work in Canada because we didn't have the wolfsbane, but that's different now."

Erin shrugged. "I'm still not going to grab it. I don—" Her cell phone rang, and she let out a breath of relief. "Saved by the bell."

"What do you mean 'saved'? Apart from me and Dane, who even has that number?"

"Frank does." She shook her head. "But this isn't him. I don't recognize this number. I sure hope it's not Jonathan Stratton. In fact, I can't think of anyone other than Frank, or you, that I want to talk to." She clicked on the answer button and put the phone against her ear.

"Hi Erin. Victor here," a deep voice said.

Without responding, she hung up on him.

"Well, that's rude," Pauline said.

"It was Victor."

"All the more reason not to antagonize him. Come on," Pauline said as she started waving the silver knife in front of Erin's face. "We need to know if it worked, especially if Victor is starting to become impatient. Before you know it, he'll show up here with his pack to drag you to their little commune."

Erin sighed. "Fine, just put it against my upper

arm."

Without any hesitation, Pauline did as she'd told her to. As soon as the silver blade touched her skin, she felt a burning agony flash through her body, leaving her gasping for breath. Tears filled her eyes, and she doubled over. She fell to the ground, blackness threatening her consciousness.

Through the haze of pain, she saw Pauline ripping the knife from her arm. She screamed as the knife tore off a piece of her skin.

"Oh God. I'm sorry, I'm sorry," Pauline repeated over and over again.

Erin took a moment to catch her breath, waiting for the pain to diminish. "It's okay," she finally said. "You were right. We had to know."

Pauline examined the wound on her arm. "I'm so sorry. But it should close up quickly, right? Thanks to the werewolf super healing powers."

"I already had those thanks to my leopard."

"*Thank you, Erin*," Leila said.

"No. Thank *you*, Leila."

Her smile vanished. She peered up at Pauline. "So obviously the wolfsbane potion in combination with the spell doesn't kill the werewolf." She closed her eyes. "I'm doomed."

She felt Pauline's hand on her shoulder. "Don't give up. How about if instead of killing the werewolf, we try to hide it?"

"Like my mom's invisibility spell?"

"Yes, but you can't walk around invisible all day. It's more like a glamour spell, making people see what we want them to see, only not just visually. We need to involve all the other senses too. And if the werewolves are trying to smell an animal on you, we just have to make sure that they smell the leopard instead."

Erin pointed at the silver knife. "Can we fool objects too?"

"Hmm, I doubt it. But werewolves wouldn't make you touch silver, right? They wouldn't be able to hold it themselves."

"They might wear gloves. I really think it will be impossible to trick them, especially because Victor already knows."

"Then we'll only fool the others. Erin, stop thinking like that. I won't let them take you away!"

"You won't? But if I'm gone, you'll have this amazing apartment all to yourself," Erin joked.

Pauline got up and grabbed a piece of paper. She grabbed Erin's good arm and pulled her up. "You're my friend. I won't abandon you. Here, sit down, and help me with that spell."

Pauline first wrote down a list of key words and then tried to link them with words that rhymed. Erin came up with a few.

"Okay, what rhymes with 'hide'? Bride, pride...?" Pauline suggested.

"No, don't use 'pride'! Before you know it, instead of a pack, I'll have to join a pride."

"A pride of leopards?" Pauline giggled. "Isn't it a pride of lions?"

Pauline's giggling compelled hers, and Erin found she enjoyed being around her roommate. "I don't know. Let's look it up online."

They struggled to write grammatically correct rhymes, but Pauline thought that the elements wouldn't care about that.

"It's the intent that matters."

It took them less than thirty minutes to come up with a spell. Erin stared at the thin piece of paper.

What if it doesn't work?

"Are you sure we should burn the herbs?" Erin asked "Shouldn't I eat them instead? I'd hate to waste the wolfsbane."

"Don't worry. It's not a waste if we're inhaling it. I thought that since we're trying an elements spell, we should treat the herbs like incense, so it represents air. Why don't you sit down on the floor? Clear your mind while I prepare the circle."

Erin sat on the ground with her eyes closed while listening to Pauline fill a glass with water before putting it down beside her. She heard a match being lit, and the smell of burnt herbs soon suppressed the scented candle that Pauline had placed on her other side. Then she positioned herself in front of Erin.

Erin opened her eyes and discovered the incantation lying on her lap. She read it several times before looking up, meeting Pauline's intense stare. A lot depended on the success of this spell.

"*Good luck,*" Erin's mother whispered.

She inhaled, and slowly breathed out as she called upon her magic. She nodded at her friend, and together they started their recitation:

"*With eucalyptus, myrrh and wolfsbane times three,
No longer shall others sense a part of me,*

We seek to hide,
The wolf inside,
No one will smell,
The wolf with this spell,
No one will touch the werewolf's fur,
Instead, they will hear the leopard purr,
The werewolf's taste will be concealed,
When called upon, a cat will be revealed.
This cloak will not be lifted,
Into a werewolf will I never be shifted,
Not even silver can tell,
What's been hidden so well,
Hide the wolf, hear my plea,
As is my will so mote it be."

The smoke from the herbs had thickened and surrounded them. As the smoke began to slowly cover her skin like a gray blanket, she felt its energy, raising goose bumps along her flesh.

A smoke screen.

The smoke didn't touch Pauline. Her roommate was staring at her with awe when she moved her hands, and the smoke remained glued to her body.

Did it work?

Pauline began thanking the elements, and hopeful, Erin joined in. The smoke weakened until it faded away.

Pauline took down the circle in silence while Erin waited for her limbs to start working again.

Impatient to find out if the spell had been successful, she forced herself to stand up. Her legs were trembling, but she managed to take a couple of steps before she let herself drop on her bed, face down.

She felt the bed sag when Pauline sat down beside her.

"You okay?"

When she nodded, Pauline continued, "I see Willow in front of the window. Shall I let her in and see how she responds to you?"

"Will you save me if she attacks me again?"

Pauline chuckled. "Of course." The mattress rose as her roommate opened the window. Erin turned around, lying on her side to watch her orange cat jump inside. Pauline closed the window.

Willow's first stop was her food bowl. Never before had Erin felt more anxious to get her cat to stop eating. Next stop was her water bowl. Pauline, who was still standing in front of the window, sniggered.

Erin raised her eyebrows. "I hope you won't find it amusing when my cat lashes out at me again."

Pauline shook her head. "Be quiet. You don't want to startle her."

Willow glanced up from the water bowl and watched Erin intently with her green-gold eyes. She meowed before getting up and padding toward the bed. Erin held her breath when the cat leaped onto the bed.

Her first instinct was to cover her face, but she didn't want to frighten Willow with any sudden movements. She slowly lifted her hand and held it in front of the cat's face. The cat started to rub her face against it.

Erin smiled and began scratching Willow behind her ears.

The cat purred and stretched out next to her, pressing her heavy frame against her stomach. The rumble of Willow's purr was a soothing sensation against her skin.

She looked up at Pauline, who still hadn't moved as if movement may break the spell. Her roommate's eyes were bright with wonder.

"I don't think Willow's ever let me pet her for this long before," Erin whispered.

"It makes sense to me. She's probably greeting you as if you've just come back from a long absence. She missed you."

Erin stilled her hand on Willow's fur. "But how long will this work?"

"You should probably repeat this ritual when the moon is at its weakest and then see Victor. I wouldn't risk going there when it's close to the full moon."

"This means we should do the ritual again about eleven days from now and then call Victor."

"Alright. Just in case, drink the potion too," Pauline said. "I think we need to be extremely careful not to show even a hint of the werewolf when you meet with them. If you do, I doubt I'll ever get to see you again."

They'll probably never forgive me for trying to trick them.

TWENTY

S he was in a large room with about twenty rowdy people, mainly men. They had surrounded a female figure, calling out "Ms. Sloane" again and again.

The brunette had crossed her arms over her chest and defiantly raised her chin, but she couldn't hide the terror in her blue eyes. The skin on her face was so pale, it was almost white, and her lips were clamped shut in a flat, tight line.

She walked up to the woman, and their eyes met. Her gaze reminded her of that of the rabbit caught in the headlights. "Ms. Sloane," she heard herself say in a masculine voice. "I'm not doing this because I seek to punish you. In fact, it pains me to admit that this is my fault. I have neglected you."

The woman shook her head frantically.

"No, no. It's true. You've never known how valuable you are to me because I never showed it, and that's why you applied elsewhere. But I can't have you leaving me, Ms. Sloane."

One of the men behind the secretary grabbed her hair and ripped out the clip holding her bun together. The woman screamed in pain as the man clearly tore out several hairs too.

She aimed her gaze at the man holding the clip. "Now, what did I say? Did you not hear me say that this woman is valuable to me? Unlike you. Throw him out. I'll deal with him later."

She pointed at the table beside Ms. Sloane. On it were a dildo and a syringe. "Ms. Sloane hasn't made her choice yet. But whatever happens, I won't let any of you lay a hand on her. She is precious. Do you understand me, Ms. Sloane?"

The woman's cheeks turned red with embarrassment, and as she lowered her gaze, she saw tears of defeat running down her face.

"Have you made your choice, Ms. Sloane? Margot?"

The woman glared at her. So she wasn't completely broken. *"I think I can call you Margot tonight, don't you? After all, I'm about to see a different side of you, and so are we all."*

"Pick the dildo," a blond man shouted. She saw the man's gaze roam provocatively down Ms. Sloane's body and back up again.

"Down boy, let the woman decide. If you don't mind me making a suggestion, I would recommend the dildo too. I don't want to risk damaging my secretary. I worry that the heroin might harm your brains. You know what it did to your brother. But if you're forcing me to make the decision for you, it will have to be the heroin."

Ms. Sloane stared at the objects on the table with her fists clenched at her sides before raising her eyes. She sneered at her. "Go to hell."

"Erin. Erin, you're dreaming." A warm hand shaking her woke her. She blinked while looking up at Pauline's concerned expression.

"Are you okay?" Pauline asked. "I heard you mumbling. And it sounded like you were in pain."

Swallowing hard, she closed her eyes in horror. "Thank you for waking me up. That was horrible."

"You want to talk about it? When I was little, my mom told me to talk about my nightmares so it would be out of my system, and I wouldn't dream about it anymore."

"That's nice."

"Yes or maybe they just wanted to make sure that I would sleep in my own bed and not climb in theirs." She smiled briefly. "I'll go for nice. Sorry, we were discussing your dream."

Erin sighed. "I'd rather not discuss it at all, but I'm afraid I must. I've been dreaming about Jonathan Stratton, about *being* Jonathan Stratton. It reminds me of the dreams I had about being Dane, only being Dane didn't seem nearly as twisted as being Stratton."

"It must be a side effect to the blood bond. I wish I could help you, but I don't know anything about it. I don't suppose you want to talk to Dane about it."

Erin snorted. "Right, I can just imagine what his solution will be. Only this time he can gloat because I would be asking for it."

"That's plan B then. I'll try to do some research first and see what I can find. But will you be okay with being tied to Jonathan Stratton for the time being?"

Erin shivered. "I don't know. It's as if I got a

glimpse into the soul of someone so evil that I feel corrupted just by sharing his thoughts. That poor secretary! No wonder Ms. Sloane never smiles. He's keeping her captive, terrifying her into submission."

"Maybe you can talk to her. She might be able to help."

"I don't know. He has probably terrorized her so much that any thought of rebellion has been vanquished."

The way Ms. Sloane had glared as she told her tormentor to go to hell flickered through her mind. "But she might want to fight back."

Maybe he hadn't crushed that woman's spirit. But what if he has? I haven't dreamt the entire event.

"On the other hand," Erin continued, "she might try to warn him about my intentions. I'll have to think about it."

Pauline yawned. "You're ready to try to fall asleep again?"

"I should. I just hope I won't dream about Stratton anymore."

"Try to think happy thoughts," Pauline suggested as she turned off the lights.

Happy thoughts.

Automatically she conjured the image of Dane to her mind. Thinking of him until she fell asleep, where he continued to haunt her dreams.

Jonathan Stratton's wrists were captured with one hand and pressed against the wall. Dane Lynch pinned his hands

above his head, holding tight as he lowered his mouth. Dane nibbled on his bottom lip, before drawing it between his teeth.

"I said, no biting," he whispered in a female voice. His lips throbbed, and Dane pulled back a fraction. He stared at him, flashing him a wicked half grin, shaking his head.

While one hand continued to keep him captive, the other began to explore his body. The strap of his dress was lowered, uncovering a small, yet perfect breast. Dane cupped it, stroking the tight rosy pink nipple with his thumb. Stratton felt his body curve against Dane's, shivering.

Dane's mouth moved down, kissing his body until he reached the breast, placing his warm mouth on the taut peak, grazing his fangs over the flesh, and he could hear himself moan.

Dane smiled up at him, eyes blazing, watching his response as his large, broad hand slid down to his knee before slowly raising the hem of the dress, lifting it, until he uncovered white cotton panties. He slid his hand underneath them, cupping him, after which he started rubbing. He lifted his hips against Dane's hand until Dane withdrew his hand and put his fingers into his mouth.

"Hmm, I want to have more," Dane whispered, watching him. "Can I have more, Goldilocks?"

Jonathan Stratton woke from the worst dream he'd ever had, and he'd been a vampire for nearly five hundred years, so he'd had his share of bad dreams. He had also never experienced a blood bond where he dreamt of being his slave before.

With his previous blood slaves, he had caught the occasional emotion whereas they had been consumed by an almost obsessive need to please him. That was what he had envisioned when he had proposed sharing a blood bond with Ms. Holland.

But she acted like no blood bound slave he'd ever had. Instead of being upset to leave his company when he'd offered her his private plane to take her home, she'd accepted it quietly. He hoped that it was because she had still been in shock over Dane's betrayal, and that the begging would come once the shock had worn off.

But he also realized that her lack in submissive attitude could also have been caused by her father's ritual that had given her part of Altman's powers. Perhaps Altman made her more resistant to vampires. That would be a disappointment.

Sharing another dream about her time with Dane would be worse. This dream was unexpected, a surprise, and he didn't like surprises unless he was the one organizing them.

Watching Dane pleasuring her had disgusted him. When he closed his eyes, the image of Dane's possessive gaze reappeared in his mind.

Dane sure acted keen about bedding her.

Stratton's lips pursed in thought.

I bet he intended to keep her. He's probably a bit upset that I took her away from him, maybe even devastated.

He smiled in satisfaction.

And if I were to sleep with her, it would probably really upset him.

Without any hesitation, Stratton picked up the

phone.

"Uh, hello?" a female voice answered.

"Erin, I hope you had a pleasant flight. I would like to invite you back here soon though."

"Mr. Stratton?"

He frowned. "Yes. Were you expecting someone else?"

"It's nearly five o'clock in the morning. I was asleep. I wasn't expecting anyone to call."

Irritated, he clenched his hand around the receiver.

She's definitely not acting the way a blood bound slave should.

He struggled to suppress his anger and tried to keep his tone pleasant. "I'm sorry. There are no clocks in Las Vegas, and as you probably know, vampires keep different times. I'm just eager to get to know you better, especially now that we're sharing blood."

"Uh, I—uh…"

He chuckled. "I've surprised you. Good."

You've surprised me too.

"Think about it. I'll ask my secretary to call you back soon so we can arrange something. I'll show you around town. We'll go to a nice restaurant, and we'll go dancing. I'd hate it if your time in Las Vegas was tainted because you'd discovered Dane's betrayal here."

"I-I uh, no, it's just been a bit hectic lately. I could use a bit of quiet now."

"So no dancing. Just some dinner then." Before Erin could reject him, he said, "Great. That's settled.

It'll let you go back to sleep. Pleasant dreams."

Only not too pleasant.

Dane had been fighting to keep his anger under control, but he'd lost the battle. Ever since Stratton had kicked him out, a violent haze blurred his vision. It had been lifted briefly during his interaction with Erin, but after she had told him to leave the previous night—especially after he'd opened up to her—all he felt was an overwhelming fury.

He still couldn't comprehend how his attack on Stratton could have backfired so horribly, but what stared him in the face was betrayal.

She picked Stratton over me.

Not that he accepted her choice. He grabbed his phone.

"Good evening, Dane. I had been expecting your call."

"I don't want to talk anymore. I'm hereby officially challenging you."

"A fight? You want to be the next Master Vampire of Las Vegas now?" Stratton sneered. "Are you sure you want to fight me, *old friend*, when in fact, I'm much older than you?"

"But unlike you, I'm not surrounded by bodyguards all the time so I'm forced to keep fit."

"I'm not going to fight you, Dane. I don't want you to die. I want you to witness what happens next."

Dane ground his teeth together so hard that he worried he might be breaking them. "I'm offering you a fair fight." He kept his voice low.

"Fair? Like you were fair to Ms. Holland when you did the blood exchange? Like you tried to kill me the other night, unarmed? Besides, I don't do fair myself either. You'll find out soon enough."

Stratton hung up before he could respond. A red-hot rage exploded inside him, and he roared in fury. Brock opened his door and stared at him in shock.

"Do, um, do you need my help with something?" he asked.

"I want to blow up Stratton's house," Dane muttered.

"A-are you sure?" Brock looked a little uncertain, but Dane knew he would stand by him if asked. "Didn't you say that Erin now shares his blood bond? What if you accidentally kill her?"

"I say let her burn."

"Really? You really want to kill Erin?"

"Oh, never mind," he snapped. "Just forget it."

Brock opened his mouth. But after Dane narrowed his eyes on his second-in-command, Brock turned around, leaving Dane alone with his anger.

How dare she join Stratton!

After she had seen that recording, she should have come to him.

"You should have come to me!" The echo of his words, charged with suffering, lingered in the room.

He understood that she'd been hurt and that breaking the blood bond hadn't been a rational decision. She didn't even know Stratton. Had she known him, she never would have accepted to bond with him. It had been her way of lashing out at him.

He hurt her so she had hurt him back.

It still hurt.

Strange.

The blood bond was broken, but he could still experience that same curious sensation, that constricting feeling settling around him. He had opened up to her, and now even after their physical connection had been severed, she still had an effect on him.

I hate this vulnerability. I hate her.

I love her.

Damn.

TWENTY-ONE

The aroma of tantalizing food hit Pauline's nostrils as soon as she opened the door to Erin's apartment.

"I hope you're hungry," Erin said with a big grin on her face. "I made lasagna."

Pauline returned the smile. "My favorite." Over the past couple of weeks, she had started to think of the tiny apartment as if it was *their* apartment even if Erin had never asked her to contribute to the rent. She hoped that her aid with the cleaning, the werewolf curse and possible cure for the blood bond would encourage Erin to let her stay, not because she needed a roof over her head but because she liked her company.

Unfortunately, she was afraid to bring it up, worried that Erin would reject her.

Maybe not knowing is worse?

"So was Mrs. Beauchamps watching you again while you cleaned her house?" Erin asked as soon as they both sat down to eat.

"Yes. I swear that woman is trying to find fault with my work. Maybe she prefers to do the cleaning herself."

Erin grimaced. "I can't imagine why."

"I actually think it's quite fulfilling. It's just too bad that it doesn't pay more." She cleared her throat. "I uh, I understand I should probably be looking for another place to stay. You probably think it's too crowded in here."

"Yes, it is," Erin agreed.

"I'm sorry." She sucked in her breath to keep the disappointment from spilling out.

"Hey, I'm only kidding. Don't worry," Erin said, tapping Pauline on her upper arm. "It's just that I have been thinking of moving out of this place too."

"You have? Not to live with Dane or Jonathan Stratton?"

"What? No, not after those nightmares! No, I actually thought that if we both chipped in, we could move to a better place together. If you can live with my mess."

Giddy with relief, Pauline said, "No, but I would be very happy to teach you how to clean it."

Erin gave her a black look.

She giggled. "Okay, maybe I could do it for you and pay less rent." She wanted to shout with joy. "I can't wait to search the ads. Have you thought about where you'd like to live?"

"We should probably wait and see what happens after my call to Victor tonight before we start making plans." A small, sad smile lifted the edges of her mouth. "The werewolves may not let me go."

Pauline shook her head. "If Victor keeps you as his prisoner, I'll open that forbidden notebook of yours and go black magic on his ass."

She laughed. "And this time, I'll let you use it. Victor may not care about that though. He seemed so eager about me joining him. I'm actually surprised he hasn't tried calling me again, but maybe he's waiting for the full moon."

"Yeah, but we're not. I just hope he won't make you wait till then."

"Only one way to find out… After I finish my meal," Erin said.

Pauline had just lost her appetite. She wondered how her roommate could eat with the threat over her head.

What if the pack can't be fooled?

Victor wasn't answering his cell phone. Erin's mouth was dry as cotton while the seconds passed like hours. She caught Pauline staring at her, and she turned away.

"I'm sorry. Do you want some privacy?" Pauline whispered.

The sound of the phone ringing was interrupted by a moment of silence. "Erin?" Victor said.

Her breath caught in her throat before she could get her voice to work. "Hi Victor, I hope you're alright."

"I'm great, especially now that you decided to call me. Does this mean that you're finally ready to meet the pack?"

She sighed. "I didn't think I would be able to talk you out of it. I don't want to risk you kidnapping me again."

Victor didn't respond. She could picture him pressing his lips tightly together, forcing himself to be quiet, for a couple of seconds.

"I'll pick you up." Unable to deny he had kidnapped her once, she hoped his way of trying to hide his shame was by sounding all business-like. His discomfort made her feel a bit more empowered.

"No thank you. I'd rather take my own bike."

So I won't depend on you to let me leave.

"You should probably take some stuff with you, like clothes and a tooth brush. Do you think you can carry it all on your bike?"

"I'll be fine."

Since I don't intend to stay for more than an hour anyway.

"When will you get here?"

This time, she did look at Pauline. "I can be ready to leave in about thirty minutes, so I'll be there around nine."

"We'll be waiting for you," he said before he hung up.

"It sounds like it went well," Pauline said. "Do you think anyone else was listening in on the conversation?"

She shrugged. "I'm not too worried about that. I was careful not to confirm anything he said, but I couldn't outright deny anything either. I didn't want to risk warning him of our strategy."

Pauline grinned as she picked up the wolfsbane. "I think we still have the element of surprise."

Erin got up and sat down on the ground,

mentally preparing herself to perform the ritual of hiding the werewolf again. Her palms were sweating. "I just hope it's going to be enough."

Erin's heart thundered in her chest as she rode further into the dark woods. She was already ten minutes late and was worried about starting off on the wrong foot. She would antagonize Victor that night. But for her plan to succeed, she needed some allies too. Arriving late was not the way to get them. Then again, she probably wouldn't have scored brownie points by killing Quentin either. She just hoped nobody knew about that little incident.

She could hardly breathe with the way she pushed herself to ride her bike as fast as she could. She was about to cry in despair when the first house appeared.

"Halleluiah," she whispered.

"*Calm down, Erin,*" Altman said. "*You need to have a clear head for this.*"

"*Right,*" Leila said. "*Try not to get emotional when you're a cat about to meet a bunch of dogs who probably want nothing more than to tear you apart as soon as they smell you. I feel like we're entering enemy territory.*"

"That's because we *are* entering enemy territory, Leila," Erin said.

"*What if Billy tells them he's the one who attacked you?*" her mother asked. "*If both Billy and Victor confirm that you should be a werewolf, they might keep you, at least until the full moon. What if the magic wears off before then*?"

Erin sighed. "Well, then I'm fucked."

She reached the end of the road, where four large men were waiting in front of a large wooden house, observing her every movement. She recognized Victor and Crispin.

Pauline had shown her several pictures of the alpha. Well-built with military-short hair, he was watching her with shrewd, cynical brown eyes.

She gasped for air when a fifth man joined them. He had gray hair, and she remembered him as one of the werewolves who chased her a couple of months ago.

Fear gripped her.

He knew I was a leopard shifter with a wolf inside. What if he recalls my smell?

She turned her head, struggling to control her emotions. She couldn't afford them sensing her terror at discovering a third obstacle. She could feel them watching her as she locked her bike around a tree. She couldn't risk Victor hiding the bike to stop her from leaving. Even in leopard form, she could never outrun a pack of werewolves on the hunt.

She shook her head.

What am I thinking? I can't outride them on my bike either!

Her head pounded, but she forced herself to smile as she faced the men. Victor grinned wolfishly at her, revealing all his white and pointy teeth, and the uncomfortable feeling increased.

One of the men lifted his nose, sniffing the air as she approached them. "I smell cat, not wolf," he growled.

Victor frowned. "I told you she could also shift into a leopard." He walked up to her, and before she could protest, he put his arms around her.

"Relax," he murmured when she stiffened. "I won't let them attack you." She glanced up at him, the expression on his face one of concern and care.

But who will protect me from you when you decide to attack me yourself?

"Just because you're rubbing your scent on her, won't make her smell like one of us," the angry man continued.

Victor turned away from the others and put his hand on her back. "I won't have you chase her away. Wait with the interrogation. Let me show her around first."

Victor guided her down the street, and while nobody responded, she noticed Crispin narrowing his eyes on them. She hoped it meant he was starting to doubt Victor's claims.

"This is where my aunt lives," Victor said, pointing at a large white house. "Whenever I get here, she lets me stay."

She swallowed the lump. "It's big."

He smiled. "Yes, we like our space. In spite of werewolves generally living in a pack, each family here has a house with a large area around it so they can also enjoy some privacy. With our excellent sense of hearing, it's damn hard to keep anything a secret."

She nodded politely, wondering how long she had to wait before setting her plan in motion. It appeared that she didn't have to wait long since a familiar face walked up to them, Billy Blair, the intern.

He stared at her, the horror on his bearded face as clear as if it had been written across his bald forehead with a neon-colored marker.

"Oh my God, Erin," Billy said, his moist brown eyes bulging from his head. "Don't tell me—" his voice laced with guilt.

Her belly clenched as Erin shook her head emphatically.

Please don't apologize. You'll ruin everything.

She took a deep breath, trying to still her panicked thoughts and tried to smile.

Okay. Showtime.

TWENTY-TWO

Victor saw the shock on Billy's face. "Hi Billy. I didn't realize you met Erin before. Wait, is he the reason that you're a werewolf now?"

He could smell Billy's fear pouring off him, confirming his suspicions.

Should I kill him or thank him for biting Erin?

If Crispin found out, Billy would wish he were dead.

Maybe as a thank you, I'll stay quiet.

To Victor's surprise, Erin tapped him on his arm. "I'm sorry, Billy. Victor thinks I'm a werewolf. I only decided to visit your pack tonight hoping that the others would cure him of his delusions before he did something drastic. Especially because I have heard these stories about the awful lives female werewolves have."

Billy looked as confused as Victor felt.

What's going on?

Erin met his gaze and shrugged. "I know Billy from before he was bit because he also works at the hospital."

The truth slowly dawned on him. She raised one

NICOLE LECLERCQ

of her eyebrows at Billy, and Victor narrowed his eyes on Billy when he saw the young man nod.

"I'm really happy to see you looking so well, Billy," she continued, ignoring him. "I heard about you getting bit and was worried when you didn't return to the hospital. I hope you don't miss your old life too much."

Billy rubbed the back of his neck and stared at the ground. "Ah, yes. I uh, I miss our conversations, of course, but I like it here. They don't have a doctor, so I feel really needed. When our kind gets hurt, we usually can't get medical help because we become all instinct, and doctors could get hurt. I'm now strong enough to help them anyway."

He felt his anger begin to boil and had to clench his teeth to prevent himself from railing at them.

Erin smiled. "That's great, Billy."

"What hell are you trying to pull, Erin?" he hissed. "You can't just suddenly declare that you're not a werewolf."

"Listen," she said calmly. "I know that you want me, and that you'd like me to be like you. But just because you wish it, doesn't make it so. I'm not helping you by feeding your illusion."

Billy approached her, put his nose against her neck and took a deep breath. He glanced at Victor. "She's not a werewolf. I can smell she's a shifter, but definitely not a werewolf."

"Shut up, pup," he snarled. "What do you know about recognizing smell?" He grabbed her arms in a steely grip and saw pain flash across her face.

I hope it hurts.

He sniffed the air around her, and then froze, peering down at her as shock, confusion and anger surged through him.

"What the hell have you done?" he spat.

A sardonic little smile played around her mouth. "I don't know what you're talking about."

"You bitch! You think you can fool me, fool all of us?" He shook her hard, causing her jaw to snap shut loud enough for him to hear. "Ungrateful bitch, I protected you from being exposed during the team building, and this is how you repay me? Do you know what Stratton had on you? He had footage of you eating Doctor Quirkhart! Do you know what he'll do if he gets his hands on me?"

Her eyes caught his with a wide, confused gaze. "Jonathan Stratton has this footage of me?"

"Yes, you stupid bitch! I can't believe you still haven't figured out that Stratton has been the one sabotaging you all along. Who do you think arranged for your old psychiatrist to visit Hope Acres?"

"It doesn't make sense. Why would he do that?"

"Because he's a sadistic fuck. How do you think he got this footage, and that I ended up at your team-building event? I saved your ass by deleting the footage on that USB."

She pulled herself from his grip and glared at him. "Well, I'm sure you didn't decide to help me out of the goodness of your heart. What else was on that USB?"

"What the hell is going on here?" Crispin asked. He had brought the entire welcoming committee with him.

"That bitch is pretending that she's not a werewolf!" When he realized that he was bellowing, he took a deep breath.

Crispin scowled at him. "That *bitch* seems to have a point. You're the only one here who claims that she is one of us."

"Anton knows she is one," he gritted out. "He told you about the leopard he'd run into a couple of months ago."

The gray-haired man shook his head. "If she's the one we saw—and I'm not saying she is—then it doesn't matter. It's obvious that she doesn't carry the wolf."

"Billy knows she's one too. Admit it, Billy." His voice cracked.

"No, s-she isn't," Billy stammered.

His blood ran cold. She was making him look like a liar.

What if Crispin kicks me out? I'll have no protection against Stratton.

"She's lying," he roared. "She did something, with that witchy friend of hers. She's trying to trick us, again."

She stood perfectly still during his rant, making him look like the irrational one, but he noticed her fisted hands.

Not as cool as you'd like us to believe, eh?

Her smile faltered as he stepped closer, her gaze swinging immediately to his cousin for support, for protection *from me*.

Circling her, he taunted, "You think I don't know what you did at Camp Happy? How do you think they will react if I told them, hmm?" Realization was dawning on Erin's pale face, and the tension between them grew. "Not so brave anymore, hmm? And you think you managed to subdue your wolf with a little spell? You think you're safe because it's not full moon. That's why you're here tonight, isn't it?"

"I'm here tonight instead of the night of the full moon because I thought you'd be calmer now if you were confronted with the fact that I'm not one of you. Y-you're so eager to see me as a werewolf."

"And I will," he vowed. "There is one thing that will always work even without the full moon. Don't you feel her close to the surface tonight?"

He took out his pocketknife, and before Crispin could knock the weapon from his hand, he cut open the skin on his chest. He could hear the others growling, but he only had eyes for her.

Let her try to suppress the wolf now.

She fell to the ground and screamed when the contractions started.

"What the fuck have you done," Crispin shouted. Startled, Victor watched his cousin as he began to shift.

"I'm giving you evidence," he said. "You refused to believe me. Now, you see that she's shifting too. Blood is calling it out."

The beast inside of Victor also clawed to the surface. He shuddered and braced himself for the violent rearrangement of bone and muscle when his cousin's heavy body slammed into his, and he hit the floor. He howled in anger.

"Get off of me," he growled.

"No. Look at her," Crispin snarled.

"W-what?" He struggled to turn his head, but when he did, he understood Crispin's anger. Erin had shifted into a leopard, hissing at the growling werewolves who had surrounded her. Disaster gripped him with a relentless fist.

"Everyone, back off right now," Crispin ordered. His teeth had turned to fangs, and he struggled to speak. "If you need to fight, then fight my cousin. I won't let you kill this woman."

Crispin let go of Victor and moved away. "Don't move," Crispin told Erin. "If you run, it will trigger their hunting instincts. Let Victor run instead."

He then turned to Victor. "Victor Nichols, you're banished from now on."

Those words caused the werewolves to direct their aggression at him instead. Panic flooded him. He needed to get out of his human skin and escape before he was torn apart.

"Run," Crispin commanded.

He felt the wolf inside him rise and break free. He ran.

Erin waited for the sounds of the chase to quieten before allowing herself to return to her human form. The leopard fought to stay in control of her body. As a human she would be defenseless against the pack, but Erin hoped that Crispin would find it easier to handle his pack if she was human.

299

TOUCHED BY DARKNESS

Pushing herself up on weak and trembling arms, she put on her torn clothes. Her hands shook when she unlocked her bike. In the distance, she heard inhuman sounds of howling and yelping echoing into the night, and she felt her eyes burning with guilt. What if they killed him because of her lies?

She got on her bike and rode as fast as she could. Her heart pounded too fast for her lungs to match the beat, but she couldn't risk slowing down.

What if after they kill him they decide to chase me too?

Twigs cracked here and there, and blind panic and fear hit her.

"*Calm down*," Altman said.

"*Yes, if they do decide to come after you, I'll do the hiding spell again*," Erin's mom said. "*You know what? I'll do it right now.*"

Her mother's hiding spell had been effective before, and Erin's fear of getting torn apart by the werewolves diminished.

"*And have people see a bike moving on its own?*" Gideon sneered. "*Like that won't draw anyone's attention! I'm sure it will make a great addition to Jonathan Stratton's collection!*"

Gideon probably meant it as a joke, but her throat tightened down with anger at the very idea. "Do you think he's watching me now? I can't believe that he was responsible for Doctor Quirky kidnapping me, unless Victor lied when he said that."

"*Victor did help Doctor Quirkhart abduct you, and you were being sabotaged during the team building,*" Altman said. "*Maybe he targeted you because of your relationship with Dane.*"

"I can't believe we share this blood bond. How am I supposed to get rid of him?"

"*I doubt any magic can break that bond, but we could try*," her mother suggested.

"*Just try my death spell*," Gideon said.

"*I wouldn't. Right now, Stratton is happy to just play with you. If you seriously attempt to kill him, you have to make sure you're going to succeed. Because after that, playing alone will not satisfy him*," Altman warned. "*I'm sure he has protected himself against dark magic. Many men have tried to kill him.*"

Dane tried.

She noted with irony that a few weeks ago she had attacked Dane over trying to murder Stratton, whereas she was now considering doing the same thing.

"*I think you should get in touch with his secretary. She'll have a lot of dirt on him. You just need to convince her that she'll let you use it*," Altman said.

Erin groaned. "Can't I just tell him that I know what he did and that he should leave me alone?"

She heard Gideon laugh. Annoyed, she clenched her hands around the bicycle handlebars, wishing it were the warlock's neck instead.

As soon as Erin got home, Pauline was there to hug her. "I'm so relieved you made it! Tell me what happened!"

"Um, well it worked. Victor got so upset that he cut himself to force me to shift, and I did."

Pauline gasped. "Into a leopard, I hope."

"Yes. There I was, surrounded by werewolves eager to sink their teeth in a cat. Fortunately, Crispin suggested they sink their teeth into Victor instead."

"Did they?"

Erin thought about the yelping sounds she'd heard in the forest. "I think so. I just hope they didn't kill him. He was actually quite nice to me when I first got there."

Pauline grimaced. "On the other hand, if he survived, he might want to get even. You've just gained an enemy."

Erin snorted. "As it turns out, I seem to have gained two enemies tonight. Victor told me that Jonathan Stratton has been the one sabotaging me during the team-building event. And worse, he's the one responsible for Doctor Quirkhart kidnapping me. He has footage of me killing him and wanted to show it during the team building."

"What! Why the hell would he do that?"

Erin shrugged. "I don't know, maybe because he's a sick fuck? Although, I'd say he's more like a bully."

"A bully with money."

"Do you know why bullies bully? It's because they're afraid, insecure."

Pauline moaned. "Oh no, please don't romanticize him."

"I'm just saying. Maybe we can use that against him. He likes to humiliate others. What if we return the favor?"

"Who is 'we'? Can't you leave me out of this?"

Erin nodded. "Sure, I actually meant someone else."

"Dane?"

"Hmm, I'd rather not join forces with him at the moment. No, there's someone else I know who might want to be free of him too, his secretary."

Pauline looked horrified.

"I need to trust that she won't run to him with my plan and hope the number I got isn't a direct line to Stratton." If it were a direct line, she would be forced to meet him.

She took the business card Ms. Sloane had given her and dialed the number. Her mouth was dry as cotton.

Please answer, Ms. Sloane.

As soon as the phone started ringing, it was picked up. She bit her lip, her heart blocked her throat, thundering loud enough to make her entire body tremble.

"Mr. Stratton's office."

"Ms. Sloane, I—"

"Ah, Ms. Holland," the secretary interrupted her. "He's been expecting your call. I'll put you through."

"No, wait!" she cried in despair. "I need to talk to you. You'll want to hear what I have to say."

Silence answered her.

I'm too late. She's put me through already.

She suppressed the instinct to disconnect and waited for Jonathan Stratton's taunting voice.

Instead, she heard Ms. Sloane say, "What?"

TWENTY-THREE

"Could I just say again that this is a terrible idea?" Gideon asked.

"No," Erin said through gritted teeth.

"Couldn't you have done this over the phone at least?" he continued.

"No, he has to know we're serious." Besides, it was too late to change her mind. She was already in the limousine that Jonathan Stratton had sent to pick her up from the airport. Maybe Margot had arranged the limo. The dark-tinted windows didn't let in the tiniest bit of light, and she pressed a button to open them. It didn't work.

"And by 'we', you mean you and his secretary, only his secretary won't be here today?"

She frowned and pushed the button a couple of times. When nothing happened, she slid to the other side and tried to open the window there.

"If you ask me, that secretary is the smart one, letting you fight her battle."

"Shut up, Gideon. I could never have done this without her."

"Technically, you still haven't done it," Gideon

taunted.

"*You should have gone to the police,*" her mother said. "*I'm sure that writer's family would like to know what happened to him and where to find his body.*"

"*The moment she goes to the cops, she loses her leverage,*" Altman said. "*Stop putting doubts in her head. This is the worst timing ever!*"

Deep breath. Relax.

"Why won't this window open? What's the point of having windows if you can't open them?"

"*Stop playing with those windows! You need to focus, Erin,*" her mother said. "*You don't need to go through with this. The cops could put him away for life or sentence him to death.*"

She peered up at the roof of the limousine. She should be able to open that window. She eyed the buttons near the sunroof that she had yet to try.

"*He could still do a lot of damage behind bars,*" Altman warned. "*Besides, I'm not confident the cops could put him away, even with our evidence. His money can buy the best defense.*"

"*Are you gonna tell him straight away or at the end of the date?*" Leila asked. "*He probably organized an amazing night.*"

The window between the chauffeur and herself went down. The driver looked at her in the reflection of his mirror. "Yes, ma'am?"

"Hi. Uh, I tried to open the windows, but the buttons don't seem to work. I'm starting to feel a bit claustrophobic in here."

"I'm sorry, ma'am. It's Mr. Stratton's car. The windows don't open for security reasons. We're almost there, or do you want me to stop now? Get out for some fresh air?"

She let out a deep breath. "No, never mind." She worried that if she got out of the car, she would be too scared to get back in.

No, let's just get this over with.

They drove through a high fenced gate with several cameras pointed at the entrance. Unlike Dane's mansion, Stratton's house was surprisingly modern with large black windows. From the outside, it appeared as though the lights inside were turned off, but she expected the windows to be similar to the ones of her limo.

At least, I hope so.

She wouldn't want to confront Stratton in absolute darkness.

Her breath caught in her throat.

I don't want to confront him in a well-lit room either.

The door of the limousine opened, and as she stepped outside, a gust of wind hit her, and chills marched down her spine.

"*Good luck, dear,*" her mother whispered.

She walked to the front of the house, and before she could ring the doorbell, the door opened, and a man who appeared to be in his late fifties let her in. He led her to an empty office next to an indoor swimming pool. With its thick carpet and stunning artworks, she recognized the Dalí painting Margot had mentioned. Wealth oozed from the walls.

She was staring at the pool when a deep voice behind her said, "You're wearing jeans. How disappointing, not even the pretense of a nice night out."

She turned around to find Jonathan Stratton dressed to impress in his tailored tux, watching her. His steel gray eyes held no laughter in their depths.

She folded her arms across her chest as she faced him. "Well, when I found out that you were the one behind Doctor Quirkhart's actions, I lost any interest I might have had in ever going out with you."

He smiled at her, a white disturbing smile. "So Victor has blabbed. Yes, when he suddenly refused to answer my calls, I understood that Victor had decided to abandon ship."

"He's not the only one," she said in a tightly controlled voice. "Why the hell did you have Doctor Quirkhart kidnap me?"

"Yes, I suppose some people could say I owe you an explanation. The thing is, I don't really give a fuck about what people say."

"Do you do that with all your employees, terrorize them just for kicks?"

"No, not all." He grinned at her without amusement, the flash of his teeth promising aggression. "Only the special ones like you."

A shiver shot up her spine. "So how did you know I was 'special'?"

"You're determined to find answers, I see." He shrugged. "Fine, I knew who you were because I've been watching you for twenty years, ever since your father tried to lure me to the Devereaux Church to perform the ritual that killed Altman instead of me." A cruel little smile twitched at the corners of his mouth. "You see, your father offered me power beyond my imagination. I was detained, so he took Altman to replace me. You can imagine my surprise when I found out that he had intended to kill me. And how frustrating that I couldn't get even since your dear daddy had disappeared, not that I've given up my search. But what fascinated me was that out of all those powerful creatures, you were the one to survive."

"That had nothing to with power, and everything to do with the fact that I was too young to lift a sword and stick it through my own heart." She was unable to hide the bitterness in her voice.

"Could be. Still… You were the one to survive and get everyone's powers. It made me wonder what would have happened if I had been there and been the one to survive instead. What were these powers, and how could I use them to suit me? Having you work for me with the powers—one of them being what your father tried to steal from me—is very satisfying."

"And the kidnapping? He could have killed me! You wouldn't have been able to use my powers then."

He shook his head. "I knew you'd fight Quirkhart and win, just as I had faith in you when I sabotaged your team building. I wanted to see what you were capable of, so I could use you to the best of your abilities. But I admit, maybe some of my tests were a little bit payback for what your father had intended."

She frowned. "It's not as if I cooperated with him. My father wanted me to die too."

"I don't care. Your father isn't here. You're the next best thing, and I must say that it's been a pleasure seeing you in action. Watching you eat that psychiatrist was amazing!"

It was his mirth that had her grinding her teeth. "Well, you won't get to see me in action again. I quit," she spat. "And so does Margot."

The laughter died abruptly in his eyes. "Margot? Do you mean Ms. Sloane?"

Her chest tight, she took a deep breath. *Here we go.* "Yes, we both demand that you let us go."

"Making demands now, are you? Is that all?" Stratton asked casually, though she could detect the amused edge to his tone.

"No, I want you to also leave Frank and Victor alone."

He smiled at her, but the cold smile didn't reach his eyes. "Not Dane?"

"No. He's a big boy. I'm sure he can look after himself."

He laughed a cold, humorless sound. "Now, why would I do that? Do you think you can fight me? Will you eat me if I don't?"

"Oh, I don't think that'll be necessary," she said coolly. "The one good thing about this horrible link between us is that I now know your secrets too. I have evidence of your involvement in the disappearance of Mr. Tennant."

His relaxed mask dropped, and anger flashed in

his eyes. She caught him glancing at the Dalí behind him. Margot had told her about the location of his safe.

Keeping her voice light, she swallowed down nauseating dread. "You can open the safe if you want to, but you won't find what you're looking for. Margot helped me get your trophies."

He straightened the cuffs of his perfectly pressed shirt as he took a step in her direction. "And you think you'll live to use this evidence against me?"

He was studying her with an intensity that made her draw a shaking breath. Steeling her resolve, she raised her chin. "You might kill me, but then the evidence will miraculously end up on the desks of Detectives Stevens and Hill."

"Maybe I'll just risk it," he said as he lunged at her.

Shock tore through her, and for a moment, she was stunned. He grabbed her by her throat, shoving her hard against the wall, his fingers squeezing painfully tight. Thrashing wildly, she opened her mouth to scream, but the only sound that came out was a wheezing whimper.

Panicked, she clawed at her throat. White spots danced in her vision.

Baring his fangs, he grinned down at her. He was a chilling sight. He leaned his face in close to her ear and whispered, "Strangling is so intimate don't you think? Although not as intimate as eating someone, I suppose. I could suck you dry of course. What are you saying?"

His hold on her throat loosened for a second.

The air hissed through her lungs when she sucked in a shaky breath. She focused her gaze on his. She knew she only had one chance to enthrall him. If she failed, he wouldn't let her speak again.

Heart hammering, she concentrated on pouring all her energy into her voice and called on Altman's vampiric power.

"You will unhand me. It hurts you to touch me."

He released her as if stung. She stepped away, for a second when he caught her again by her throat, pushing her back into the wall.

"Amazing!" He laughed. "Yes, this hurts, but I won't let a little pain stop me. I've lived over five hundred years and have survived worse."

He squeezed, her hips bucking wildly as he dug his sharp nails into her skin. "This isn't Altman's power, you know. He could never put a thrall on a vampire. But your father could get vampires to do things, and you can too." The wonder in his tone caused a tremor to ripple along her spine. "So much power... Such a pity to kill it, especially if I can still use it." His voice didn't hold any kind of menace, only a matter-of-factness that was far more terrifying.

"Such big golden eyes you have," he continued as her lungs started to burn in need of oxygen. "It's like your father is staring up at me."

He released her, and she collapsed on the ground. She took deep breaths.

"I can sense your father in you." When she stiffened, he continued, his tone mocking, "Don't be offended. It made me realize I shouldn't act recklessly. Yes, I'll continue to have you working for me, but not at the hospital. I'll find something a bit more useful."

She glared at him. "I'd rather die and have Margot go to the police with the evidence."

"Don't challenge me," he warned. "Do you really want to die? Ms. Sloane too? How about your witchy roommate, your colleague and Dane? Be glad you entertained me tonight. It was a nice little performance. You don't want an encore. Give me back my little trinkets, and I'll let you and my secretary off with a warning. Ah, you doubt me. I see it in your eyes. Shouldn't I let you go then? You can try to fight me, but that would annoy me. Annoy me enough, and after I kill you, I'll kill your friends too. You can try giving my treasure to the police of course. But again, if you release it, you'll wish you were dead. I'll first punish all your friends, and you'll be last, knowing you could have stopped it. Do you really want to risk it? Do you believe the police could protect you and everyone you care about? Everyone can be bribed or intimidated. Evidence can be replaced, you know."

She could risk herself and maybe Margot, but she could never forgive herself if Pauline and Frank got hurt because of her stupid plan. *Gideon was right. It was a terrible idea.* "Okay." She sounded hoarse.

"Goodbye, Ms. Holland. I'll let Ms. Sloane contact you about your new job. You should be happy! You're getting promoted."

She couldn't form the words to thank him. She merely nodded and turned around, ready to leave the room when he said, "Wait, I almost forgot, we still have the matter of our blood link to discuss. I'm afraid it's not working out."

"No shit," she mumbled.

He sighed. "So disappointing. You're not at all acting like a proper blood slave."

"B-blood slave? W-what?"

"Oh yes, I may have embellished the reason behind a blood exchange a bit. It was never really about protection. Well, I can't speak for Dane Lynch, but I don't really give a fuck about your protection."

She had to swallow past the lump in her throat to talk. "So what do you give a 'fuck' about then? Hurting Dane or is it about me acting like your 'proper' blood slave? How was I supposed to act? In love?"

Like I loved Dane?

He shivered theatrically. "Heaven forbid! No, I just wanted you to follow me blindly."

She narrowed her eyes at him. "I'm glad I got my vision back."

He shook his head. "As my creature you should have been eager to please me, to give me whatever I wanted. Instead, the only thing you gave me was a fucking nightmare."

"Not for long," she muttered.

"Back to Dane Lynch, eh? Do you think he will take you back?"

She didn't answer and walked out of the office on wobbly legs. During the ride to the airport, she could hear Stratton's question echoing in her mind.

Will he take me back?

TOUCHED BY DARKNESS

A loud clap of thunder vibrated the air as Erin rode her bike to Dane's house. She stopped to glare at the sky, and a fat drop of rain splattered on her forehead. She hadn't thought to put on a raincoat when she left her apartment. She'd been far too preoccupied to think about something as trivial as protecting herself from a bit of water. Quickly the rain settled into a blinding downpour.

She sighed.

Why couldn't he agree to meet me at my apartment?

She wouldn't turn back. She squinted her eyes, got back on her bike and peddled as fast as she could through the rain-blurred street.

Great, now I'll have to ask him to recreate this blood bond with me while I'm looking like a drowned rat.

Fortunately, she had almost reached her destination. She saw Dane's mansion when a streak of lightning lit up the quiet street, followed by a rumbling so close that it caused the hair on her arms to rise.

She stepped off her bike and shivered. Her fingers were nearly numb as she pushed the buzzer. She expected to hear a voice, but the gate to the courtyard opened without anyone welcoming her.

A gust of wet wind struck her in the face, and she pressed her lips together as she walked through the gate. She locked her bike and saw the gates close behind her, trapping her inside.

She sucked in her breath, remembering Dane's threat the last time she had visited his house.

I will let you go for now. But the next time you enter my house, I will not.

She stared at the mansion and frowned. From the outside, it looked as though all the lights inside had been switched off.

Are we alone? Doesn't he want anyone to witness what is about to happen tonight?

The wind howled past the deserted building.

Unlike her previous visit, the garden appeared to have been neglected. Her feet crackled amongst the dead leaves and grass on the path. The hedges hadn't been trimmed in a while either.

The door was open. She stuck her head inside the dark, spacious hallway.

"Hello?" she called out. Utter silence answered her. No squeaking of the floors, no voices, no footsteps. The alarming quiet was ghostlike, and she could feel panic welling up.

"*Maybe you're better off staying connected to Jonathan Stratton,*" she heard her mother say.

"*Don't be such a chicken! You've just faced a pack of werewolves and Stratton. What's one more vampire?*" Gideon sneered.

"Dane?" she tried again.

"I'm in the basement." The words were low, almost a murmur of sound.

His bedroom.

Heart hammering, she went down the stairs and entered the darkened interior of the room. A fire blazed in the hearth. In the firelight, he looked like a dangerous adversary, far too seductive and strong to be trifled with.

"*Don't let him intimidate you,*" Leila said. "*Get mad. He wanted you to be his blood slave. You're just lucky you weren't affected the way Jonathan Stratton said.*"

He was standing in front of his four-poster bed watching her intently. His penetrating gaze made her feel naked.

"Hi," she said as she rubbed her arms. "What's wrong with the lights? Trying to save on your energy bill?"

His eyes narrowed, and annoyance flashed through them. "You're not afraid of the dark, are you, or are you cold? Maybe you should get out of these wet clothes."

She felt that a few strands of hair were stuck to her brow, and she pushed them from her face. "Thanks, but I'm okay."

He took a step in her direction. The creaking of the floor echoed as loud as a gunshot in the room, and she had to force herself not to run.

Get mad, she told herself.

He gave her a look so hot it would have melted steel. "Are you sure? I wouldn't want you to catch a cold."

She took a deep breath, sucking down a burst of fear and let anger fill her. "Stop playing games with me. Jonathan Stratton told me the purpose of the blood exchange. As a blood slave, I was supposed to give you whatever you wanted. You expected me to act like a puppet."

He frowned. "So you now believe everything Stratton tells you. How nice it must be to have a connection with someone so trustworthy. But if you're so happy with Stratton, why are you standing in my bedroom? Want to spend the night?"

Embarrassment flared. "I uh, I can't stay long. Pauline's waiting for me."

He grinned, his smile decidedly feral. "I'm sure she understands you're staying here. After all, we have some making up to do, right? That's why you're here, isn't it?"

Apprehension gripped her.

This is not going well.

"Um, not quite. I'm here because I need your help."

His blue eyes were cool. "And why should I help you if you're not here to make up with me?" His voice was so cold it had icicles dripping off it.

Fighting nausea, she said, "Because I wouldn't have needed your help if you hadn't forced that blood bond on me in the first place."

His gaze was without mercy. "You chose Stratton over me."

"Yes. I was upset, not thinking clearly." Her tone was strained.

He walked up to her and stuck out his hand. She told herself not to flinch as he brushed a stray tendril of hair from her face. "And now you *are* thinking clearly. Now, you want to be connected with me." His voice was as soft as a lover's sigh, playing along her nerve endings like the caress of fingertips.

Her whispered, "Yes," sounded shaky.

His eyes devoured her, causing her skin to pebble and her breath to hitch. The silence stretched between them until she wanted to scream.

"Please. I don't want to be in Jonathan Stratton's head anymore."

"You said that we were over. You told me to go away."

He's going to make me beg.

She cleared her throat. "Please."

"If I do this, you'd be in my head again. I'd be in yours. I won't let you reject me again after this."

A knot of fear formed in her chest. "It's n-not romantic."

You're just the lesser of two evils.

She couldn't say her last thought aloud, but his scowl made her believe he could read it from her expression.

Her heart sank. "R–remember I never would have bonded with Jonathan Stratton i–if you hadn't... Unless, you want me to stay bonded with him?"

Dane didn't move a muscle as he contemplated Erin while she stood motionless in the dim light of the bedroom. She looked utterly exhausted. He saw the flicker of doubt on her face, and he knew he could ease her mind. He would never allow her blood bond with his enemy to continue, but he resented her only wanting the bond with him to break her connection with Stratton. He still loved her, and he wanted her to admit that she loved him too. If he broke off the blood bond with Stratton, he would get to hold her in his arms again, but he didn't want to do that with her acting as if he was some kind of monster to be scorned.

He pushed the corners of his lips up into a smile, and he noticed the heat filling her cheeks.

Not as immune to me as you'd like, Goldilocks. And with the blood bond, it would be even harder to resist me.

"If I do this, what will I get in return? I don't want to be linked to someone who's going to complain about it."

He saw her throat work as she swallowed. "I won't complain. This time it's my choice."

He nodded. "Your choice, remember that." He caught her waist in a solid, unbreakable grip, and he pulled her against his hard body. He breathed in her alluring scent.

"I'll be back inside," he whispered against her skin. He held her tight with his right hand as his fingers on his left hand trailed along the sensitive underside of her arm. He dragged his teeth across her skin until he nipped at her earlobe. She gasped.

"And you want me inside you, Goldilocks," he said, his voice low and seductive. His hand slid briefly, teasingly, over her left breast before finding its way across her stomach.

"You want me inside," he repeated. "Your choice," he breathed in her ear.

She whimpered. His teeth scraped the nape of her vulnerable neck before sinking his fangs deeply into her jugular. Her flavor burst onto his tongue, and the taste of her went straight to his cock. His hand moved downward and cupped the mound of her sex. He held her up when her knees buckled.

He enjoyed the shivers racing through her as

lightning bolts of pleasure and pain shot through her body. He held her tight as he drank deeply from her.

He told himself he had to make sure that enough blood would be exchanged for the bond with Stratton to break, but realized it was an excuse. Her blood quenched a thirst he hadn't been able to satisfy ever since he had first tasted her.

He continued to grind his palm against the sensitive bundle of nerves at her center when she threw her head back, crying out as her orgasm flooded her.

Reluctantly, he slowed down, licking gently at the last drops of blood before withdrawing his mouth from her neck.

Knowing that the blood loss would make her feel lightheaded and dizzy, he lifted her in his arms and lowered her gently to the bed before she collapsed.

He sat down beside her and unbuttoned his shirt.

She opened her eyes. They clouded for a moment in confusion when she took in his naked chest. He got out a knife when she frowned.

"Not the chest." Her voice cracked, and she licked her lips. "S-Stratton, he—"

He understood and agreed. He didn't want anything of tonight to remind her of Stratton. Instead of letting her drink from his chest, he cut open his wrist. He lay down on the bed and pulled her onto his lap, gathering her in his arms. He lifted his wrist to her mouth.

He registered her instant tension, how she was warring with herself to put her lips on his wound.

"I can enter your mind, so that you're not aware

of this."

"No," she muttered as she pulled his wrist to her lips and sucked hard.

Her mouth on his skin, her tongue licking up his blood, it had an erotic effect on his body. He closed his eyes and pressed the full length of his erection against her back. His free arm moved to her stomach. He let his hand slid under her moist jacket, and his fingers drew circles around her belly button.

She moaned.

Paradise. *The only way this could feel better is if we're both naked, and I'm buried deeply inside her.*

He let her drink for several minutes before he took his wrist away. He moved it against his own mouth, licking the wound closed using the healing agent in his saliva. They continued to lie on the bed, and he savored the feel of her body against his.

Too quickly, she sat up, jerking away from him. His hands slipped slowly, reluctantly off her skin.

He thought about warning her not to move too quickly, but secretly he hoped that she would fall down, punishment for leaving his embrace so soon after the blood exchange. She left the bed and gripped the top of his desk to steady herself.

He frowned.

So eager to leave me.

He watched her stumble to the door before he snapped. He left the bed, chasing after her. He grabbed her, hauling her against him and ravaged her mouth, kissing her as if it were the last kiss they would ever share.

His tongue delved deep into her mouth, staking

his claim. In seconds, she was returning his kiss with lusty kisses of her own. He waited until he knew she had surrendered completely, that she was his before he pulled away from her. His kiss had her panting and gasping for air. She stared at him in shock. With a trembling hand, she touched her swollen lips. Victory surged through his veins.

"I'm back inside now, Goldilocks," he murmured. "Your choice this time."

She spun around and fled.

He let his laughter follow her out of his house. "Too late, Goldilocks," he called out.

She was upset now, but he didn't care. It was too late.

I'm in your blood again. If you fight me, you'll be fighting yourself.

In time, you'll accept me.

THE END

AUTHOR

As a child, Nicole always wanted to be an actress. However, her only shot at becoming the next Meryl Streep was during her one-second appearance in Paul Verhoeven's film 'Black Book' where her shirt got ripped off her body. After that, she decided to focus on her writing career instead.

When she's not writing, she spends her time as crazy cat lady, playing with her cats Buffy and Garfield. In addition, Nicole's hobbies include trying to chase tornadoes (although she still hasn't seen any), fantasizing about villains (isn't Lex Luthor far more interesting than Clark Kent?), and most of all reading stories somebody else wrote.